LAF – Life After Felix

LAF

Life After Felix

Elaine Durbach

www.elainedurbach.com

Author: Elaine Durbach
Cover Design: Abigail Rothman
Hat Drawing: Rick Parker
Book Layout Design: Linda Lombri, *Lombri Writes!*

LAF – Life After Felix

ISBN-13: 9798985883121 (paperback)
ISBN-13: 9798985883138 (ebook)

Acknowledgments

Thank you, first of all, to the people who inspired me to embark on this sequel by asking what happened to Sally and her companions in *Roundabout*. I'd never planned to write a sequel, but their questions made me realize that those characters were still telling me their stories.

A crucial circle of friends and one cousin read my early drafts. Each shed a different light, depending on their expertise and/or cultural background, always with encouragement. Special gratitude to Lisa Trusiani and Helene Thorup-Hayes for reading and re-reading multiple times, always with enthusiasm. And thank you to gifted author/artist Louise Berliner for being a true patron of the arts.

For their professional skills, thank you, Mimi Michel and Abby Kanter, and the ever patient and persistent Linda Lombri. You guys gave this book a polish that makes me proud of our product. Thank you too to ingeniously creative Abby Rothman for creating a cover that captures so much of what lies within, and to Rick Parker for the wonderful central image.

Ever and always, thank you to my husband, Marshall Norstein, for giving me the nurturing base from which I can explore my flights of fancy, and to our son, Gabe, for opening my heart and stretching my mind.

Dedication

Roundabout was dedicated to my late sister, Jan.
This book is dedicated to her daughter, my amazing niece,
Emily Roberts, whose ongoing tough-minded, soft-hearted support
and extraordinary generosity have made this publishing venture a
reality. Thank you, beloved Pem!

$$\sim \; 1 \; \sim$$

When you have loved someone your entire adult life, how on earth are you meant to go on without them?

Just move on, Sal. You have so much to live for.

Easy for you to say, Felix; you did "move on."

Not by choice, and you know it.

Crazy lady here, talking to her departed lover—but not out loud. I'm not that crazy. Hearing him inside me. Feeling the love I doubted for so long. Still arguing with him.

Why are you so afraid?

Who says I'm afraid?

But he's right, as usual. I am jittery. That agitation prodded me out of bed this morning and out here into the garden way earlier than usual. Usually, I cling to sleep as long as possible.

It's hot already and the plants look dusty, neglected, like me. How could I let this happen? Cape Town is in a drought, so we're not supposed to use hoses. That thought is enough to make me want to retreat indoors. But, driven by guilt, I find the hand shovel under a pile of rusty implements and clumsily start chiseling into the hardened soil. Carve small hollows around the stems the way Jacob taught us, and—with a pitcher filled in the kitchen—dole out cautious portions of water. Hoping it will soften the soil, allow nourishment to reach the roots.

Yes, I know, I should have been doing this all along.

When Felix was here, we gardened together. It was a delight, even when we bickered over what to plant or how to prune. "Dabbling with nature's alchemy," he called it. In all the decades since we'd last lived together, way back in our youth, I hadn't cultivated anything larger than a window box of petunias. He hadn't either, till he asked me to come stay with him here in this ramshackle old cottage. He'd let the plants grow wild, the same way he'd let the ocean mist rust the window catches and the lichen spread over the roof tiles. But together we were making progress.

. . . till Felix died, in the middle of the night, eight months ago. Almost nine.

The shovel goes still, half immersed in mud.

Left me with no warning, no goodbye. Just a final flare in his marvelous brain—and gone.

We'd only had five years together this time around. It wasn't enough. A hundred years wouldn't have been enough.

I was grateful every day of those five years.

Me too.

~ ~ ~ ~

For all these months, hibernation has seemed the safest

option. I've hugged my loneliness like a shawl, doing my best not to care about anything, except the cats. Mergatroid and Skelm keep me company. Most days, unless my neighbors come by, I talk to no one except them—and Felix.

I'm not into the supernatural, haven't ever gone to seances or anything like that, so what is this? Are his words just projection on my part, knowing him so well that I can predict what he'd say in any situation? But then what of the times when he catches me by surprise? Or when he nags me in a way he never used to?

Like about lightening up? You really need to. Sometimes, I think you love me more in absentia . . .

Nonsense.

Well, maybe. I did adore Felix in person, but his absence etches each detail of what is missing, every quirk and precious quality. Is it ever possible to appreciate someone with this intensity when they're alive, with you, face to face?

I pine for his physical presence. Talking to him helps, but I long to have his breath in the air I breathe, his warmth in our bed, his arm tight around my waist, making me dance a silly jig. I still pour two cups of coffee each morning, so as not to see one alone on the table.

As the coffee brews, I write in my diary. I can see Felix writing in his journal, meticulously tracking the discoveries and ideas that filled his waking hours—as if he knew how abruptly it all could end. His entries were filled with passion, just like those he wrote way back in his youth, before we met, when he was traveling the world. I read and reread those volumes, hearing his voice in the impetuous scrawl.

My entries are more mundane. I record my days so they don't merge into grayness. But there's been so little to record—that is, until the day before yesterday.

The first encounter, was that only forty-nine hours ago?

~ ~ ~ ~

One hour till the second encounter. Trying to distract myself with this gardening, wanting to stall, to still the thrum of anticipation. How has this person already wrought such tension?

The water seeps away as if it was never there. Should I cheat and use the hose? Can't, still too law-abiding. The marigolds and crimson bougainvillea will probably survive, but the petals of the yesterday-today-and-tomorrow, mauve, purple, and white, crumble as I touch them, releasing nostalgic sweetness, like a cheap perfume.

Ridiculously, tears well up and trickle down the side of my nose. I wipe them away with muddy fingers. I should go inside and clean up. Maybe he'll call and cancel. I hope so.

As I stand up, Jacob calls a greeting from over the fence, his mahogany face gleaming with sweat. This is his day to work at Edith and Roxie's next door. He used to come once a week to help us with the garden. I can't afford to pay him these days, but when he has time, he still stops by to check on me. He has a wonderful way of conveying sympathy without pity

Jacob came to Felix's wake/memorial—whatever you want to call it—as did a motley collection of other guests of all races and ages. The event ought to have been far sooner. Felix's priest buddy, Bob Halpert, kept nagging me, though neither of us belonged to his flock, me being Jewish and my beloved a total freethinker. "You need closure," the minister insisted. I disagreed, but I knew I owed it to all those as shocked as I was by Felix's sudden departure.

So, when his children came to visit from the States, my wonderful sort-of stepkids Joanie and Trevor, and Joanie's husband, Eric, I finally gave in. We did the deed together. It was a rollicking, drunken affair with lots of singing. We even choreographed a little dance, the kids and I, a brief piece to honor—and mock—their father, playing with the hats that were his trademark. It was the kind of party Felix Barnard would have loved.

That was the last time I've danced. And despite Bob Halpert's assurance, the party provided no closure. If anything, the gap loomed larger. A week later, Joanie, with her pregnant belly just starting to show, departed with her guys, heading home to America. I was left alone, hearing only my tinnitus and the wind rattling the windows—and occasional teasing taunts from my ghost lover.

I've tried to dance to lift my energy, as I've done all my life. You don't need to be happy to find pleasure in rhythm, but you do have to let feelings flow through you, and that has seemed dangerous, as if something might tear.

Other than walks down to the sea or up the mountain, I've kept busy with tasks. Fixing this and that around the house. Sifting through Felix's stuff, giving away or throwing out whatever I can bear to part with. Trying to work on our long-delayed book, his and mine, about the benefits of dance. The fixing has gone quite well, the throwing out not so well, and the writing? Not well at all.

What else can you expect?

With the writing, or from the unexpected visitor?

~ ~ ~ ~

As I wash and dress, memories from Wednesday flicker through my mind, still intertwining disbelief and wariness.

It was around mid-morning. I heard the ding-dong of the front doorbell. Opened expecting to see the mailman or a neighbor, and there stood—Felix?

Ground and sky swirled around me, and I had to clutch the door handle to keep from falling. A man with a white Panama hat was smiling down at me. His cheeks creased the right way. He tilted his head the right way, peering inquiringly. Even the lilting timbre of his voice was right.

For one glorious, breath-stealing moment, the impossible seemed possible. A great gust of relief filled me.

Then he whipped off his hat with an "Oops, sorry, ma'am!" That shook me awake. Felix would never have said that. And he'd have kept his hat on. The hair was thicker, more blond than gray. The eyes were different—not tiger topaz, more of a sea blue, or green. Hard to tell, and I was too flustered to decide.

I just croaked, "Yes? What can I do for you?"

"Are you Sally Paddington?"

"That depends. Who are you?"

The wind was blowing so hard, his answer whisked away from my ears. I had to brace the door to prevent it from slamming shut, and the buxom, peeling mermaid above the lintel rattled on her hooks.

"May I come in?" he shouted. "It's kind of hard to talk

like this."

"No." I was still reeling, trying not to stare—not to look at him straight on, because I wanted so much to recapture that first blissful illusion. "I don't let strangers into my home. What do you want?"

"It's a bit awkward. A long story. What if I buy you a cup of tea at that café around the corner?"

It was a reasonable suggestion. With half my mind I recognized that. The other half was tumbling into the past, tripping over an echo; Felix said almost exactly the same thing all those eons ago, standing in line to register for the new college year at Rhodes University, back in Grahamstown. I could still feel the tingle that shimmied through me and the feeling of a passage opening to the future.

I told the man to give me a minute and closed the door, leaving him outside. Considered donning a bra and changing out of my jeans and Felix's gray T-shirt, but instead just put on my green glass pendant, like a talisman. Tried to get a brush through my knotted white locks and gave up. Twisted my hair up instead, and with trembling hands fastened it with the first thing I found, a red clip that used to match my color.

Copper Girl, relax. It's okay.

Felix loved my hair when we met. Used to pull the pins out of my tight, neat knot so the waves would tumble down. He'd wrap the strands across his fingers and watch the light glisten off them. When at last we were together again, when my hair had faded to peach and then beyond, he didn't seem to notice the difference. I was still his Copper Girl.

So, who is he? I asked the air.

Find out.

Of course, Felix would say that. I closed the front door and went to the café with the stranger.

On our way down the street, we passed Jacob, still trimming the hedge. He waved, and then did a double take, staring open-mouthed at my companion. I nodded, knowing what he was wondering, and waved back. I hoped he hadn't noticed the flush burning in my cheeks.

The man beside me had put his hat back on, though he had to hold it to withstand the gale. In the periphery of my vision, he looked utterly familiar. More real than real, almost glowing. Not quite as bowlegged as Felix, but with the same rolling cowboy gait that made my guy recognizable from blocks away. A wave of longing rippled through me, mingled with sharp curiosity.

"In case you haven't realized, I'm Humphrey Barnard, Felix's brother," he said as we set out down the street. I had guessed that already, but the confirmation reverberated through me. We'd never met before and I hadn't seen a clear picture of him in years, yet I knew every plane of his face.

Humphrey? That came as a shock. Felix always called him Boet or Boetie, Afrikaans for "brother." Joanie and Trevor referred to him as Uncle Boet. The youngest of the three boys, I remembered, was Matthew, but I had no idea what this middle son's real name was. Ridiculous, yes, but Felix seldom spoke of them. In the early days, he just called them "the Neanderthals." He didn't talk about his two sisters either. It was a part of him that mystified me and still does, something oddly detached in a man who was warm with everyone else.

Now, that name proved to be the first hurdle to our communication. When I heard it, I'd burst out laughing. In my defense, I was a bit hysterical, but who calls their child Humphrey? I asked that as we faced each other across a table in the café.

"The same people who named their first daughter Olivia, after their favorite movie star," he replied, "and their first born after a cartoon cat."

So that was where "Felix" came from. I'd always wanted to ask and—like with so much else—was too circumspect to push for answers. "Perhaps, before they became who they became, they were impetuous kids with a sense of humor," this son told me. And here was another difference: Felix never said anything that charitable about his parents.

Why had Humphrey come? If I remember correctly, in ancient Jewish lore it was incumbent on a man to marry his brother's widow. My education in these matters is sparse. It shouldn't be, given that my parents, both Holocaust survivors, subjected me to Hebrew school. But neither they nor I delved deep into the Bible.

I learned more from Felix, steeped as he was in Evangelical teaching that he had largely rejected. It was he who told me the bit about brothers, that it was to ensure the dead man's line continued if his wife hadn't yet borne him any children. But what if the widow and brother-in-law didn't like each other? And what if she was way past childbearing age? Such a loopy notion, yet it yammered in my brain.

Humphrey certainly hadn't come with the aim of luring me into holy matrimony. Come to think of it, Felix didn't either; he and I never bothered to get married. Both too burned by unsuccessful attempts during our years apart—two on his side, one on mine. So, I'm not legally his widow, and this Barnard surely had no intention of filling his sibling's shoes—or bed. I couldn't imagine what had brought him to me.

Our tea arrived along with two oven-warm muffins. Humphrey inhaled deeply before taking a bite, relishing the aroma just as Felix would have. My mouth was so dry I couldn't face eating anything. I gulped the too-hot Darjeeling instead.

"Who were you named after?" I asked.

"Humphrey Bogart, another of their favorite actors." He licked crumbs from his lips. The corners of his mouth curled, just like those others I knew so well. I almost reached a fingertip to touch them. "Long story—for some other time."

There'd be another time?

He went quiet, staring at me as if wondering the same thing. "Your eyes are the same blue as my hydrangeas," he murmured. "Do you grow them too? Felix told me the two of you had become hotshot gardeners." I shook my head, admitting how negligent I've been. "I doubt that," he said. A flicker passed through me, as warm as a sip of whisky.

"We were learning as we went. But that 'long story' you mentioned . . .?"

"Oh yeah, as I was saying: my folks planned to emigrate to the States, and they thought it would give us kids a leg up to have famous namesakes."

"Felix never mentioned that. He just told me about his own adventures there, you know, before he went to Rhodes."

"Yeah, he had a great time there. I suppose that's why he went back after you two broke up." Humphrey gave me an odd look. "Didn't you meet up in the States years later, like by pure chance, at some big conference in California?"

Everything around me went pale. What could he know of that encounter, or its consequences? Felix, for certain, would never have shared any of the details, and I had no intention of doing so either.

Instead, I asked, "Why didn't your folks ever go to America?"

"Not really sure. I think, by the time they could afford to, they'd lost heart. Been through too much loss. My mother just wanted to huddle in her nest and guard her remaining chicks." I knew what he meant, but still was shocked by his openness.

A hush settled between us. Humphrey circled his mug with both hands and said, without looking up, "I suppose you want to know why I'm here."

I shrugged, suddenly wary. Why was he avoiding my gaze? Perhaps not so open after all. The words blurted out: "Felix left everything to his children, to Joanie and Trevor."

Humphrey shoved away from the table, leaning his chair back on two legs as if to distance himself from me. "Shit, that's not why I came! I don't want his damn money, if he had any. On the contrary—"

Old Sally—well, young Sally—would have apologized and tried to smooth things over, but this Sally didn't give a stuff. I've definitely become more blunt as I age, and the isolation probably hasn't helped. "Don't get all huffy with me," I snapped. "What am I meant to think, you turn up like this without calling or texting? You didn't bother to attend his memorial party."

But I didn't want him to leave without telling me why he'd come. Didn't want him to leave, not so soon. My heart was thudding, maybe from the over-steeped tea. He let the chair drop forward again, and I sucked in a deep breath, relieved.

"Fair enough," he said. "It's complicated. That's why I didn't call first. I had to be in Cape Town for work, and I thought I'd give it a try. Rented a car for the day and came. Helga, my wife, said I should phone before or write or something, that it was rude to just show up, or that I might drive all this way out to Kalk Bay and find you'd gone off to America. Isn't Joanie about to have her baby? Helga said you might want to be with her for the birth. I know she's not your daughter, but . . ."

This guy was a chatterbox. So many words. Felix could talk up a storm if he was discussing his theories about healing and motion, but about personal stuff he was always terse. Humphrey lifted his mug, realized it was empty, and signaled for a refill—and then waved his hand, a change of mind. He's nervous, I thought, and softened. And he's married, and he knows about Joanie's pregnancy.

It's true, I've been thinking of going to the U.S., if I can scrape together the money and the courage to leave my cocoon. I'm not really comfortable around babies, haven't been for a long time, but I love Joanie and she has been nagging me to come.

"You're in touch with the kids?" I asked.

"Now and then— since Felix brought them to visit Mom

after my father died. He wouldn't come while the old man was around." I remember that saga, how their father reacted to the fact that Felix's second wife was Jamaican.

Humphrey grimaced, then continued: "Joanie tells me she's closer to you than to her actual mother. That Deidre sounds like a bitch. Helga says I shouldn't judge, that I don't know how Felix might have hurt her, why she divorced him, but that doesn't excuse her being a lousy parent. Wife number two, Trevor's mom, now she's a different story."

I like Nellie too. I remember feeling like a pendulum; one moment he annoyed me, the next I was nodding in agreement.

"So why *are* you here?" I demanded.

He dipped his head and sighed. "I wasted too much time. And there's stuff I need to straighten out about Felix and my mom and our family before it's too late."

"Too late? Are you dying?"

He looked up and then guffawed. "Aren't we all? Thank the Lord, no, I'm fine. You really don't mince your words, do you? You're not what I expected. Joanie always said you were such a lady."

"So, what do you mean, 'too late'?" I'd gone through losing one Barnard brother; if this one was likely to exit soon, I didn't want anything to do with him. My breath grew rough. This wasn't a joking matter for me.

"I have to be back in the city center for a meeting later this afternoon," Humphrey said. His voice went low. "Actually, it's you I was worrying about."

"You've had a strange way of showing it." The waiter paused beside me with a tray of dirty dishes, and I clunked my mug onto it. Another pendulum swing. I wanted to leave, to get away. It's true that in the first weeks after Felix's death—even the first months—I'd contemplated suicide. It seemed to offer a sweet relief, a way to follow him. Some days it still feels like a good idea, but I've never told anyone. Humphrey couldn't possibly know, though the way he was looking at me now with those eyes the color of sea, it was as if he did.

"I don't mean you're going to die," he said. He laid his fingers on my wrist. I shivered. "Joanie said something about you maybe wanting to close this chapter, to move on. I thought you might move back to New York, that I'd lose the chance to meet with you."

I jerked my hand away. "She thought that? I never wanted to leave." It came out sharper than intended. "We sorted that out before they went home to America."

"Like I said, I've only had sporadic contact . . ."

"I was surprised you didn't come to the memorial. Joanie said she invited you all. Your brother and sister came. I don't understand why you didn't." I was on the attack, angry with him, perhaps for the letdown after that initial moment of dizzy euphoria, thinking he was Felix.

"Hey, lighten up," he said. "There's a lot I expect you don't understand." I snorted. Bad enough to have a ghost say that. We glared at each other.

He broke away first, and I saw him glance down at the pendant rising and falling with my panting breaths. I laid my hand over it.

A voice came from above: "Sally Barnard—I mean Paddington! What a lovely surprise. So nice to see you out and about. And—oh, my goodness, you must be—Peter? Or was it Paul? One of the disciples. Felix's brother?"

"Yes, but not the disciple one, Matthew. It's Humphrey, actually." He got to his feet and held out his hand. "And you are?"

It was the minister, Bob Halpert, recently become my buddy too. He was clad in black, as usual, but he'd swept up to us with such blithe benevolence, I could almost see his wings. I frequently spot a halo in the gleam around his bald head. Eyes wide, he pulled up a chair, and turned our duel into a sunny circle of pleasantries. Humphrey sat up straighter, his demeanor respectful. Bob asked about Port Elizabeth, where Humphrey lives, and about his work in marine biology, and about poachers and conservation, and on and on.

I wondered if the big brother had opened up with Bob as readily as the younger one was doing. I know Felix shared secrets he wouldn't discuss with me. I should have pushed harder for answers when he was around, sought to understand the wounded parts of him. Hard as I've tried to make my peace with those blank patches, they still bother me. Perhaps that's why his ghost hovers, because I nag him with questions.

And now here was this guy, this very-much-alive family member, who simultaneously was making things better and worse.

Finally, Humphrey looked at his watch. "Excuse me, Sally, Reverend Halpert. I must get going. I've got that meeting in the city. Sorry. This is nuts."

"Can you come back tomorrow? You never finished telling me why you came. And I have some things of Felix's that you might like to have."

The moment the words came out my mouth I wanted to grab them back.

"Not tomorrow. We have an all-day conference in Stellenbosch." I turned away, looking for a waiter to pay. He said, "How about the next day? I'm meant to fly back first thing on Friday morning, but I can take a later flight. Please?"

I was about to tell him I was busy, that it wouldn't suit me. My guard had gone up. But I wasn't busy that day, or the next, unless you count my feeble attempts to work on the book. And, more urgent, I also have a conference I should be preparing for, unless I can squirm out of it.

But Humphrey was looking at me like an eager boy, almost pleading. "Yeah, you can come on Friday," I said. "Same time."

Forty-five hours to wait.

~ 2 ~

Ocean glimmers way down below, dotted with the lights of tiny ships. And above, if I cup my hands like blinkers to shut out the cabin glow, I can see a scattering of stars. In this droning nowhere space between continents, shouldn't it be possible to distill some perspective?

While those around me sleep or watch movies, I have taken out my diary and started writing, trying to sort out the jostling impressions of these past few days. Most entries have been about as exciting as this one:

> *Slept badly, then couldn't wake up. The cats got me out of bed. Paid bills. Cooler weather. Walked from Kalk Bay to Muizenberg and back. Hope I'm tired enough to sleep better tonight . . .*

OR . . .

> *Roxie & Edith insisted I come with them and the pugs to the farmers market. Fridge empty so I went. Used to*

love the market, now it's too crowded. Skelm slipped out the garden gate and disappeared. Strolled back at dinner time. I wish he wouldn't escape like that.

Now I have more than I can squeeze onto the Friday page, from the lame attempt at gardening, to the visit, to the shared ride to the airport. I write for a while and then lay down the pen. My fingers caress the pendant hanging against my breastbone. The glass is warm and smooth, and links me to Felix and to a time without him, when he and I lived far apart in that country I'm flying toward.

Another memory rises—of green eyes the color of this glass, looking into mine earlier today—and whatever clarity I've conjured fractures into a spiral of pleasure and guilt. After all these months of craving what's passed, it's odd to be obsessing over a fresh experience. Hard to believe that the memory that makes my breathing catch was just this morning.

Such nonsense! The whole thing is out of the question, verboten, ludicrous. I'm not interested.

That's what I told my old college friend Angie when we had our weekly call on Wednesday, just hours after Humphrey's first visit. She harrumphed—as she is wont to do. "Verboten? Bullshit. He sounds hot, precisely what you need. I haven't heard you this buzzy in a long time. So, he's married? Don't have an affair—just a little flirtation. Where's the harm in that? But don't go falling in love, okay?"

How could I fall in love? I'm not even sure I like this man. Felix didn't—or certainly not in our student days when he and I first met at Rhodes. He rebuffed all my attempts to go with him to visit his family, though they lived only two hours away.

He insisted that I would detest his siblings. His parents, I gathered would frown on me because of my religion.

The passenger next to me on the plane, a round-faced American with a tie-dyed T-shirt and badly cut gray hair, is chatty. I'd hoped to be seated alone. It's overwhelming being among all these people after my months of solitude, but this guy is pleasant enough. He introduced himself the moment we settled into our seats, and offered me some of his duty-free chocolate, the dark kind I love. Told me he's an accountant— not what I'd expected from his appearance—and started to ask what I do. I accepted one piece, but put on the headset, as if eager to listen to music while I write. He took the hint and selected a movie, an animated French comedy Felix and I both adored, and subsided into his own space, chuckling quietly.

I could be watching the same movie, but it hurts to remember how it made Felix chortle, and me too. Can't remember when last I've laughed out loud like that. Glad my seatmate has left me in peace, I sip my whisky and try to summarize the happenings still sifting through my brain.

~ ~ ~ ~

The call from Joanie came about three hours after I'd fallen asleep on Wednesday night. I floundered about, trying to find the phone. The ringing stopped. Still disoriented, thinking it was a wrong number or an obscene prank, I lay back down. But something made me sit up again. Checked who'd called and my heart began pounding. The screen seemed to waver as I tapped on her number.

"Joanie, are you all right? What has happened?"
"Sally, will you come?"

Sitting upright then—toes burrowing into the pile of the shaggy bedside rug, trying to calm down and listen. Fully awake, hyper-alert. Silence on the line, and then a sniff and a stammer. I whispered, "The baby? Joanie . . .?"

"He's not all right."

"Sally?" A deeper voice replaced hers, her husband, Eric. "It's okay, sweetheart. Take it easy. I'll tell her."

"Eric, tell me what?" I wanted to climb right through that little slab in my hand and across the world.

"Joanie went into labor early this morning," he said. About three weeks early—that shouldn't be too serious, from what I've heard. Or it might be. I held my breath, waiting for his next words. Eric's a capable guy, an architect, very cool and methodical, but he was struggling to sound matter-of-fact.

They only moved into their new home in Portland a few months ago. Did they even know where the closest hospital was? Silly question: Eric would have researched the best places on day one.

"We got to the medical center around midday. Everything was going smoothly, her blood pressure, his heartbeat. The baby came out all right, six and a half pounds, small but not too small. He looked perfect, so beautiful, with all his fingers and toes. He seemed fine, but then they noticed something not quite right about his reflexes. They've got him in the pediatric ICU, hooked up to all kinds of machines."

Joanie must be frantic. Eric said, "She's very anxious—we both are—but physically she's doing okay." That, at least, was reassuring. It gave me space to focus on the baby.

"What's his name?" Just last week, he was a fuzzy, black-

and-white scan and a vague due date; now here he was, a member of the family. I almost didn't want to hear a name. That would anchor him as a person, another focus of love—with this awful, unexpected fragility. Exactly the kind of vortex of emotion I dread these days.

"We haven't been able to decide. We thought about Felix, but it feels too soon. What about the Jewish way, with his initial, a name starting with 'F'? Frank, no. Or Fred? Sal, wasn't that your father's name—Frederick? Joanie's nodding. She likes that. Do you?"

Choking on tears, I bleated out a "Yes." My father escaped death in Nazi-controlled Europe and went on to live a good, happy life. It's a survivor's name. That thought was like oxygen. I loved that the 'F' linked Felix and my adoring Pops.

Eric handed the phone to Joanie, and I heard her say, "Of course. How could we not have known that? He's Freddie." For the first time, her voice had a ring of maternal confidence.

"Will you come, Sal?" she asked again. "Even if it's just a quick visit, just to meet Freddie?"

"What about Deidre?"

"Mom's coming tomorrow, but probably only for a day or two, on her way to some investment shindig. She'll be gone by the weekend. Please, I really need time with you."

"If I do, it can't be for long," I told her. "I'm supposed to speak at a big dance conference here next month."

That sounded so phony. Am I really going to go through with it? I pressed the heel of my free hand against my forehead, to push away the thought.

The dance conference was my suggestion, an international

exploration of the therapeutic power of dance. I mentioned it to Mary, my professor friend, a year ago, over sundowners on our patio. Blithely promised I'd help her organize it. She suggested I give the opening address. I demurred. Felix, alongside me in that mellow evening glow, pushed me to agree to speak. He said it would revive a part of my career I'd sacrificed to be with him. I started to deny that, but Mary backed him up. Within weeks the higher-ups had given her the green light, and she began pulling it together.

Like another life. I felt so strong then, but now the prospect makes me nauseous. It's around the corner and I have nothing to say. Have been wishing there was a way to back out, but people are coming from all over the world, many of them because I persuaded them to. If I could just think of a brilliant speaker to take my place . . .

"A conference? That's wonderful, Sal," Joanie exclaimed. "It'll give you such a boost. But still come, please, please."

Trying to be practical, the way I used to be. If I give that address, the speaker's fee will replenish what an airline ticket would take out. Ugh, such a mercenary attitude! What inspiration will it offer when I'm in a dark auditorium, facing hundreds of dance experts?

"I'll get to you as soon as possible," I told Joanie.

Realized after I'd rung off that I should have told her about her uncle's visit. But she had so much else on her mind. And given that I planned to be on a flight the next day, who knew if I'd ever see Humphrey again?

~ ~ ~ ~

If my original plan had worked out, I'd already be in

Portland with Joanie. I pick up the pen again to write that in my diary, but thoughts are darting this way and that. Close my eyes and try to continue an inner stock-taking.

With Christmas just weeks away, planes were full. My travel agent couldn't find me a seat on a direct flight to the U.S. on Thursday, the day after Joanie's call. I could have flown via France or Japan, but that would have cost more and taken longer. Instead, she got me on this Friday-night budget special to New York, with a connection to Oregon. Two-week maximum stay, but it will have to suffice.

Just as well I had that extra day. So much to sort out—with Mary at the university, and a roofer scheduled to replace some tiles, and—most important of all—finding someone to feed my furry housemates.

If I had my way, there would have been five cats in the house. When Mergatroid presented me with four kittens back in the autumn, I wanted to keep them all, the whole fluffy, squeaking bunch. It felt cruel to separate siblings. But my neighbors conducted an intervention; they said I was projecting. So, reluctantly, I let three of the kittens go to new homes, and held on to only one. Trevor named him Skelm, Afrikaans for "naughty" because he seemed wilder than the rest. Also, it worked really well as a call: "Sksskskselm!"

But what to do with them in my absence? My neighbor June offered to have her eight-year-old feed them, and I know Samantha would be reliable, but an even better solution presented itself: Jacob popped in yesterday to say hello, and he agreed to stay in the house with his wife, Nomse. Normally, he travels in from Guguletu to his clients in the area. It takes hours on buses and trains. "It'll be like a holiday for us," he said. With Jacob around, my home will be safe from burglars and the cats will be cared for. My plants might even thrive.

And then there was Humphrey. If I left on Thursday, how would I tell him not to come on Friday? We hadn't exchanged phone numbers. Joanie was the one who'd been in contact with him, but given everything she is dealing with, I couldn't ask her to go hunting for his info. True, a sensible woman might have tracked down Helga and asked for her husband's cellphone number, but that thought made me cringe.

She sounded like such a scold. Plus, according to Humphrey, she had taken Deidre's side against Felix, suggesting he might have treated her badly. Flimsy cause to dislike the woman, I know. And face it, if Felix treated Deidre shabbily, I was part of that betrayal. It was just once with me, but once too often. I don't think Deidre knew about what happened, but still . . . Did Helga?

~ ~ ~ ~

That "once" was part of the California encounter Humphrey mentioned over tea on Wednesday. As I packed last night, the surprise of that moment again made me gasp. I pushed back thoughts of Deidre, and questions about what Humphrey knew, and instead reveled in the pleasure on the flip side of that guilt. The memory stilled my hands.

There again was the sunbaked restaurant terrace in Hollywood, my files in front of me, the iced tea, my blue sun hat. The heat was melting the tension I'd carried with me from New York, from the gray winter days and the chill of my marriage. Trying to put aside the hurt my husband, Charles, had inflicted the day before. Trying not to think about his blustering confession of infidelity—his first, he claimed—and to focus on my notes. I had to prepare for a talk that evening about Southern African dance traditions, as part of a multidisciplinary symposium on movement.

Out of nowhere I heard, "Copper Girl, what are you doing here?" I looked up and there he was, my Tiger Man, laughing in astonishment.

Delight and lust and longing. Weighed down by the memory and buoyed by it even now, wondering again what it meant to Felix, and what he told his brother about that day.

Fate? Destiny? By wildly unlikely coincidence, my old sweetheart was taking part in the same symposium. From our worlds-apart fields of study, his in physiology, mine in music, our paths had come together. Whatever the forces at play, our joy outweighed all other considerations.

The suitcase in front of me stayed splayed open, half-filled, as I peeled back those layers within. Ancient history until recently, talking with Joanie when she was visiting me in Kalk Bay, when she asked if I had ever been pregnant.

That consequence . . .

I tried to block her questioning—but I should have tried harder. After all, this was about her father cheating on her mother. But she was pregnant herself and had confided in me. The precious sharing unstitched my resolve. She ferreted the story out of me and seemed unsurprised. "You two should have stayed together then," she said. "You were so dumb."

~ ~ ~ ~

As I went back to packing, I was suffused with an entirely

new prickle of guilt and longing. Have I learned nothing in all these years? Now, with my notebook on my lap in this airplane seat, lit by a circle of light, I'm writing down these thoughts in an effort to gain clarity, but what if the wrong person opens my diary one day? —or if this nice guy next to me sees what I'm writing? I'm embarrassed to admit the truth even to myself.

The fact is that last night, the chimera of Felix blurred into the colors of his brother. The gray hair or the blond? Brown eyes or green? Was I seeing Felix's smile—or Humphrey's? On some way-down layer of the barely conscious, in my touch-deprived flesh, or maybe in the gut brain that does its thing quite independently of the intellect, I was imagining Helga's husband's hands.

Silly old bat. Humphrey surely wouldn't look at me, I told myself. He and I are about the same age, but his wife is probably ten years younger and still gorgeous. In any case, it shouldn't matter. Nothing was going to happen between us. So why the daydreaming, imagining being close again to that wiry, familiar-unfamiliar body, feeling those calloused hands on my shoulders, moving down my back?

Eleven hours till he returned.

With all the pre-trip preparations to handle, I dragged my mind to a safer subject, the baby and Joanie and Eric. But that wasn't safe either. Picturing that fragile mite tapped right into my fault line of terror, the possibility of another loss. I shoved aside the suitcase and curled into a tight ball on the bed, my arms wrapped around my head. Fending off thoughts of Felix, and that other long-ago loss, of the child he and I conceived.

How can I help now? What do I need to understand?

What triggered Joanie's early labor?

Not that unusual, I gather, and she had been very aggravated. Crazy to care so much about politics, but she had been fretting about the outcome of the general election in America. Even with her swelling belly, she had marched from door to door, campaigning to ensure "that monster" didn't win. And he did win, beating the candidate she so badly wanted to see in the White House. "It can't be true," she kept saying after the results were confirmed.

We in South Africa have been astounded, but it's nothing like the shock I've been hearing from friends in the States. And Joanie had been pessimistic in a way I'd never heard her before. "What kind of world are we bringing our child into?" she asked me last Sunday, just days before the baby's arrival. She's intense at the best of times, and she was raging on the phone. Had it been enough to send her body into crisis mode?

Give my daughter a hug from me, the ghost beside me said as I finally slid under the blankets. Still just on one side of the bed, still unable to use his pillow and spread out.

Tell her she needs to calm down.

I nodded an inner yes. Will her baby be all right? I asked him.

Our Freddie will flourish, he assured me. *Tell Joanie.*

Nice alliteration, and he seemed to approve of our name choice. Not enough to ease my anxiety, or Joanie's, if I ever find a way to convey the message, but good to hear anyway.

And give my brother a hug too, the bum.

~ ~ ~ ~

The "bum" turned up at the cottage around ten this

morning (only twelve hours ago?), with flowers in hand—actually, a few minutes before. Another totally unFelixlike action. For all his obsession with dates and the passage of the years, he was laissez-faire about time. "Felix o'clock," his friends called it.

Was my visitor really glittering, or was that aura charged by my longing for his brother? From the radio in my living room, I could hear a song Felix was always humming, "Here Comes the Sun." It felt like a benediction from him.

Humphrey's unexpected punctuality caught me unready. I had showered after gardening and put on a white cotton dress and applied mascara and a slick of coral lipstick but had not yet clipped back my hair. My visitor did a double take when he saw me. He gave a long, drawled "Wo-o-w!"

Like an adolescent, I blushed. "Yeah, well, I clean up okay—if you don't check my fingernails."

I thanked him for the flowers—a hideous arrangement of dyed purple carnations in a pink vase shaped like a begging poodle. He muttered an apology, something about that being all he could find on his way from the station. I was relieved; at least this wasn't his taste—and touched that he'd bought them for me.

He had taken the suburban train from the city center, he told me, for the pleasure of the view of the coast along the last few stops. Most visitors avoid the trains these days, leaving them to those with no other option. You have to be willing to take a chance on dicey maintenance and even dicier security. I was impressed. It seemed like an open-minded thing to do, less racist than I expected, judging by Felix's old accusations. But those were from long ago. I really didn't know this guy at all.

The next words out of his mouth knocked me back: "Ugh, it was disgusting in that carriage!" He shook himself as if to shed contamination.

I recoiled. "It's hot, and who knows what work those poor passengers have been doing," I said over my shoulder, "or if they've even got running water in their homes. You try staying daisy fresh under such conditions." I ushered him into the house grudgingly, no longer clear why I'd been so eager to see him.

Humphrey stepped in front of me. "Whoa, Miss High-and-Mighty, hold your horses. Did I say a word about the passengers? It's obvious the trains aren't getting cleaned properly. Maybe they don't have enough money for maintenance because rich folks like you don't use public transport. How do you get around?"

"By car, or on a motorbike," I murmured. Heat had flooded my face again.

His annoyance vanished and he stared at me in astonishment, his eyebrows almost lost under the wave of hair that flopped across his forehead. "A motorbike? You?"

"Yeah, a Harley. What's so strange about that?"

I welcomed the change of subject. "Come, I'll show it to you while the water boils."

I set the vase on the mantlepiece and took him out to the side of the house, where the big old beast hunched under its cover. He helped me unhook the ties and pull the canvas back, exposing it in all its jet-black glory. The paint doesn't gleam the way it used to, but it still looks good—an achievement, given the many years of sea air it has endured. Humphrey ran his hands over the tank and the handlebars, nodding approval. "Felix let you ride it?" He was clearly astonished.

"Didn't let me. It was my decision, after he died. I used to have my own bike."

He stroked the glossy leather of the saddle. "You know what happened with our sister Joanne?" he asked.

I gasped. "Yes, some of it. Not the whole story."

Through my entire relationship with Felix, he never mentioned her name. And the motorcycle was landmine territory. No matter how I nagged, he refused to take me on it or to explain why. And here I was with his brother, just hours into our acquaintance, with the taboo swept aside and the topic wide open. Our intimacy had accelerated from zero to sixty.

"You should have heard Felix when I started riding," I told him. "In the beginning, he was like a lion with a thorn in its paw. He snarled at me—really snarled, 'It's not a game, you silly woman. People get hurt on these things.' I thought it was just chauvinist nonsense. I knew nothing about your sister, until a few months ago when Joanie told me about Joanne."

"You know Joanie is named after her?" he asked.

"Yeah, so I finally learned. How old were you when she died?"

"Thirteen." He had turned away from me, but I saw his shoulders slump under the smooth white shirt. I wanted to reach out and stroke his back. "I'll never forget that day." He spun around. "You know Felix wasn't hurt? Hardly a scratch. It might have been better if he had been injured."

"Come inside," I said. "Let's have that coffee. Or would

you like something stronger? We don't have much time. I need to finish my packing."

Humphrey looked up in surprise, and I told him where I was going and began to fill him in on Joanie's news. I told him the little I knew about Freddie, and that her mother was coming but only for a day, and Joanie wanted some moral support. The pendulum had swung back again, and I was liking him.

He opted just for coffee, and we sat facing each other across the pitted wooden surface of the old table. "Tell me what happened with Joanne," I said. Joanie had shared all she knew, but it wasn't much.

"Felix wasn't supposed to take her on his bike. My folks had forbidden him." He pushed his hair off his forehead, and for a moment it stood up like a boy's. "But apparently, she was in a big rush to get to a date, and she pleaded with him. He tried to tell Mom and Dad that, but they wouldn't listen. The police brought him home all covered in blood—Joanne's. He was crying so hard, I could hardly make out what he was saying, and my father was yelling at him. My mother was wailing. Felix kept saying, 'She begged me to take her. She begged me.' She was alive, in the hospital, with a broken spine. Died slowly over the next six weeks.

"And then Felix was gone too, kicked out. Or headed off to Cape Town by his own choice. I never knew. My father just kept saying, 'Good riddance to bad rubbish.' It was almost as if he was glad to have an excuse to push him out. My mom was a wreck."

There was a long silence. Gulls were crying in the distance.

A train passed, its horn like a long groan. Tears prickled. Why the hell had I put on mascara? I blinked hard but Humphrey had seen. "Are you crying for him, or her, or our family?" His voice was very gentle.

That made it worse. After all these months of coping, of stay-strong, tamped-down toughness, his tenderness melted me. Tears flooded down my face. "All of you," I said. "And for him and me, and the stupid years of misunderstanding, not knowing about that hurt."

"And he still carried the guilt?" Humphrey was staring at the table, tracing the wood grain with his finger. "When we were kids, I worshipped him, though we fought a lot. And then he left. I was pissed off with him for going, for killing Joanne the way my father said, for leaving me behind with Matt and Olivia. They weren't much comfort, and I was angry with everyone and everything for a long time. I didn't understand what it was all about—maybe I still don't. I'm really hoping you can help me."

For the first time, I reached out to him. He took my hand in his. The warmth felt wonderful. "I will if I can," I said, "but how? There's so much I'm only now starting to understand."

We went on to chat about this and that, as easy with each other as old friends. I told him how I sold my bike last year because my gammy knee was acting up, making it painful to ride, how the break from dancing seemed to have helped it heal, that and lots of walking, and how now I can ride without a problem again.

"That's really great," he said. "I ride too. When I'm depressed, there's no better therapy." I agreed. Even told him about the pleasure it gives me to feel what Felix felt, the very specific vibration, the balance, the power.

"You really miss him, don't you?" he said. And again, tears clogged my lashes.

~ ~ ~ ~

The whisky on the plane is better than the plonk favored by Reverend Halpert that, very fortunately, Humphrey turned down. By the bottom of my second glass, I'm too buzzed to carry on writing in my diary. Mr. Tie-Dye laughed his way through his comedy and has dozed off, his head almost on my shoulder. To my surprise, I don't mind. His hacked hair smells rather nice. I rest my head the other way, supported on my palm, trying to surrender to sleep. I have a very long day ahead, with a five-hour layover at Kennedy Airport before my connecting flight.

I'm not sure if she'll make it, but I emailed my beloved sister-friend Libby, who said she will try to get in from Connecticut, to keep me company between flights. We haven't seen each other in the six years since I reunited with Felix, way too long. We have a lot of catching up to do, and I don't want to be a sleep-deprived wreck. As it is, she has been worrying about me since his death, convinced I've turned into a hermit. She thinks I should move back to the States.

"You could meet someone new—when you're ready. You still have good years ahead of you," she keeps telling me. We're the same age—met when I came to America to do my master's at Boston University—but because I remained childless and footloose while she had children and then grandchildren, she assumes I'm less worn down. If life is experienced in moments of concern, as the biologists say, in a way she was right. But grief has pushed my clock forward. I've been telling her I'm not interested, that there'll never be another man in my life. "I've dried up," I told her.

I believed that, but then Humphrey appeared. A smile creeps across my face as I relive this so-long-ago morning.

~ ~ ~ ~

He and I sipped our coffee and talked about kids—my not having any but loving Felix's, and his four—four! —all more or less independent now, and how I came to stay in the cottage. I'd have skipped that topic, but Humphrey taunted me about Felix's will and the nasty comment I made on Wednesday. I explained how Joanie and Trevor insisted they didn't want the house sold and wanted me to stay in it. I was overjoyed. I rent it from them, and they've promised they'll come out for vacations. Eric and I plan to do renovations together.

"That's wonderful, a good arrangement," he said. It is, and I'm very grateful. And then he asked, "What did you want to show me?"

It was silly, really. I wanted him to see his brother's hat collection, with the Indiana Jones one similar to his white Panama, and maybe some of the family photos I'd put up on display.

Felix kept his pictures stowed away, along with all his old calendars, but after he was gone, I created a collage of them on a corkboard. It's above my desk, and whenever I stall with our book, there's his face to light me up, young and old and in between. I've put up a few of his early pictures of me too, in tutu and toe shoes, hair scraped back in a bun, the

"Bunnington" of old. (No one except my college buddies call me that these days—and even they haven't lately, since they've come to see me as a widow.)

Looking at that array, I feel Felix nod at me or shake his head, nudging me to get a move on.

What's holding you back? he has asked. *We have good stuff here, kiddo.*

The whole endeavor might be for naught. My New York publisher, who was eager for another book, turned his back on nonfiction and these days only handles novels. My agent has retired. I have no idea what to do with the manuscript—if I ever manage to finish it. But Felix seems to trust me and believe in the book—in sharp contrast to our initial conflict about it. It was one of our worst clashes. And though I still don't fully understand what happened back then, his faith has kept me going.

The hats are arrayed on a rack that runs the length of the attic. I led the way, climbing ahead of Humphrey up the steps I finished repairing only recently. They used to be so rickety, it was a gamble each time one ascended. Felix promised to fix them, but he wasn't very handy. I'm better with tools and get satisfaction from a task well done. I was telling Humphrey that as we reached the top and entered the room. It was bathed in morning sunshine. I turned with a sweeping gesture to indicate the wonderful view across the ocean, and almost whacked him. He was close behind me and was caught by surprise. He looked like a mischievous kid.

"You have a very pretty rear view—nice legs," he said.

"That's a bit forward, isn't it? And here I was thinking that you were admiring my carpentry."

"Oh yes, that too. Nice work." He smirked, and I found myself grinning also, though I tried to look disapproving. As I turned back to the window the fact registered that my "rear view" had pleased this man. A glow spread up my neck. I wanted to back up, to feel the warmth of him against me. Resisted with difficulty. And instead leaned across my desk to open the diamond-paned windows wider so he could see the full sweep of the bay, with the misty mountains rising in the distance.

"This used to be our storage room," I told Humphrey. "I didn't realize how superb the view was until I started spending time up here, sorting through all Felix's stuff." I was waffling on like an airhead. "And oh, there was a lot. Your brother was a pack rat! I've disposed of most of it, but I kept his hats. They were a part of him, like a record of his travels, with a chapeau from every chapter, so to speak."

He was standing alongside me now, peering at the photos. I mentioned how odd it always seemed to me that Felix had no childhood pictures. "It was as if his life began when he left home, went to Cape Town, and got that job with Dr. Latimer, doing research. That's when he got a camera, isn't it, and started recording everything? I have no idea what you and your siblings looked like as kids, or your parents when they were young."

"They were good-looking. Look." Humphrey took out his wallet and splayed two small black-and-white prints between his thumb and forefinger. One face was instantly recognizable—a young woman with light eyes and wide cheekbones, their mother, Elsabet. The resemblance to him and Felix—and to Joanie—was unmistakable. The other was of a man with deep-set eyes and a dark moustache, like an old matinee idol—their father, I assumed.

"Matthew and the girls looked like him," Humphrey said, as if he'd read my mind. "I wanted to be like him—strong and in charge, till I began to see what it did to my mother, the price she paid."

"The price? You mean, like with Felix, sending him away?"

He stared at the picture cupped in his palm. "She seemed afraid to argue with Dad, to contradict anything he said, no matter how much crap he talked."

I remember reading something to that effect in Felix's old journals, a frustration about her passivity. He certainly didn't expect subservience like that from me or the other women in his life. On the contrary, and just as well.

"Was it her religious belief that a wife had to obey her husband?" I asked Humphrey, leaning closer to see her face again.

"Maybe," he said, "or something between them, a deal they'd made with each other. Helga and I go to church—our children were baptized—but we're not blind believers like my folks."

He tossed his head as if to clear it, and turned to the lineup of hats, reaching out and touching each one. There was the swashbuckling Indiana Jones number Felix was wearing when we bumped into each other that day in Los Angeles, a clown hat with a pompom, a sombrero from Mexico. And there was the smart brown fedora he bought and never wore. I can see him in it though. He set it on his head in the store, admired his reflection, and then gave a yelp as he took it off, because the staple holding the price tag had caught in his hair.

"May I put it on?" Humphrey asked.

On impulse, I said, "You can have it," and handed it to him. As the hat passed through a ray of sunlight, a strand glinted inside the crown. I almost drew my hand back, to clutch at that filament of Felix—but Humphrey took it from me, and I said nothing. He set it on his head at a jaunty angle and turned to me with eyebrows raised, his mouth curling in a querying smile.

I wasn't smiling. I was dizzy, floating, just staring up at him, lost. He took off the hat, leaned down towards me. For a frozen moment I saw that beautiful mouth and wanted with all my being to reach up, to meet his lips, but I turned my face away and drew back, gasping.

"My bad," he said. Color had flared up the sides of his face. "I'm sorry." He gave a grunt of laughter. "My big bro would kill me if he saw that. But you are lovely. I've been picturing you for the past two days, remembering the curve of your cheekbones, seeing the blue of your eyes. I've been counting the hours till I could be with you again.

"Felix always did have good taste in women—and a way with them. I remember girls coming to our house looking for him, even when he was really young."

And there it was, the darn pendulum. I really didn't need to be reminded of Felix's way with women. But my skin was tingling from my thighs to my breasts to my face. I wanted the pressure of him against me so much that I was having trouble standing straight.

He was a hypocrite though, professing to be religious and then doing that. On the other hand, I didn't mean to transgress either—and look at me, just as bad.

"When last did you see Felix with anyone?" I managed to ask. I couldn't remember which woman he was living with when Humphrey visited him in the States, or who came with Felix to visit the family in South Africa. Whoever it was, the comparison didn't matter; Boet found me sexy—and that has left me feeling more alive than I have in a long time.

"How are you getting to the airport?" he asked. "Want to share a taxi?"

~ 3 ~

Should I tell Libby about the little brush with Humphrey? She and I sit nattering over lunch. It might shock her though, given that he is married, and she is such an upright citizen who—to the best of my knowledge—has slept with only one man, her husband, Doug. But it would make her happy to hear I'm still open to such things.

We ask our waiter for an array of starters to share, pickled herring and crispy fried pierogi and eggplant caviar, followed by blueberry blintzes. It's exactly what we used to order when I'd bring her to this Russian region of Brooklyn. "Jewish food," she used to call it, true-blue WASP that she is. For me, it's the stuff of nostalgia, the food my Polish mother would make in her new life in South Africa.

Libby looks lovely, still dimpled and girlish, though the chestnut hair has gray roots, and she has gained a few pounds. She was waiting for me as I came through customs and past eager relatives and limo drivers holding up name cards. She used to urge me to color my wild mop too, to keep it red, and she looked a little shocked by how white-haired I am. But that didn't make her hug any less enthusiastic.

"Who was that shaggy fellow in the rainbow T-shirt helping you with your luggage?" she asked. "He looked smitten."

"Oh, nonsense! Just a nice guy, being kind!" I said. "He's also flying on to the West Coast and he shared some delicious chocolate." Aiming to sound offhand, but I had registered his attentiveness. Chatting in the last hour before landing, he told me how he let his granddaughter cut his hair, and that he was a widower. I told him I'd also lost my partner and was going to see my new sort-of grandson. More open than usual; the Humphrey effect? There's still a lingering frisson from—was it just yesterday?

"When do you have to check in for the Portland flight?" Libby asked. She grabbed my luggage cart and offered to take my shoulder bag, but I held on to that. In it was a fragile gift for her, a fabulously kitschy shell ornament of the kind she collects, and two boxes of the South African rooibos tea she loves. "Do we have time to go have lunch somewhere nicer than these fast-food places, maybe at one of your old favorites?"

"We've got five hours," I told her.

I was nervous about leaving the airport, inclined to avoid possible delays with traffic or parking, anything that might make me miss my connection. But her suggestion was enticing. I was hungry for a glimpse of New York and my old haunts. So, we found the car and wove our way onto the parkway.

With the worry about the baby, I hadn't anticipated such eagerness. The place names on the big green and white boards, the speed signs in miles instead of kilometers, even the ugliness of the towering, redbrick apartment blocks—all of it was pleasing in its familiarity. Even the roar of the elevated train line, casting its shade over the bumbling traffic on Brighton Beach Avenue, gave me a thrill.

~ ~ ~ ~

Now, in the restaurant, at my request, Libby produces a fat plastic booklet of photos of her kids and her grandkids. "I promise I don't carry it all the time," she insists. "I popped it in my bag so I could show you my darlings. I wish you could see them in person." They are beautiful, one and all, and all beaming, except the youngest, a solemn toddler staring impatiently at the camera with his fierce blue eyes. It brings me back with a jolt to the fact that I don't know how Freddie is doing.

With an apology to Libby, I find myself a quiet corner of the restaurant and switch my phone from airplane mode and try to dial. But I can't get reception or Gs or whatever the hell it needs. Wrong calling plan? When I look to see if there are messages, all that show are old ones from yesterday. What if Joanie is trying to reach me?

At Libby's urging, I dash out into the teeming street in search of a phone store. A passerby with a heavy Israeli accent points one out to me and kindly offers to take me there, clearly assuming I'm a clueless foreigner. I thank him and escape, and within minutes, guided by the bored but efficient customer service person, have access to the ether. With a beep-beep-beep the phone updates. Messages pour into email and Facebook and wherever.

There are three missed calls from Joanie and one text message. It reads, PLEASE PLEASE CALL ME WHEN YOU SEE THIS! Shivering on the sidewalk, regretting that I left my coat in the restaurant, I listen to the most recent message, but with the rumble of traffic and jabber of passing voices, I can't make out anything except, "Sally, I'm sorry."

I step back into the warmth and quiet of the phone store, nod a thank you to the service person, and play it again. Joanie has a groan in her voice. "You mustn't come. My crazy mother is here after all. She's gone batty over her grandchild and doesn't want to leave. I told her you were coming, and she threw a fit. She really is worried about Freddie. Has already called all the top doctors in the city and made appointments with half a dozen. Sorrysorrysorry."

I press reply and listen as the number dials. It's busy. Try again, and again no luck. I text instead: It's fine. Don't worry. I'm with my friend Libby. We'll make a plan. Will call you this afternoon.

Despite that matter-of-fact tone, I'm reeling. All the rushing, getting catapulted out my safe haven, bracing for the encounter with the baby, longing to hug Joanie—that's come to nothing? What am I doing here?

Libby, of course, says I must come stay with them in Greenwich. A naughty smile makes her dimples deepen. "That's really awful about her mother—but I'm so glad. I get to have you to myself for a real visit." And then, because she is much nicer than me, she says, "You know, being a grandmother myself, I have to say I sympathize a teensy bit. This is her first, isn't it? I don't understand why you can't both be there—that seems mean—but if I were her, I'd want to stay around."

Fair enough; I'm just the unofficial stepmother. I didn't meet Joanie till she was a teenager, when Felix turned up in New York with her and Trevor on a quick visit. That day at the Natural History Museum still glows in my mind. We clicked from the start, but I know blood comes first. Plus, Deidre is a highly successful businesswoman, willing and eager to splash her wealth around. Without her, they would be battling. Money has been tight since Eric started his new design practice, and if Freddie has problems, her assistance might be needed even more.

Suddenly, I'm exhausted. Jet lag or sleep deprivation or whatever, I struggle to finish my lunch and limp back to the car. We return to the airport and Libby waits in the car, double-parked, while I plow through the crowds to go cancel my Portland booking, assuming it'll be easier face-to-face. Doesn't work out that way. They say they can't refund that portion of the ticket. Getting ratty now, I insist that if they won't give me my money, they should be flexible about the booking. Maybe I'll still get to use the ticket. They agree, but just for ten days. If I want to fly after X date, I'll have to pay for a new ticket, which I can't afford.

All I can think about is laying my head on a soft pillow in a darkened room, but it would be smarter to stay awake a few more hours, to get in synch with U.S. time.

I excuse myself right after dinner with Libby and her Doug. Ensconced in their cozy guest bedroom, I write in my diary, and then check my email one more time. Nothing from Joanie. But there is one from "HBarnard," which she forwarded. The name brings a flutter. Wide awake again, I stall, checking out some Facebook posts from friends, and go over a couple of unimportant emails, before letting myself read what Humphrey has written. It could just be a brisk "Go well" or "Give my niece my regards."

Or maybe it's about his reason for visiting me in the first place. Bizarre that we didn't discuss that back then. And those are his first words, kind of:

> Never diid get aroumd to telling you why I came lojking for you. 2 lonmg and complcted to write (and my typing is 2 lame). It's to do with Felix & my mon and old family shut.

So much for autocorrect. Felix always had his turned off. He'd bark, "I don't need some algorithm deciding what I mean to say!" And apparently Humphrey feels the same despite his lack of typing skill. Shut—or shit? Mon—mom? And what about the "before it's too late" part at our first meeting?

There is a second email from him. I click on that, hope rising again. It would be nice to read that he enjoyed meeting me, or he's sorry the visit was cut short.

Actually, it did get prolonged a little; we shared a ride to the airport, as he suggested. Realize with a jolt that I haven't given it a thought since leaving Cape Town, as if a censorship sticker has been pasted over the memory. Too much to absorb? Too many contradictory currents? Now I let myself sink back, as if into an imagined story. Feeling again the cushiness of the backseat of the car, how he reached for my hand, and I let him take it. He leaned forward and kissed me. I kissed him back.

"This is weird," I said to him. "We've only just met. It's so new, yet this feels totally natural. I'm not usually so easy."

"You, easy? —I bet you've never been." He laughed and added, "But in a way this isn't new. I've known about you forever, Felix's amazing redhead dancer."

"Oops, and then you meet this reality."

He shook his head and kissed my fingers. "Still amazing." His tone made me glad I was sitting, supported by the car seat.

We were teasing one another about our vastly different taste in music when a colleague called him with some urgent question. Humphrey winked an apology and proceeded to respond in detail. I started to pull away, but he put his hand on my knee, as if to keep me close.

When he rang off, he looked into my eyes and said, "Where were we when we got so rudely interrupted?"

He was just leaning towards me—I could feel the warmth of his breath and was lifting my face—when his phone buzzed again. I hoped he'd ignore it, but he glanced at the screen and answered, turning to stare out the window as he listened. Evidently, it was his wife, wanting to know why he wasn't back in Port Elizabeth yet. A cold heaviness settled in my stomach. I gathered she wasn't at home either, but he said nothing about meeting me and spun her some story about having to tie up loose ends from the Stellenbosch conference.

The airport was a milling chaos with hordes hurrying in all directions. I nearly ducked back into the car. Humphrey saw me cringe and seemed to understand. He grabbed my luggage cart and led the way to the international check-in area, clearing a path for me right up to the counter. Once there, he turned and cupped my face between his hands, and asked, "Will you be all right?" Then very slowly he kissed me again. I put my arms around his neck, not wanting to let him draw away, until I heard the clerk's brusque "Ma'am, sir, can I help you?"

Humphrey gave me a rueful grin, one last peck on my forehead, and strode away towards the domestic departures. As the clerk flicked through my passport and tapped on his computer, I stared over my shoulder, watching until the white shirt disappeared in the crowd.

~ ~ ~ ~

There's nothing tender in his email, just one question: When will you be back? Ihave a mtg in CT in a fewweeks.

That's enough to raise a silly smirk. How embarrassing—to be this old with the ego of an eighteen-year-old! It's not much, but maybe that's all he's comfortable saying, given that he was asking Joanie to forward the email to me, and she might read it.

Almost too sleepy to stay upright, I undress and pull on a sleepshirt. I take off my glass pendant and slip it into a little velvet pouch. At home, I hang it on a hook by the bathroom mirror, alongside the leather cord with a small, perfect abalone shell that I strung for Felix. I've brought that with me too.

Thoughts are flip-flopping between memory and dream and doubts about this whole expedition.

The piece of glass on my pendant came from a beach south of here, past Cape May. Such a beautiful place. Divorced and fiercely focused on my career, I went a couple of times a year for working holidays. I'd give talks on dance at a local college and at a senior center, or the high school.

I longed to have Felix with me, but he was still living on the West Coast and was on his second marriage, to Nellie—had been for some time before I got divorced. When we did meet up now and then, hard as it was sometimes, we kept the contact strictly platonic.

In my leisure hours in Cape May, I'd prowl the deserted beaches, sifting through the sand in search of translucent pebbles. The tourist literature called them "Cape May diamonds," fragments of glass, apparently from broken bottles, worn smooth by tides. Others might prize the clearest pieces; my treasures were those clouded with a blue-green haze.

I had a bowl of them in my little apartment in Brooklyn, left behind with so much else when, at last, Felix asked me to come be with him in Cape Town. It was right after his first aneurysm. As he told me later, facing death made him push aside his fears and reach for what he wanted most. I caught the next available flight.

The only piece of the sea glass I brought with me was this teardrop. Felix wrapped it in silver wire and threaded it on a chain. He said it was to remind me that now I was safe in his embrace. "No more tears," he said. I had no such poetic theme for the shell I gave him, except that it reminded me of him—rough on the outside and beautiful on the inside. He wore it all the time.

When they came to take his body, the paramedics asked my permission and then gently removed the abalone necklace from around his neck and handed it to me. There was no ring or watch, just this.

Sleep dissolves those thoughts, blending with them. I dream of wafting along a beach with Felix's spectral presence beside me. I struggle to feel the grit of the sand below my feet and will his to have weight too, to prove he is real. I look down at the warm hand holding mine and realize with amazement that the man beside me is sinking into the sand with each stride. I can hear the crunch of the grains. This is no ghost, and when he looks at me his eyes are the color of the curling waves.

~  ~

~ *4* ~

onday morning, I accompany Libby on a shopping
expedition to find stocking stuffers for her children
and grandchildren. Everyone gets a stocking in this household,
me included, she insists.

Greenwich is a mixture of bleak and festive, the skies
colorless and the trees skeletal, but the stores and streets and
homes are all a-twinkle with red and green and gold. Here and
there I spot the blue and white of Hanukkah decorations. You
can hear Yuletide music bouncing out of every doorway.

Libby asserts that it's not all that cold, but I am freezing.
Thinking I'd be heading straight to Oregon, it didn't dawn on
me to pack my winter gear, other than my old down coat. My
nose and toes go numb. "Your blood is still thin. It'll get
thicker," Libby pronounces. No idea if that's medically valid,
but I've gratefully accepted her loan of a woolly scarf and
gloves and a hat.

The cold is helpful in a funny way; it pushes aside the jumble of emotions still vying for dominance. All day yesterday, I vacillated between anxiety about getting to Portland, and whether I should have come at all, and delight at being with Libby and Doug, away from the solitude of Kalk Bay. In a way, this sojourn feels *bashert*—meant to be. It's given me a chance to adjust to being out in the world again.

In these months since Felix's exit, invitations have come from various friends—from Angie in Grahamstown, from dance colleagues in Johannesburg, from Maria in Spain. But to all of them I've been adamant: I wasn't ready to leave my burrow. And yet here I am, energized by the frivolity, wanting to go places and see people.

Look how I'm moving on, I try to tell my ghost, but he hasn't made himself heard since I crossed the Atlantic. Testing me, to see if I can spread my wings alone? I think I'm doing pretty well.

To Libby's surprise, as we stride arm in arm back to the car, I suggest we head into New York, to the Big Apple at Christmastime, at its most hectic. "You're really sure you're up for it?" she asks. "You said you've been a total recluse. Even we locals find it a bit much."

Back at the house, we comb through vouchers for special deals at Broadway theaters, and finally find tickets to a matinee performance of *The Nutcracker* at Carnegie Hall. What could be more festive?

Libby takes my mood as a positive sign about the future. She broaches the idea of me coming back to live in the States. She says, "Look how good you feel here. You always fitted in like a native, as if you'd been here all your life. We'll introduce you to new people, help you find a job if you want one." The idea sounds so much more feasible than it would have back in Kalk Bay. I still have the condo in Brooklyn Heights, bought after my divorce from Charles. It's rented out and very small, but it's still mine. I could reclaim it.

"And maybe, maybe you'll meet someone," Libby can't help adding. I nearly tell her about Humphrey but hold back.

Instead, our conversation turns to his niece and her baby. Doug is a doctor, a family GP, not a pediatrician, as he has emphasized to me, but he is curious to know what is wrong with Freddie. I have only a rudimentary idea. In my jetlagged state after arriving, I took notes on what Joanie told me, guessing at the spelling of the medical terms that tumbled from her mouth. I've read those to Doug.

Freddie doesn't have cerebral palsy or spina bifida, that much seems clear. But something seems to be amiss with his neuroskeletal development and—or—his digestive system. They can't narrow it down yet, but the upshot thus far, Doug agrees, is "failure to thrive." That's a term I understand, but it's infuriatingly vague.

When she called yesterday, Joanie said, "They can't work out why he doesn't want to feed—not from the breast or from a bottle. My boobs are bursting, but he sucks for a moment or two and then turns away." The nurses are making her express milk, to relieve the pressure but also to keep it coming in, for when he does decide to feed.

"But each time we get some milk into him, he starts crying," she said, choking up. "It's heartbreaking. He sounds like a little kitten, mewling. He's in pain." She started sobbing and that made me tear up too. I long to hug her—yet when I think of her child, I'm almost glad I can't be there. A wall of terror goes up when I think of opening up to him. Rather not start bonding with him if he is going to leave us, if there's going to be another awful wound.

~ ~ ~ ~

Mid-afternoon now, midday in Portland. Joanie has said not to call in case her mother is around, rather to text her when I want to talk, and she'll call back as soon as the coast is clear. So, I do that. Then pace around my room, waiting.

I check out the books in the bookcase—mostly old family favorites, like *Curious George* and *Goodnight Moon*. They're not what I grew up with; my parents were into the classics and hadn't yet discovered more recent English-language children's literature. I got Hans Christian Andersen and the Brothers Grimm.

On the bottom shelf, among the big, illustrated volumes, I spot my first book, *New Steps*, published way back when I was married to Charles. A different life—both of us teaching, attending concerts, entertaining our friends and his family. Chatting now and then with Felix, trying to keep thoughts of him way back in my mind.

I settle into an armchair and flick through the pages. Its handsome cover is dog-eared, which delights me—proof of much handling. For years it was displayed on the coffee table in their living room. Libby was so proud of it, and I was too. It opened doors for me, to give lectures and workshops on different dance traditions from around the world and how they can be used to introduce children to other cultures. Because of that book, I traveled to countries I might never have visited, and met amazing dancers and educators.

Felix liked it, but with reservations. He thought my text was too theoretical, that I hadn't included enough of my own experience and my views on the therapeutic power of rhythmic movement. He suggested I do another, more personal book. I loved the concept but didn't have the time to undertake such an ambitious project.

And very soon after that, life turned upside down. Charles and I split up, and I lost my job and my home. Without *New Steps*, I don't know how I would have found my footing again.

It wasn't until a few years later that the idea for *Next Steps* emerged. Felix and I were chatting on the phone, as we did every few weeks. He was uncharacteristically down, fed up with his job and feeling uninspired. It hurt to hear him so glum. "What if we do a book together, combining your research and my teaching?" I asked. "What if we team up?"

There was a long moment of silence, and then Felix bellowed, "Yes!"

I can still feel how my cheek pushed up against the phone at my ear, my smile wide enough to ache. I don't know who came up with the title, he or I, simply remember our excitement, fizzing like champagne out of an uncorked bottle.

Frustration lifts me to my feet and drops me back into the chair. The early winter gloom, so different from the golden midsummer evenings I've come from, creeps into my bones. The room is already dark enough for the stars stuck onto the dark blue ceiling to glimmer into view. If I strain to see, I can make out a few here and there, but the constellations are incomplete.

Not only did we have this potential work partnership, but for the first time in so long, we were both single. Nellie had left Felix for a younger man. He seemed okay with it. "What chance did I stand? He's an ebony Adonis," he told me. But he sounded lonely and ready to move on. Life felt lush with possibility.

We arranged that he would fly out from San Francisco and meet me in postcard-pretty Greenport, out on Long Island, to start weaving together our ideas. It was the perfect setting, I fancied, for the last chapter of a romance novel, the lead-up to a "happily ever after" ending.

Except, of course, that isn't what happened. We screwed up. I try to block any further memories, but they hover into view like the stars above me, dim and jagged. If things had worked out, we might have had much more than five years together. And I wouldn't be struggling now to write our book by myself; it could have been in bookstores long ago.

You were so obstinate, I tell the absent ghost.

I know what his response would be and almost hear it: *Not half as obstinate as you.*

We began quite calmly, laying out our respective ideas. Two intellectuals, both passionate about our fields. But field turned into territory, which turned into turf. Seemingly out of nowhere, each turned defensive. I thought he was obsessing over statistics; he accused me of haphazard improvisation in my approach, said it could cause injuries. That infuriated me. The arguing spiraled, drawing on older and older charges that had nothing to do with dance or therapy.

Were we too rigid—or too afraid? I wanted to hate whatever had skewed our usual harmony, but who could I blame?

Two very bruised people said goodbye that Monday morning. Though we did eventually get back in touch, the book project was derailed, and so was the flirtatious bond between us that had nurtured my hope for so many years.

The regret still stings, as sharp as if it were yesterday. I have to remind myself that eventually the love part came right, when we reunited in Cape Town. But the collaboration did not. Through our few years of domestic bliss, we both avoided the subject. I assumed Felix had lost interest in the book idea. Evidently, he made the same assumption about me.

I discovered how wrong I'd been too late. Clearing out boxes after his death, I unearthed a dusty cache of his files from underneath our bed. Casually at first, and then with mounting astonishment, I flicked through the pages. They were full of typed case studies and handwritten notes, all relating to dance.

Frustration percolates all over again. Working together on his brilliant ideas would have been so exhilarating. But perhaps we would have clashed again. It might have ruined our hard-won happiness. Maybe, finally, it did have to be a solo effort.

But what's the use of all his work—and mine —if, in the end, I can't get our book out into the world?

The radiator is hissing, warming the room, but I'm chilled to my core and exhausted. That book business was typical of our stupidity—in our youth and even when we were older and supposedly wiser. We would go silent, avoiding touchy topics, always imagining there'd be another chance to tackle the tough stuff.

Enough! I'm so tired of myself and my silly ego. No more hanging back with anyone. With a tug that almost knocks it over, I turn on the lamp next to me. I haven't answered Humphrey's email yet. Maybe I should tell him how happy he made me, that yes, his kiss was wrong, but I want to do it again.

This is what I know: The thing with Humphrey isn't parallel to what happened in LA with Felix. Then I thought my marriage was over. Felix said he and Deidre were only staying together because of Joanie. But this man seems entrenched in his marriage. And he has four children. Besides, did he feel anything more than a fleeting wave of lust? Maybe that's all I felt too. Maybe he's a player and a habitual flirt. On impulse, I pick up my phone. Type a cool, curt response to Humphrey's question about New Year: Plans here up in the air. In Connecticut still. No idea when I'll get home.

And then curiosity pushes its way to the fore. Honesty requires facts. I add: So perhaps you ought to tell me what the big issue was—or is. Get your secretary to type it for you—if you have one. Or do a voice dictation. Don't these gadgets do that?

I hit SEND.

~ ~ ~ ~

Next morning, the cuckoo clock wakes me with its rise-and-shine chirps. I'm too cozy under the big soft duvet to move. Dreaming gives way to daydreaming, my eyes cruising over the family pictures that adorn the walls. This room has been a haven for me before, the first time more than thirty years ago. The infant portraits draw me in most of all.

But no time to dwell on that now. Libby will be up and preparing breakfast. I should go join her.

She is setting the breakfast table when I enter, using the bright blue tea set I gave her when she got married. It bears a few nicks and cracks, but I love the fact that she still cherishes it. I help her put out toasted English muffins and some homemade jellies. My pal is her usual sunny self, and I try to match her good cheer.

To my astonishment, Libby stops what she is doing and says, "Remember when you came here after your miscarriage?" It is almost as if she has heard my thoughts from upstairs. With yesterday's resolution about honesty still sharp in my mind, I almost start to tell her the part I never shared.

Libby knows only that I lost a baby and mourned with me. She assumed it was Charles's child, and I said nothing about my own uncertainty. I didn't mention Felix, whom she knew as a lover from my college days in South Africa, someone I'd lost my virginity to. It was the kind of thing we'd confided to one another as college roommates. I had told her about bumping into him on my California trip, but not quite how ecstatic it was, or all that transpired.

She doesn't know why, a decade later, Charles pushed me out of our beautiful brownstone apartment. Doesn't know that was when he finally put two and two together about "our" lost baby. She knows only that by then he was having another affair, yet somehow managed to blame me for our marriage failing. That was enough to dim her wide-eyed admiration for my handsome professor.

"Sorry," she says, "I just have babies on my mind. But thinking of Freddie, could there be a family problem—you know, something amiss on Joanie's side or on Eric's?"

The same question has buzzed around in my head. "I wish I knew," I tell her.

"Let's see what we can find out," she murmurs. I expect Libby to call Doug for answers, the way she has always done. He is semi-retired but has gone into the surgery to see some old patients. But instead of dialing his work number, she first texts a query to their eldest, Bridget, who is a therapist working with children with developmental issues. "The young are more up to date on this new stuff," she says. There's a fleeting note of something else there. Doug is quite a bit older than she is and beginning to get forgetful. Is he no longer the authority she always saw him as?

Bridget texts back within minutes. Libby reads the message with her bottom lip sucked in and then repeats it to me. "Hm, this is good and bad. She says they've made amazing strides in understanding genes, but the sooner they can pinpoint the problem and correct it, the better. She asks if you know what tests they're doing."

The kettle whistles, and she jumps up to silence it. I spoon rooibos leaves into the teapot and hand it to her to fill. We make such a good team. I tell her, "I assume Joanie and Eric—and her mother and their doctors—will be considering all the possibilities. I need to be careful how I ask, not to sound as if I'm interfering."

I think it will be all right. Since Joanie's interrogation of me back in Kalk Bay, we've had a new level of intimacy. That communication still delights me. Is it only childless people who are amazed by how kids grow up and turn into equals and friends? Joanie can be volatile, but I adore discussing life with her. Trevor, in his laidback way, has become a pal too. I smile at the thought of them.

Libby sees my expression and smiles too. "Go get your coat," she says. "If you want to have a meander around your old Manhattan haunts before the matinee, we need to get going!"

~ ~ ~ ~

Working things backwards: The show, a holiday special, starts at 2:30. We should be there by 2:15 at the latest. Maybe get a snack before. It would be good to get to the Theater District by 1:00. We're taking the train to Grand Central. I want to pop in to see the magnificent murals in the renovated 42nd Street Library, where I used to spend hours doing research. And maybe we can go see the skating rink at Rockefeller Center, if the crowds aren't too dense.

On the train, Libby is accosted by one of her many cousins, delighted to see her and eager to catch her up on family news, the deaths and weddings and births. My mind drifts to Libby's question.

Maybe my little one didn't fancy the mess she or he would have been born into. By comparison, in this way at least, Freddie is blessed: Joanie and Eric cherish each other. Charles and I certainly didn't any longer, though both of us believed that with the right attitude and effort—and a hefty dose of forgetting—we could still forge a happy family.

For so long, I'd been hoping to get pregnant. Now, at last

the miracle was happening, but my joy was undermined by uncertainty. How would my husband and his raven-haired clan respond if this red-haired daughter-in-law produced a white-blond child (like Felix's little girl)?

I decided to have an abortion. Made an appointment and went to a clinic, but I couldn't go through with it. Body and mind were already in mothering mode. I was in love with my child.

And then fate decided the whole thing. It ended with a heartbreaking, bloody mess. We had no idea why. "It's just one of those things," the doctor said. "Try again. Next time, it will go better."

There would be no next time. Years later, confirmation came that Charles was sterile and that my baby must have been Felix's, a fact that comforted me even as it broke apart my marriage. Her brief existence was yet another bond with my beloved.

~ ~ ~ ~

Back in the city where I lost my baby. Back where every day brought challenges and lessons. From passersby in the street, like on every TV channel, I hear fragments of anxious political talk. When I left six years ago, there were still posters up that spoke of new hope. Now headlines quote this president-elect who talks about reclaiming America's past glory.

But otherwise, to the eye, all is fine, a wonderland of twinkling abundance. I've forgotten how to dodge the hurrying masses, and I keep getting jostled, but it's exhilarating, even having to navigate the icy slush at every intersection.

Libby wants to buy me a new winter coat as a Christmas gift. The turquoise one I've brought with me is fraying around the cuffs. She says it's older than her kids and it's time for something new. So, we dip into tastefully sparkly Saks Fifth Avenue, and I reluctantly agree to try on some options, as long as I can find the same blue as the coat I'm wearing. Libby makes me choose a woolly hat too, because I've been borrowing one from her to shield my frozen ears. It's a vibrant orangey red, and on impulse I buy myself a silky Indian scarf that combines those shades. I haven't worn this much color since when? Last summer, I reckon.

Walking out of the store adorned in my new finery, a reflection from a mirrored pillar beams back a pleasing illusion: In this color, with the red hat concealing my unred hair and the pompom on top like the ballet bun I used to wear, I look almost like my long-ago self.

The show is fabulous. We come out bubbling with praise for the costumes and the vivacity of the dancers and gossiping about the couple sitting in front of us who looked like illicit lovers. We wrap up again and head to the exit, dipping and swaying together, remembering the music.

And then, as we weave through the chattering crowd, a figure up ahead does a double take. An elderly woman, a little hunched but very elegant with a lacquered helmet of snowy hair, is staring at me. I realize who she is because I recognize the younger man beside her, equally well groomed, with a lurching limp. I freeze, my heart going into overdrive. The woman yanks at her companion's arm, doesn't point, but she thrusts her chin forward to direct his attention.

Libby is a few steps ahead of me before she realizes I've stopped. She loops back with a questioning smile, turns to see where I'm looking and gasps, "Charles?"

It is as if the long memory trip from this morning has manifested these people, but I should have anticipated their presence. The family always had season tickets. We would come together to almost every show.

Can I dodge, dash away as if we haven't seen them? That would be childish and rude—though my ex-mother-in-law is the one who cut contact with me. I wanted so much to stay in touch, to explain to her that I had only transgressed once. I loved her and Ben and their big, affectionate brood. They were the family I'd always craved. The loneliness without them was terrible. But I understood their loyalty to Charles, and I knew he would never tell them the whole truth. In her eyes, clearly, I was a betrayer, a cheating hussy.

I clutch at my pendant as if it contains my self-respect, but all the confidence from years of teaching and travel and life experience has evaporated. No Humphrey glow, just a bereft sort-of widow with no money and no idea what she is doing back in the city where her life once got ripped apart. The milling throng of New Yorkers are Ethel's people, her allies. They would be sure to take her side against this foreigner.

She is tottering forward, her face as blank as a mask. "Sally? It's good to see you." I'm still puzzled that she has recognized me till I remember how I look in the red hat and blue coat. We go into a stiff, tentative hug. She feels much smaller than before, birdlike. I'm scared to squeeze her—and already she has pulled back.

Libby and Charles are shaking hands, exclaiming how well each looks, making polite noises. And then he turns, and we greet each other.

"Sally."

"Charles."

The ushers are trying to herd us out so they can start preparing for the evening audiences. We head into the chilly twilight and stand hunched in our coats, commenting on the performance. "Let's go have a cup of coffee," Ethel says. It's an instruction more than a suggestion, to Charles as much as to Libby and me. There is a purposefulness to her tone.

"I know a good place across Broadway. Ben and I used to go there all the time," she says. Adjusting to her pace, we make our way down the block, wait for the traffic lights to halt the lanes of yellow cabs and long, lumbering buses, and cross the avenue painfully slowly. Could it be that she doesn't remember what happened, that she has a touch of dementia? I'm half hoping for that, but since she has remembered who Libby is and is bright-eyed and determined, it seems unlikely. The density and rush-hour noise are an assault for which I no longer have the requisite armor. I plow through it, dazed, following my ex and his mother.

Facing each other across the table, Ethel scrutinizes me. With the hat off, my white hair is probably a matted mess. I make one futile attempt to smooth it back. I definitely have no lipstick left on.

"You have aged a lot," she states. "And you're too thin." I laugh. She has also aged a lot, though I'm too polite to say it. But Libby is shocked. Fierce in my defense, she says, "Well,

Sally has been through an extremely hard time. She's been working very hard on her new book, and—poor girl—she's still getting over …"

Ethel tilts her head with an inquiring look of sympathy, and I know what the next words out of Libby's mouth will be. That mustn't happen. If we mention Felix, the goodwill we're all trying so hard to maintain will shrivel. I kick her ankle under the table, and she stops with a look of indignation.

"Life!" I exclaim, and add, my Jewish roots surfacing, "Who doesn't have *tsuris?*" Fairly sure of the reply, I ask, "Ben, has he …?"

Charles reaches for his mother's hand, saving her from answering. "Dad died last year—almost exactly twelve months ago. It was a long time coming, though. After all his suffering, a blessed release, wasn't it, Mother?"

She nods, her lips pressed together. I am sad, fighting back tears. What right do I have to cry for a man I last saw twenty years ago or more? I remember him as cheerful, dapper, and domineering, always ready with advice, but always kind. I never considered bypassing Ethel, but it's possible that if I had contacted him directly, appealed to him, he might have insisted that she see me. He was the one person she bowed to. But I didn't reach out.

I just say, "I'm sorry. Long life." And she nods again.

To lighten the mood, I say to Charles, "How is Dorothea? And your son? He must be all grown up." This time, Ethel steps in, evidently to help Charles. He is looking everywhere but at me, casting about the room as if finding a waiter is the most urgent mission in the world.

She says, "Dorothea is in Switzerland."

A waiter comes to our table. Libby and Ethel ask for coffee, I ask for hot chocolate, thinking it will help thaw my chilled hands. Charles orders the same—and then shoots me a sly look that makes my stomach lurch. His hair is a dark metallic gray—that men's hair coloring probably—and he has developed jowls, but his face is still very expressive. I know what he's thinking. Our very first date, I invited him to my place for hot chocolate.

"I want marshmallows on mine," I declare, one-upping the nostalgia.

Libby chirps, "How lovely! I adore Switzerland. How long will she be there?"

Ethel snaps, "Too long. She's staying there, living very nicely at Charles's expense."

He frowns at her. "Mother! Jason is there. He's studying at the Jung Institute. She feels he's too young to be abroad by himself, so she has relocated for the duration of his course."

"Oh my!" Libby exclaims. It's the perfect response, conveying neutral surprise that can be taken as shock or disapproval, depending on one's own view. Mother and son both glance at her with gratitude. She breezes on, asking if they have a photo of Jason. "I'd love to see him!"

I'm curious too and doing my best not to display very old antagonism towards Dorothea. There's a woman sitting across from us who reminds me of her, big-bosomed, with big hair and a big voice, occupying her space with the same air of sturdy entitlement I liked in Dorothea. She and I were buddies for years. As the secretary in Charles's department at City

University, she was the source of all the best gossip. Whenever I called in search of my husband, she would first fill me in on the latest—that is, until he and she became the topic *du jour.* Probably the whole department and the departmental spouses knew before I recognized why our chitchats had ended.

The woman across the way has received her dessert, a piled-high pavlova, and is digging into it with voracious determination. I hear at the back of my mind fragments of the phone call when the penny dropped, Dorothea yelling at me that I was wasting my time trying to win Charles back, which I wasn't. I had dinner guests seated just a few feet away in my cramped studio apartment, earnestly trying to make whispered conversation. What a sucker I'd been. "Wrong number!" I told them and hung up on her.

"Oh, my goodness, who does he look like?" Libby asks, all warm innocence, holding up the snapshot Ethel has handed her. "Maybe your eyes, Charles? Or is he more like his mother's side? My children all turned out like carbon copies of Doug. I might as well have been their stepmother!"

Charles is watching me. I feel it like heat as I peer intently at the photo. The boy is very handsome, with his mother's bold features and full mouth. Of course, there is nothing of Charles there; Jason was a sperm-donor baby.

So much is crisscrossing between us—without a word uttered. I might have had a child too if Charles hadn't refused to seek medical help throughout our years of hope and disappointment. He was so sure the problem wasn't on his side; therefore, it must be on mine. I would have been happy to adopt, but he ruled that out too. "You never know what you might be getting with someone else's ancestry," he'd say.

Really, I'm glad for him that Dorothea was more forceful, that he finally got to experience fatherhood. Jason sounds smart and looks healthy. And I have gotten to experience parental love of a wonderful kind with Trevor and Joanie. And now, if I can get to see Freddie, hopefully I will get to enjoy grandmotherhood—of a kind.

But Charles doesn't know all that. He is looking directly at me now, his eyes still brandy brown, though not as intense as they were. This silence is new; he used to hold forth continually, center stage in any group. Is it his mother's presence or his wife's absence that has deflated him—or mellowed him? Like the flute theme that threaded through the bassoons in the show, I hear again the enthusiasm of our first conversations, my pleasure in his earnest intellectualism, his pride in my dancing. We did love each other once upon a time.

His eyebrows are raised in the middle, giving him a contrite look. Is he signaling guilt, regret, pity? Perhaps regret, and maybe pity, but certainly not guilt. Anger is spreading up through my chest. I want so much to tell him that everything turned out fine for me. It did, aside from my beloved bursting an artery, and now this baby being sick.

Ethel looks at her son and then at me. The next moment she blurts it out: "You know, Sally, if you persisted a little harder to sort out your fertility problems, you could have had a boy like that. My son could have stayed happily married. Instead, he got snatched up by that *shiksa*, and now he's stuck paying for her to live like a queen in Zurich!"

"Mother!" Charles barks. "And she's in Basel."

"Sorry, Elizabeth," she says to Libby. "But she's a bitch, and you know it, Charles!"

So, Ethel doesn't know about the insemination. I wonder if Ben did. For all its warmth, this family was riddled with conflicts and secrets. And evidently some things haven't changed. I remember reading somewhere that old age doesn't alter people, it just makes them more fully who they've been all along. That is, of course, if dementia doesn't dismantle their minds. The Ethel I knew would never have spoken so bluntly—but it's not out of character; she always let you know exactly how she felt.

But right now, she is including me in her condemnation, and I am dying to respond. If she and I could talk freely, I could explain. Maybe we could recapture the rapport we had. When my beloved Imma died of cancer far away in South Africa, she was the person who called every day to see how I was doing, took me out for cheer-up sessions, made sure my birthdays were still special. Losing her was another bereavement.

She must be in her late eighties, even early nineties—I've lost track—but maybe it's not too late. Even long-distance, she and I could still be friends. But Charles is signaling that they need to get going. And Libby is getting anxious about us missing our train; she is always home in time to feed Doug. She also wants to get started on holiday baking and decorating.

"How long are you here for?" Ethel asks as Charles helps her into her coat.

"I don't know. It's complicated," I tell her.

As Charles goes to pay, Ethel suddenly grabs my hand.

"I want to talk to you," she says. "Give me your number." I dig in my bag for a page of notepaper and write my cellphone number and email address. We haven't actually mentioned where I'm living these days, just that I'm visiting with Libby.

"You're writing a new book? What is it about?" Ethel glances over her shoulder at her son, still busy at the cash register, and whispers, "I still have your other book, you know. It's very good. Do you have a publisher for this new one? I know an agent who might be interested, the daughter of a friend. Perhaps I can introduce you to her."

I'm too stunned to say anything, and Charles is back. We say our goodbyes and they leave. I don my new blue coat and pull on the wool hat, tucking my hair under it, and put on scarf and gloves. All the palaver of winter that I haven't had these past six years, but in this stunned state of mind, the old movements click in automatically. Libby hails a cab, and we make it to Grand Central with minutes to spare for our train, squeezing our way through the home-going commuters and Christmas shoppers with their bunches of bags. It isn't until we flop onto our seats that I realize I haven't uttered a word since leaving Charles and Ethel.

Libby is looking at me with wide eyes. "I don't know what was going on there," she says, "but it was like being in the middle of a Eugene O'Neill play. Everyone was talking in riddles. Why didn't you want me to tell them about Felix?"

This dilemma again: If you believe in honesty and the value of telling the truth, just how important is it to share the whole story?—to let the chips fall wherever? If I want Ethel to have the full picture, isn't it even more important to come clean with this beloved friend, this woman who has stood by me through so much?

"You might not like me as much after this, but you deserve to know," I tell her, raising my voice to be heard over the thrum of train noise. "I'm going to tell you why Charles divorced me." I brace myself to begin, but just then two men slide into the seats next to us. She is looking at me eagerly, but I shake my head, and say, "I will tell you. But not here, not now." Not sure if it's out of cowardice or discretion, or simply emotional exhaustion.

~ *5* ~

Snow has blanketed the garden beyond my bedroom window. A pristine layer covers the lawn, almost blue in the shadow cast by the towering cypress trees. As I watch, the sun grows brighter, edging each shape with a line of silver and turning the vista into a medieval woodcut. I could stay right here, in bed, propped up against the pillows, doing nothing but stare.

A tentative double tap at my door breaks the reverie. "Are you awake?" Libby elbows her way into the room, clutching a tray laden with plates and food. "If the mountain won't come to me, I'll come to it," she declares. "You've awakened so early every morning till now, I got worried." She pauses. "Are you all right?"

"I'm fine, just not ready to move. Maybe the jet lag is wearing off. Took a long time to fall asleep last night and couldn't surface this morning. Maybe it was the eggnog Bridget brought. I loved doing the tree with her kids."

Stalling, dreading the conversation I promised her days ago—that she seems to have forgotten all about. But it's true we had a good time last night, stringing up tinsel and hanging all the ornaments, each fragile treasure unwrapped from its nest of tissue paper and greeted with the question: "Who knows where this one came from?" The grandkids were competing to answer or turning to Grandpa Doug for help. He is the family recordkeeper and arbiter of all things historical. A couple of times I saw Libby tip her head, give it a little shake, and then shrug. If he said this bauble came from Great Aunt So-and-So, it did; if he insisted the green elf or the little tin Santa were purchased on their honeymoon in London, she agreed.

I watched them interact in awe, impressed as always by how effortlessly they mesh. There was a time when it upset me, the way she elevated men—even her own son over her daughters— just as her mother did. I had to bite my tongue when I was around them, though I noticed that her daughter doesn't. A couple of times Bridget butted in to correct her dad.

Libby returns, carefully toting two mugs of coffee. She dabs butter on a muffin, dollops on jelly, and hands it to me as if I'm a kid, before doing one for herself. I balance the plate on my comforter-covered lap, already spilling crumbs as she bounces onto the edge of the bed. This is a messy idea, but we're giggling like children.

"This afternoon let's go sledding," I say. I haven't been for years and years. What better way to forget about everything except cold and speed?

The park is Christmas-card perfect. The white panorama

is dotted with Crayola-colored figures trudging up the hillside or zooming down it, squealing or roaring with glee. Doug has come along, and the three of us, each toting some form of sled—metal and wood classic for him, Styrofoam bellyboard for me and inflated vinyl tire for Libby—make our way to the crest. First Doug, then Libby launches into a descent.

I wait, taking it all in, inhaling deeply, feeling the echoes of past winters. There is no Felix in this; we never experienced proper snow together. The memories are of my first winters in Boston as a student, open to everything, learning how to survive and thrive, with Libby as my guide, and then with Charles as my partner. He had—still has—that limp from childhood polio, and it made walking in snow extra challenging, and he didn't enjoy skiing, but he was a master sledder. I was taught by the best.

With a mental thank-you to him, I hurl myself headfirst down the slope. For a few glorious seconds, there's just the swoosh of passing whiteness and gathering speed, before a bump flings me off balance and into a tumble that won't slow, round and round, down the hill. I land with my face pressed into icy froth, no idea which way is up. I flip over and lie there utterly free—of gravity and worry, past and present.

Okay, it's been a long time. This requires full attention. I brush myself off, grab the cord on my snowboard, and slog back up the incline, impatient to try again, this time with balance in mind. Libby, in her bright pink snowsuit, flies by me, and I meet with her moments later down below. Puffing and panting, we head together back up to the crest.

Five slides—or, rather, the five treks back up the hill—are

all I can handle. The downward part I could do all day once I get back the technique. But with hands and feet frozen and snow coming in horizontal squalls, we agree we've had enough. On the way home, Doug pulls into the drive-up window of a Wendy's and orders hot chocolate for all three of us. We park and sit in the car, with our rosy cheeks and noses, just for a while not going anywhere, as carefree as kids.

~ ~ ~ ~

Back at the house, Libby notices a message for me on the house phone. It's from Joanie. Apparently, she was unable to reach my cell. She has left a message asking me to call between two and three my time, when she's sure her mother won't be around.

When I check my phone, I see an email from Humphrey, all in bold type. It's taken him long enough to answer. I feel petulant and excited at the same time, with a wisp of premonition that this message will convey more than the previous one. As I wait for it to appear on the screen, I summon up the image of his clear, smiling eyes and his mouth with the twist at the corners. My body remembers that first moment in the attic, feeling the warmth all the way down my back, my butt, my legs, knowing he was right behind me, aroused.

Hi, Bunnington. (haha isn't that what they called you at universsty? Because you've got such cutte buns?) Sorrry this has taken so long. I have ben trying to work out that voice dictation thing you mentioned but I haven't got it right. I'm trying to type more careffuly.

I'm grinning as I decipher his words. There's something

touching about the effort evident in those lines, even with that dumb old nickname (inflicted because of the way I wore my hair, still a would-be ballet dancer back then —not because of my rear).

When r you coming back? I askd that before. Is Joanie's baby doing all right? Great if you get to see them but I misss you. It was amazing being with you. Stay warm. Have a good Chrstmas. P.S. Can we talk?. That stuff I came to see you about. is hard to write it with two fingrs.

For a few minutes, I let the glow seep in, the sweetness of having my interest reciprocated. It wasn't just my imagination. Or if it was, it's in his imagination too. As for why he came to see me, right now I don't much care.

I wait till a few minutes past two o'clock and call Joanie.

Freddie is doing better. His weight is holding steady, and he isn't crying as much. The doctors have agreed to let them take him home. Joanie is thrilled. Her mother has hired a live-in baby nurse, and once the obstetrician has done a final checkup, he has promised they can leave. For now, she is relaxing in the ward, waiting. I tell her about the sledding, and she's envious, says they haven't seen a real winter in ages.

And I tell her about meeting Charles and Ethel. It feels like weeks ago.

"You all sat and chatted as though everything was fine?" Joanie asks.

"I don't know how you could do that. It's so civilized. I'd have told his mother right there what a scumbag her son was, how he had no right to kick you out!"

Talking of people who're angry, it's been on my mind to ask what Deidre's problem is. "So, why does your mother hate me?" I venture.

I hear her groan. "It's my fault," she sighs, "me and my big mouth. She and I had an awful fight around the time of the elections. She started with how maybe that idiot would be good for the economy, that her shares have already gone up because there is more confidence. I said all she thinks about is money, and I didn't know how she gave birth to me. She yelled something about how ungrateful I am, and I'm as deluded as my dad was. I said, 'I wish Sally was my mother,' and that you nearly were. She said, 'What the hell do you mean? Anyway, she was barren, wasn't she?' That flipped my lid. I told her you got pregnant by dad and—yeah, well, that didn't go down too well."

I just say, "Oops." Any hope I had of getting to see her and the baby, of Deidre mellowing out enough to accept my presence, has just turned to ashes. The extension on my booking expires the day after tomorrow. This whole trip was a giant mistake.

Joanie's voice is almost inaudible. She whispers, "I'm sorry. I'm an idiot, I know. But I'm so grateful you were willing to come. Just knowing you were, that you're nearer, on this continent, helps somehow. I love you."

I say, "I love you more." She laughs and we ring off.

I'm sitting on my bed, slumped with the phone in my lap, when Libby sticks her head around the door. She comes in and sits down next to me and puts her arm around my shoulders. "You don't mind that I come looking for you, do you?" she asks. I shake my head emphatically. "What's this all about?"

"Remember what I mentioned on the train the other night? I might as well tell you now, the whole story."

"You don't need to," she says. "It's ancient history, whatever happened with Charles."

"Actually, it's what happened with Felix, and it's even more ancient history—but it's not over. Does anything we do ever just go away, disappear out of the universe?"

I stand up and plant myself with my arms wrapped around my ribs.

"It's the reason I can't go to Portland. This is the story: I had a night of wild passion with Felix a few years after Charles and I got married, when he was still with Deidre." Libby's eyebrows rise. I push on. "Remember when I got pregnant and had the miscarriage? That was Felix's. Charles found out ten years later. That's really what kept me awake last night, trying to work out how to tell you."

Her mouth falls open. Something I take to be grief puckers her face. "You were the one cheating on him, not the other way around? Oh, Sally…" Her hands have gone slack, resting with palms up on her thighs.

My tongue feels paralyzed. I can't say anything. Too much is going on in her, I can see it in the blotched red in her cheeks. She must be thinking I'm not who she thought I was, not the victim but the victimizer. I don't know where to begin. Finally, I croak, "Yes, the other way around. But he was involved with Dorothea and had been for I don't know how long."

"But you—"

"Only that one time. I had an excuse. I'd just found out

Charles had been sleeping with one of his students, maybe one of a succession." My voice goes whiny; I can hear it myself. "He'd called me the day before, while I was in California, ignoring the time difference from New York, ignoring the fact that I had a big presentation to give the next day, woke me so that he could confess his disgusting behavior and demand that I forgive him."

I stop. "That wasn't really an excuse. I simply couldn't resist the desire. But for me that wonderful night with Felix was a one-time thing, pure therapy. Not that I didn't want to make love every time I saw him. Oh God, I wanted to so much. But we didn't, Libby. We never did it again, not until years after the divorce—until Kalk Bay."

"How did Charles find out?" she asks finally.

"He and Dorothea were screwing like rabbits, and she wasn't getting pregnant." She pulls in her chin at that crudeness, but listens, frowning. "He discovered he couldn't make babies—probably an aftereffect from the polio he had as a kid. And he realized that my pregnancy all those years back had to be with someone else."

She's my mother confessor, if there is such a thing, and I want expiation.

I say, "The worst is that I was dishonest with Charles, let him think I was so virtuous. I deserved his anger, even if he did worse."

"Hiding the truth can be a punishment in itself," Libby says. She is silent for a long time, and I simply wait. "I know. I had an affair too."

Now I'm the one with saucer eyes. It's the last thing I'd

expected to hear. Saint Libby?!

"Don't stare at me like that!" she squawks, rising and clutching my shoulders. "Oh my, you and I are a pair of scarlet women," and she starts giggling. "Funny, we don't look scarlet." I hug her, with a great draft of relief erupting. And astonishment. She kept such a secret from me, and I never suspected a thing.

"Tell me all about it. With whom? When?"

"Oh, nobody significant," she says. "But worse than you—we did it four times. It wasn't even that enjoyable. He was so excited; it was always over before I felt anything. I got bored. But I was so cross with Doug, it felt good just to be bad."

My eyebrows rise. She shrugs. "He and I were going through a terrible patch, fighting about everything. He hadn't touched me in months. But I felt horribly guilty. Oh, lordy, I was miserable. So, I told him, and he cried, got really upset. And he apologized to me, which made me feel ten times worse. We went into therapy—and the rest is history. It did us a world of good. I recommend a fling to all my friends with marital trouble."

That's not true; she never recommended it to me. But I love her for claiming that. I feel as light as a balloon. Snow is wafting down again outside, sparkling like a benediction.

Libby exclaims, "If only we'd had this conversation the other morning before we went to the city. I wouldn't have felt like such a clueless idiot with Charles and his mom. And you wouldn't have spent all this time worrying, you silly thing! Oh, I can't believe how much you suffered for one little transgression. You're such a moral human being."

"Me? You're the one who's moral," I say. "But I've got one more thing to tell you." I'm feeling a little giddy and reckless. "I kind of want to do it again, at my age now, with another married man."

She giggles, her hands on her cheeks. "Who? Tell me everything!"

"Felix's brother."

"Oh my," Libby says. "Oh my." Her hands are over her mouth. She peers at me, not in disapproval, but something worse—pity? I look away, start busily straightening out my pillow, smoothing the comforter. I want her to leave the room.

~ 6 ~

On Saturday, Libby and Doug have a brunch date with friends. I'm invited too, but I beg off. In desperate need of time alone. The sudden exposure to this much company and communication has been wonderful, but I feel emotionally sunburned, tender all over. The silence in the house is like a balm.

With their permission, I park myself at the family computer, full of good resolutions to work on an introduction for the book, or maybe my conference talk. Working might help still the worries and fears and desires all rattling about in my head. Always used to. It occurs to me that while the book is for Felix, the talk is really for me. Which might be why I seem utterly unable to focus on it.

The study is crowded with stuff. Libby used it as her sewing room before Doug retired. Now it is a jostling blend of their styles. Gray filing cabinets and dark rows of medical books bump up against floral wallpaper and pink carpeting. Every vertical surface is covered in framed pictures, family photographs, professional certificates, Impressionist prints.

Now, to start typing—

There are potted plants lining the windowsill. I don't know who usually cares for them, but they look as neglected as the poor flowers in my garden at home. I fill a pitcher in the kitchen and bring it back to the study. Push aside the dried debris of leaves and petals to make way for a circle of water, as if here too we need to conserve.

Plants cared for, I put aside the water, and shut out concerns about Joanie and her baby, and questions about Humphrey. Instead, I try to think of future readers, my kind of people, passionate about the blending of music and movement. Perhaps I can open with a description of how I began to teach dance, as a student volunteering with a group of ragged children in the slums on the far side of Grahamstown. Those kids, steeped in traditional Xhosa dance steps, performed with a whole-body abandon I've wished I could emulate all my life. If I can convey that joy . . . Ha! That's rich, coming from a woman who barely cracked a grin for the past nine months.

But the thought of Felix does bring a smile. When he and I first met as students, he teased me about being too serious. At twenty-one, I hadn't suffered any real heartache or any real failure. I wanted to fall in love, of course, and dreamed of it. I'd had crushes, but nobody had penetrated my defenses physically or emotionally—until this newcomer with his motorbike and big dreams.

We landed up in the same physiology class. Though I planned a sensible career as a music teacher, not a dancer, it seemed a good idea to learn what I could about body mechanisms, and almost immediately I was out of my depth.

Felix was way more ambitious. He loved the subject and was already quite knowledgeable, from his early years working as an assistant for the inventor in Cape Town, John Latimer, who became his mentor. He studied on his own too. He told me how Dr. Latimer, caring more about him than his own father had, insisted he get his high school diploma and then start a correspondence degree. He'd carried on, doing one credit at a time while he was traveling, growing increasingly fascinated by human mobility. I found his passion intriguing and sexy.

When he saw how I was floundering in class, he offered to tutor me.

Doug's big desk chair sighs as I lean back, lost in memories of the room Felix rented off-campus. The bed was way too close to his desk. We took our exploration of physiology from theory to practice, going from page to fingers to skin. Like his words, his touch opened new pathways of awareness in me.

Of course, now I wish I'd studied harder. Felix went on to get his doctorate; I stayed an amateur, learning on a need-to-know basis. If only I had a better foundation to help understand what is going on in Freddie's little structure. I should probably be more mindful of my own sixty-nine-year-old structure too, but I slip into old habits. Here I am, folding one leg under me as I hunch forward again, scanning the screen. My knee will make me pay later.

I start typing "birth defects" and "prematurity" and "neonatal development." Most of what comes up goes way over my head.

The information is out there. Keep asking.

It's the first time all week that I've heard his voice. Glad to discover my ghost travels with me, isn't just resident in our drafty old cottage. But ask what? You have to know something to guess where to look. He was a compulsive researcher, always asking questions and testing theories. Where do I begin? What can I look into that the doctors aren't better equipped to explore?

You have a unique perspective, Sal.

I do? In what way? Silence.

Stumped, I water a couple more plants, put the pitcher down on the rug, and text Joanie to ask if she's free to talk. She calls back almost at once. "The doctors have been asking us about family health history," she tells me. She is home again and sounds a little more relaxed. She can speak without a backdrop of beeping and calling voices. I've been thinking along those same lines and read her a quote from a TED talk I've just found online.

"Eric and I have both had blood taken—enough to feed a clan of vampires," she tells me, but the results could take weeks. "They don't seem to know what to look for. We're not candidates for the obvious things. I've asked my mother about her family, but she insists they're all perfect specimens. Do you know if there was anything wrong in Dad's family?"

I remind her that Felix seldom spoke to me about his family. He left home so early, he might not have known much about their history.

But then I remember Humphrey. "By the way, your uncle turned up on my doorstep a few days before I left," I say as casually as I can.

"Uncle Boet? Oh my God, isn't he divine?" she exclaims. "He's such a cool character. Different from Dad. Hey, didn't I just forward an email to you from him a few days ago? But why did he come visit?" And then she registers what has only just occurred to me. "Sal, he might know family stuff. Can you ask him?"

"I'll try," I say. "He's not much into writing. I think his fingertips are too broad for the phone keys. But he did suggest we talk. I'll see if I can reach him."

There's a six-hour time difference—no, seven because of wintertime. I email Humphrey right away, bearing it in mind and remembering how punctual he was that Friday. Between the three-hour difference with Joanie and this gap with South Africa, my head is seesawing. Why can't we all be in the same time zone? My fingers go still but one foot is tap-tapping, jittery.

"So different from Dad," Joanie said. In what way? She didn't think Felix was cool? I suppose to her he was just a goofy, adoring papa.

Give my daughter a hug from me, he said, and I haven't been able to. All over again, I get angry with her mother.

New thought: Does a priest have to keep the secrets of someone who has died? While I'm at the computer, hoping Humphrey will call, I email Bob Halpert and tell him the latest about Freddie. Felix conversed with the worthy minister about matters he seldom discussed with other people, about his early life and the rift with his family. Not sure if any of that would classify as confidential, whether Bob will feel free to share with me if something was peculiar about their health.

Aargh! A new guilt rises. A month before he died, Felix ordered one of those genealogy kits that have become popular. He offered to get one for me too, but I had no interest in it. The mere thought of a family tree thrusts up sorrow for my parents' lost world. Their repeated appeals to tracing organizations, seeking any relatives who might have survived the Holocaust, just reopened wounds. No one was found. Their pain cauterized any curiosity I might have had.

But for Felix it was different. For all his offhand dismissal of his own relatives, as a scientist he was intrigued by lineage. He loved the way ancient chromosomal threads weave from generation to generation.

Yet when he finally took that step to explore his roots, he did it in an oddly ambivalent way. Instead of spending more and getting a report from a reputable source, he answered an ad on TV that sounded totally hokey to me. It was as if he wanted answers that he could dismiss if he didn't like them. The report, ironically, arrived a few months after he went to join his ancestors.

Decided to do my research in person, I heard him say back then. Not funny!

The big gray envelope sat on the entry hall table for weeks before I could bring myself to open it. There was a brochure advertising more advanced—and more expensive—services, and a garish, multicolored chart that made no sense to me, listing this percentage of Western European ancestry and that percentage of Eastern European, with a fraction of a percent from North Africa and another from Asia. It looked like unverifiable nonsense. I tossed it out without even offering it to Trevor or Joanie.

I'm sorry, I tell spectral Felix now. Was that a mistake? It's too late to undo anyway.

A loud *dringgg-dringgg* makes me jump, knocking over the half-empty container of water. The sound might as well have been in my head, but in fact it's a real ring, the old-fashioned kind, from the phone on Doug's desk. I could let the call go to the machine, but ignoring it feels wrong. I sink to my knees with a handful of tissues to blot the water out of the pink rug, while reaching up to the receiver. It's so long since I've handled a landline phone, I dither over which way to hold it.

"Hello," I say, ready to launch into an explanation that Libby and Doug are out and I'm just a houseguest, but can I take a message? Before I can get out the words, the caller goes into her own staccato monologue: "Hello, Mrs. McDonald. You don't know me, but I am an acquaintance of your friend Sally. My name is Deidre Barnard. Can I speak to her?"

At any other time, I'm sure I would have copped to being that Sally, but Humphrey might call on my cellphone at any moment, and I don't want to talk to her. I look at the instrument in my hand, grateful that it isn't one of those video phones or Skype or something, and, still in mopping posture on my knees, in my best effort at broken English, I say, "I am very sorry, Miss, but Miss Libby she no here. Doctor Dog, he also no here. Please you call another time, later."

"I don't want to speak to Miss Libby or Doctor Dog. I told you I want to speak to Sally whatever-her-name-is."

Now I'm indignant on behalf of this well-meaning housekeeper. "Wait, lady. I get paper, pen. You say your name is Barnyard? Please, you spell for me very slow."

The voice barks something that sounds like "Oh, fuck that!" and there's a click. Thank goodness no one is around to see my expression. Can practically taste yellow feathers sticking out of my mouth, like Sylvester in the cartoons. Except, of course, that he never really gets Tweety Bird. And I haven't gotten Deidre; I've just delayed the evil hour when I'll have to find out why she called.

And now I'm stuck with the question. I write a text to Joanie: Why does your mother want to speak to me?

About to hit SEND but think better of it. If Mother Dearest is conducting a stealth sortie against the enemy, it's the last thing Joanie needs to worry about. I can fight my own battles. But how did she even trace me to Libby's?

I'm sitting flat on the rug, puzzling over that, when my cell phone buzzes. It's Humphrey, on WhatsApp, on camera, curly smile and all. And the camera at my end is on too. I have no idea why. Must have pressed some button by mistake.

"Am I getting you at a bad time?" he asks in that lilting tone of his. "This is when you said I should call, isn't it?" No wonder he's hesitating—I'm half under the desk, flushed and rumpled.

"Remember what you said about Joanie's mother? Well, I totally agree. She's a cow," I say. I dump the soggy tissues in the wastebasket and lean back against the desk, legs stretched out, and try to push my hair out of my face while holding the phone in approximately the right position in front of me.

"Hold it a little lower," he purrs. He is watching me with a puzzled smile, evidently reclining on a couch. There is light coming from just behind him, shadowing his face and outlining his cheekbone and brow and nose. It's catching the sprinkle of stubble along his jaw and the tidal pool green of his eyes. "Touch your pendant for me—you call it your 'lucky pendant' don't you?" My fingers find the smooth surface of the glass bead in the dip between my breasts.

Tell my brother I say hello, I hear in my head.

It startles me, not the intrusion or any guilt, but the risk. How can I convey that greeting? Those words could knock our sane, sensible communication into orbit, and there is an important topic we need to address. But this doesn't feel like a normal connection—hasn't from the first moment—more like some kind of gift. And the urge to test the dynamic is irresistible.

"Your brother says to tell you hello," I inform Humphrey. The image on my phone screen lurches as he props himself up on his elbow. He's furrowing his eyebrows, as if not sure he heard me right.

"Cool. Tell him I say hi back." And then he tilts his chin at an angle, so the light falls across his face and I can see he's trying to suppress a grin. "Does he know I kissed you?"

"He knows everything," I reply, liking him more. No mockery or disapproval, just playing along. It gives me space to be a heartsore widow and also respond to this chemistry. And it reminds me that these men have a bond I want to know more about.

But first there is the question that has floated over this connection for more than a week and across half the world: "Why did you come looking for me?"

"Felix hasn't told you that?"

"He'd know?" Dropping the joke, wanting an answer.

Humphrey goes serious too, his face in shadow again. "Actually, I'm not sure. I don't know what he knew. I should have asked him at Mom's funeral, and I didn't. I suppose I was angry with him, that he came then and not before, when she was so desperate to speak to him. Maybe I was jealous. And then he was gone too. But I think it's really important that his kids have the facts—if we can establish them."

He straightens up. "This is the thing: When our mother was weak, near the end, she got very worked up about something from her past. She kept asking me to tell Josie to come see her before it was too late. I didn't know who this 'Josie' was, and I couldn't get a last name out of her. I thought it was a woman at first, but Ma got irritated and said, 'You know who he is.'"

I'm baffled. "Did she say anything else? Why did you come to see me about that? What would I know?"

"I want you to think back," he says. "Did Felix ever say anything about a guy called Josie?"

I scan, sifting through memory. There's a very faint echo, but nothing I can pinpoint. "It's an unusual name for a South African. Could it be the Spanish name, José, with the 'J' pronounced like an 'H'? I seem to remember Felix mentioning a José or writing about one. You know he spent time in Spain and Argentina before we met? It could have been someone in either of those places, but then how would your mother have known that person? Why is it important?"

"There could be money involved, quite a lot, I think," Humphrey says. "My mother had a bank account she must have hidden from my father. Money had come from somewhere, but the bank won't give us any information unless we can show documentation from the sender. But it had added up. She used it to cover my dad's final medical expenses and when her own funds ran low, I think. When I asked her where it came from, she'd just say, 'It's money that was for Felix, but he won't take anything from me.'"

My head is resting against a desk drawer in Greenwich, but my mind is replaying a quite different scene from about a year ago. I see a sun-drenched patio with bougainvillea climbing to a trellis overhead. Perfume is wafting across from the yesterday-today-and-tomorrow blossoms. "You know these are also called kiss-me-quick?" Felix says and brushes my nose with a sprig. He and I slouch in our faded old deck chairs, chilled white wine in hand, happily relaxing—until we start arguing about his family yet again.

"Call your mother. You don't know how much longer she has," I say. Joanie has passed on a message from Boet that Elsabet is going downhill. I don't know why he hasn't called us directly, but the outlook isn't good. "Just tell her you love her."

"She knows that," Felix grunts. "If there's anything she wanted to tell me, she's had a long time to say it. If she didn't till now, it can't be that important. Let it go, Sally."

~ ~ ~ ~

His mother passed away in her sleep a few weeks later. Felix, to my astonishment, decided to attend her burial. His mood baffled me. Obviously, he was very sad, but he seemed agitated too. He went on his Harley and, along the way, stopped over with two different sets of friends.

He told me about those visits yet said almost nothing about the funeral and the two days spent with his relatives. I tried to ferret out more details but gave up. All Felix would say was that he wanted to see his clan. "And I did that," he insisted. "Ugly bunch." As offhand as he acted, I think he derived some kind of closure. He seemed more relaxed.

Three months later he was gone too. It was almost as if he'd known he would follow her, so why bother with last conversations?

"Sally?" the voice startles me back to the present. "You look glum. I'm sorry if this is hurting you."

"No, no, I'm fine," I say.

"Very good." Suddenly Humphrey sounds more formal. He glances to the side, as if someone has walked into the room. "That could be a lead worth looking into. I need to go, but it's been good talking with you."

"It has been nice. Thanks for calling. Bye, Humphrey."

He winks at me, and the screen goes blank.

I'm still smiling when Libby comes bustling in with bags of groceries. She spots my feet first and peers around the desk wide-eyed and quizzical. I scramble to my feet, and we go together to the kitchen and start unpacking the bags.

"How was your afternoon?" she asks. "I hope you weren't too bored."

"Nope, I wasn't bored," I assure her.

She gives me her big-sister worried look. "Did I hear you say Humphrey? What an unusual, old-fashioned name! Is he the brother?"

"Yes. And why the look? You're the one who's been nagging me to be open to new possibilities."

"He's a possibility?" She lines up bottles of soda on the counter, which reminds me about the spill. I apologize. She brushes that aside but looks me in the eye. "I want you to have love in your life again, but are you sure this isn't a little odd?"

I rearrange the bottles into a zigzag, alternate ones pushed back.

"No, you're right, it is very odd. I've tried to tell myself to forget about him. But it's not serious—it's just a pleasant little flirtation." I'm using Angie's term—it sounded so harmless when she suggested it the day I met Humphrey—but I can hear the defiance in my voice. "He makes me feel alive again. Some things he does are so much like Felix, I . . ."

"But he isn't—" and she stops herself, instead stroking my shoulder. I lay my hand over hers, glad she didn't finish what she was going to say.

~ ~ ~ ~

Bob replies to my email as I'm getting into bed. I can picture him, seated at the big, cluttered desk in his rectory office early in the morning, peering at the screen through his half-glasses, forefingers tapping away, his cherubic face screwed up in concentration. He types a lot better than Humphrey, presumably from all the years of writing sermons.

Dear Sally,

How delightful to hear from you! And good to hear that you are spending the festive season with good friends. You are brave to have gone sledding. At my age I don't think I would dare. When I was young it was different. Did I ever tell you about my time at Cambridge (the one in England)? How I loved those snowy Christmases!

I think, you have told me all about your halcyon days as a student in Cambridge—many times.

So sad to hear Joanie's baby has problems. I did struggle with my conscience, wondering if I should keep secret what Felix told me. But he was not confessing to me, and I know without a doubt he would want information shared if it might be of value. In any case, you know your fellow didn't give a fig for the rules of my profession.

I'm getting irritated now, not optimistic that he has anything concrete to share. My gammy knee is aching, as expected, so I get out of bed and pad barefoot around the room. I haven't been out for a walk today, despite resolutions to keep up an exercise routine.

You know better, Sal.

Yes, I do. Will get moving tomorrow.

I pick up the phone with a sleepy sigh and go on reading.

As you know too, Felix's youth was not happy. He did not go into detail, but I gathered that he and his father had a very strained relationship and talked very little. In fact, he implied on more than one occasion that his father might not be his real father.

Those words flare on the screen. I have to read and reread them.

Did you know that? It might be quite irrelevant, but since you have asked about family history, I'll leave it to you to decide. Felix said that back in his twenties, during his travels abroad, he sought out a person he had reason to believe might be the actual man. I'm afraid that is all I know. You mentioned he left a cache of journals written during those travels. Could it be that such an encounter was described in them?

A presence lurks behind my shoulder.

My life has become an open book, the ghost mock-complains.

Make up your mind, I tell Felix. You want me to find answers, don't you?

I'm still embarrassed about reading his journals after he died, and that comment makes me defensive. Though Felix read me bits and pieces, he was such a private man in certain ways, I never asked if I could look at them myself, not when we were students or even in these last years when we were closer than ever. But then he was gone, and what reason was there *not* to open them? Reading his descriptions of his travels was the closest I could come to having him back with me, like hearing his voice. But I don't remember any shocking revelations. No mention at all of his father—or any father. Which, come to think of it, was pretty odd. He did mention his mother and his siblings, now and then.

As I start to drift off a while later, I hear my phone ping. There's a message from Humphrey:

Can we chatjust quickly? I'm ssorry I rang off like that ths afternoon. Oh shit wer you asleep? sorry I forgot the time diffference.

Idiot—he's worse than I am. But I can't resist. Just feeling his embarrassment warms me. Try to dismiss it. Nonsense! This contact isn't about a wrongheaded flirtation, this is to help us learn more.

I duck under the blanket to muffle my voice in case it disturbs Libby and Doug, and call him, whispering when he answers. No video this time. I tease him about his abrupt hang-up earlier, and he tells me that one of his kids walked in unexpectedly.

I say, "Remember the priest we met up with in the café in Kalk Bay?"

"Reverend Halibut?"

"Halpert! I used to do that all the time. Wonderful man. He told me something puzzling." The same way Bob wasn't sure what to divulge to me, I hesitate too. I leave out what Felix said about their father not being his father, mindful of how shocking it might be for Humphrey. I just say, "He told me Felix mentioned visiting some person during his travels in Europe, someone who seemed particularly important to your family. Perhaps that's your mother's Josie. I don't know anything else, but there might be more in Felix's journals. I've skimmed them, but not read everything. When I get back . . ."

I leave it at that, and so does he.

~ 7 ~

Sunday morning, I push myself to wake earlier than my foggy mind wants to rouse. I'm definitely underslept. Something was niggling me with regard to Freddie, but the thought melted away when I tried to catch it. Some shield seems to be walling me off from full-on focus on him.

Libby's younger daughter, Susan, arrived last night with her husband and their three kids, a toddler and seven-year-old twins, to spend the holidays in Greenwich. Apparently, they decided to take an extra week of Christmas vacation, and she is delighted by the prospect of this bonus time together.

Thankfully—from my point of view—they have rented a holiday apartment nearby, but they will be eating meals with us. Come Christmas Eve, less than a week away, when Libby's son, Bradley, and his partner are due to arrive, this place will be bursting at the seams. The guys are only coming for one day, for reasons everyone goes tight-lipped about. Even Libby just sighs and switches the subject when I ask about them. I know it's not a gay/straight thing; she and Doug got past that a long time ago.

I'm scheduled to leave the day after Bradley gets here, flying on Christmas Day itself, but I feel bad taking up the guest room and yet another seat at the table till then. "You don't understand what a treat it is for me, having you here to share all this," Libby said yesterday. "I love my family, but they exhaust me. You give me strength. I can't wait for you to see the pantomime the kids put on. You'll love it!"

My heart sank just a smidgen. But I said, "You're my strength-giver too. Now put me to work. This week is going to be hectic."

Sure enough, as I descend the stairs, the children come bouncing in through the backdoor, followed by their parents. There's a great stomping of boots. Before they have shed their coats, Bridget and her gang arrive, and the cousins greet each other with ear-splitting glee. The older kids explain who I am to the younger ones, who don't remember me. I'm not real family, so they can't call me Aunt Sally, the big cousins decree, and instead dub me "Dance Sally" because I taught them how to do the Charleston and the Twist.

"Dance Sally, Dance Sally," the little ones chant.

Horrified to hear that I don't know how to make snow angels, they command me to come outside. I barely get a chance to grab my coat, hat, and gloves. The snow has grown crusty and muddy around the edges, but it still serves their purpose. Flat on my back, they have me waving my arms and legs.

~ ~ ~ ~

I wonder what my ex-gardener-turned-housesitter, Jacob, would make of me now. A hierarchical tribesman to his core, he has very particular ideas about how seniors should be treated—with great respect, and how they should behave—with dignity. Getting soaked in soggy snow while taking orders from two seven-year-olds doesn't fit that bill.

But Jacob and I have a connection almost as warm as the one he shared with Felix. When I got him on the phone first thing this morning—early afternoon in Cape Town—he sounded excited to have the long-distance contact and was full of news of the cats and the flowers and the weather. Recalling it, I feel the heat he described, contrasting with this icy angel bed.

But suddenly his tone went mournful. "Aw, Madam Sally, I forget to tell you. Bad news, very bad news." My heart fell. What could cause such grief? "Your new vase, that pink dog with the painted flowers, it fell down, broken on the floor. The *skelm* young cat, he knocked it down."

I exclaimed in much distress before I could catch myself. Hideous, yes, but my only memento of the meeting with Humphrey. I hastened to tell Jacob it was no problem, that I'm glad the ugly thing was smashed. He sighed with relief and asked when I was expecting to get back.

"In about a week, like we planned—I think."

I said nothing about the changed itinerary.

With the Portland visit blocked, I'm disoriented. One minute, I feel happy being back here, and I can imagine cancelling my return and just staying as Libby wants me to do. The next, I'm missing my home, even my solitude in it, with the sea smell and the sighing of the wind. Jacob said he and Nomse could stay longer if I needed them to.

Only one problem, he mentioned in passing: my neighbor Roxie. "She comes every day. Comes inside, looks around. Tells me she is keeping an eye on me."

I'm shocked—but shouldn't be. As unconventional as she and Edith might be as a couple, they are deeply conservative. Having the "hired help" stay inside one's house like regular guests to her must be asking for trouble. It violates the familiar social order. I didn't know what to say to Jacob other than, "I will let her know again that you are doing me a big favor."

How many times do I have to learn and relearn that people are a mixture, that even the kindest or most sophisticated carry kernels of inherited thinking and unexamined knee-jerk conditioning? In my dogmatic youth—and perhaps even more in later years—I would count people out if they displayed such prejudice. I've mellowed lately, I think, become more accepting, but it still catches me by surprise. I have those kernels of prejudice too. Even Felix did. And Roxie's not a bad person; I just need to find some way to redirect her concern for me and my home.

The twins are taking turns stretching up to brush the snow off my back when Libby comes wading out to us. She looks as stricken as Jacob sounded. "You all come inside; breakfast is ready," she calls. As we trudge back to the house, she turns to me: "I may have just done something terrible—but you lied. And you should have told me."

"Lied about what?"

"About being my Mexican housekeeper." She cracks a little

smile, but I grimace.

"I didn't lie," I declare. "And Mexican? I thought I sounded Albanian. I just said you and Dr. Dog were out."

"Lies of omission. Isn't that what you told me was in the Day of Atonement list of sins? Wouldn't that include letting a misunderstanding go uncorrected?"

Again, this honesty thing. I get a pass, confessing all these years later about Felix, but this little fib—where I felt totally justified—has gotten me in trouble?

Susan is settling her kids at the table. As I help Libby fill serving dishes with eggs and bacon and waffles, I ask: "What did Deidre say? I'm sorry I forgot to mention it yesterday. I should have spoken to her, but I just wasn't ready for her nastiness."

"Actually, she didn't sound all that nasty, once we got past the housekeeper I didn't know I had."

"You told her—?"

"No. She guessed from my confusion. She said, 'I've had enough Mexican women work for me over the years to know a fake when I hear one.'"

How embarrassing, and I'm still loath to deal with Deidre. But Libby has taken her number and promised she will have me call back. "After breakfast," I say.

"Before," Libby insists. I forget that she used to be the manager of a health food co-op and kept order among a fractious band of volunteers. "We'll wait for you. The kids will eat first, and then we adults can sit down in peace."

"Don't wait. I won't have much of an appetite." Back to the study I slink, and I call Deidre from the house phone. Still wondering how she got this number, and don't want her to get my cellphone one. It's barely dawn on the West Coast. Why is she up already and looking for trouble?

She answers before the second ring, evidently waiting for my call. Her voice is so hushed, I close the study door to screen out the chatter from the kitchen. "Could you speak up?" I shout.

"Sorry. I don't want to wake Joanie and Eric," she whispers. "I don't want them to know I'm contacting you until I know your answer."

"And why's that?"

"Look, Sally, you and I probably won't be friends, but we both love this girl. She is having a hard time, and I'm not good with this emotional stuff. It would help if you came. I can handle the practical stuff, but I don't know what to do with a screaming baby and a weepy woman and a bossy nanny giving everyone orders. I'm exhausted. If you can come, I'd like to go home. Will you come, even if it's just for a few days?" Her voice has grown louder, more forceful. "I'll make a booking and buy you a ticket."

"You don't need to do that." I make myself add, "But thank you anyway. How is Freddie doing?"

"Not good," she says. Her voice goes lower again. "Joanie insists he is putting on weight, but he's a scrawny little thing. I don't think they should have released him from the ICU. They should be monitoring him. But what do I know?"

Her snippiness puts my back up again. I thank her for calling and promise to let her know my flight details. I add, "Will you tell Joanie that you told me I could come?"

"It's not as if you needed my permission."

"Actually, I did."

"Well, we could have settled this the other day, if you care to remember."

We ring off in that mood, hostilities suspended but not resolved.

I'm just sitting down with the others when a fact registers: My special-price New York/Portland ticket has expired. I need to buy a new one, and that will dent a budget already stretched thin by this trip. Before pettiness can tie me in knots, I get up, return to the phone and hit the redial button. Deidre cuts short my explanation and my promise to pay her back, and demands, "Can you come on Wednesday? I've already checked and the flights are chockablock. That's the soonest I could get you a booking."

I slink back to the breakfast table chagrined. Not only did I have to accept a favor from my foe, I won't be around for Christmas Eve festivities. When I tell Libby, her face falls, but she perks up and tells me just what my mother used to: "It takes generosity to allow someone else to give to you. You did her a favor." In my case, poverty provided the push, but I like that angle, and the prospect of seeing Joanie and Eric and their little Freddie makes it all worthwhile. Still, my stomach knots tighter with all the cords that are pulling in different directions.

~ ~ ~ ~

The children are flatteringly upset when they hear that Dance Sally will be missing their pantomime. To compensate, I agree after breakfast to help with plotting and preparation. They are so full of ideas, it takes no more than a little sheepdog action on my part, making sure they don't stray too far from their agreed-upon direction. We sprawl on the living room rug, armed with big sheets of paper and some markers. Given all the grown-up talk of presidents and power, they decide to do their own version of King Canute's tale. To assist Diane, the eldest cousin, I take dictation, writing up a cast list of names and roles and stagehand duties. She is Canute and director and costume boss.

We are deep in showbiz brainstorming when she points out that my phone flashed. It's a text message from someone I've never heard of, and I'm about to dismiss it as spam when "Ethel" catches my eye and I start reading. It's from the agent daughter-of-a-friend my ex-mother-in-law mentioned. She is asking to see a brief outline of my book. A page or two will do, just to give her an idea, she says, and can I meet her for lunch on Tuesday, the day after tomorrow?

This doesn't make sense. I've been hoping to hear from Ethel, willing her to suggest a time to meet, and I thought perhaps we would discuss the new book. But this? Even the big-name writers don't get wined-and-dined by agents like they used to. And here is one offering sustenance even before seeing the substance of my proposal. She says only that she knows about my first book and has great respect for Ethel's judgment—that she has known Ethel since she was a child— and she doesn't know how long I plan to be in town.

Well, I'm not exactly "in town," but when I tell Libby about the message, she is so excited she offers to drive me to the city. Her daughters can come too, and they'll make it a girls' day out. "We'll leave the kids with the men," she says. "You can't pass up an opportunity like this! Your book idea is brilliant. She will grab the chance to do it."

I've always known that Libby's admiration comes more from her heart than her head. A flash of irritation rises. It's a totally unfamiliar feeling with this dearest companion, probably a factor of fatigue, but her eagerness is clashing with my desire to keep my expectations realistic. I point out that I don't have "a brief outline." I'm not ready for a meeting like this.

Her dimples deepen and for a moment she looks likely to exclaim something like "Fiddlesticks!" but instead she gives me a little shove in the direction of the study. "Tell her yes, you'll meet her for lunch, and go write up that outline. And tell her you want a big, fat advance. No, don't tell her that, not right away—but you should get one."

~ ~ ~ ~

"The booking is in whose name?" the maître d' asks. He's glossy-cheeked and genial, with a singsong Italian accent. When I tell him "Gail Tennant," he gives an approving, "Ah, *si*." He hands my coat to someone and leads me between the white-clothed tables to a round one set in a relatively quiet nook. It has a squat vase of orange-pink roses and a candle floating in a shell. Everything is soothing and classy. He draws out my chair, seats me, and signals for a busboy to pour me some water. "They will be here any minute," he assures me.

My hands are freezing—from nerves or the short walk from Libby's car to the restaurant—and I request a cup of coffee. "They"? Does she have a partner? The intimidation factor goes up a notch.

I sent Gail Tennant the outline yesterday around three. Tried to get it done earlier but floundered, kept deleting and rewriting and deleting. No response. Hardly surprising, given how late in the day it was. And none this morning. But at least there wasn't a phone call to say, "Ugh, sorry, this is awful. Forget about lunch." But she is taking this seriously enough to bring a colleague? I'm not sure whether to be heartened or even more suspicious.

As the waiter places the coffee in front of me, a young woman with a lovely, long sweep of thick, honey-blond hair approaches the table, chitchatting with the maître d'. He seats her and she says, "Mrs. Smith? Ms. Paddington? I'm sorry, I don't know what to call you."

"I've always used my own name, Paddington. But Sally will do. May I call you Gail?"

She laughs and nods. We natter about the weather and the city. She compliments me on my curls and adds, "If I had hair like yours, I'd never go near a beauty salon."

"It's so obvious that I don't?" I say. "Your hair is gorgeous."

"Thanks to extensions," she responds. "These days you can't tell who has good genes and who has a good hairdresser —except with a natural look like yours."

Feeling a little more relaxed now, I venture to ask her, "Is someone else joining us?"

"Yes, but not right away." Gail looks down, unfolding her napkin. "Shall we have a glass of wine? Oh, you have coffee already. Maybe, I'll get one too. I thought it would be good if we had a chance to talk about the book first. Thank you for sending the outline at such short notice."

Yes, and——? I want to ask. "I'm puzzled," Gail says. "After Ethel told me about you, I bought a copy of your first book. My local Words World didn't have it, but I found one at the little indie bookstore in my neighborhood. They say *New Steps* has been selling slowly but steadily for years. I'm not a dance person, but I loved it. It's beautifully done. But I'm confused about this next one."

I begin telling her how in *Next Steps*, through anecdotes from around the world, we will explore the various ways dancing can strengthen children and adults physically, emotionally, and socially. She is listening and nodding. It's what I described in the two-pager, but in a bit more detail.

"Who exactly is the 'we' you're referring to?" Gail asks. "I gather you're doing this with someone who has expertise on the orthopedic side, but you didn't specify who. Are you co-authoring, or writing different sections, or is this person simply a consultant?"

I am thunderstruck. It must have been subconscious, but I completely forgot to mention that my coauthor is Dr. Felix Barnard.

One of the first people I cited in the outline is his beloved friend Maria, wheelchair-bound but a teacher of flamenco. She also runs a foundation that helps children with disabilities learn to dance. Since his departure, she and I have become good friends. In fact, it was she who summoned me to Cape Town when Felix had his first burst aneurysm. Roxie and Edith had found her Barcelona phone number in a notebook in his pocket. She, in turn, got my number from my publisher. Without her making that call, my darling and I might never have been reunited. I wrote about Maria but didn't think to mention him? How bizarre!

And what about Winston, the star of my little group of township kids back in Grahamstown, now a distinguished academic teaching in Boston? It was Felix who helped him get on his feet again after he was shot in the back by the police during a protest in South Africa. His story is one of our best. And what of all the theories and insights I've gleaned from Felix's notes? He is the heart of the book.

Suddenly, the ramifications are clicking, one after the other. If this connection relies on Ethel's goodwill—and surely it does to have moved forward this fast—what will happen when she finds out that I'm using research from a man her son resents so bitterly? I can't imagine her risking his ire. Should I lie about his identity? Make up a fictitious expert? No way. I want this book out in the world for the good it can do, but also for Felix, as a tribute to him.

"It's really important," Gail says, then pauses, pouring packet after packet of sugar into her coffee and absentmindedly stirring. Odd for someone slim and clearly into health—a subconscious ritual as she sorts out her thinking? "If there are two of you involved, your compatibility is a critical component. Would I be dealing with just you, or both of you? Is it an equal partnership, or does one of you have final say if disagreements arise?"

Should I let on that my coauthor is no longer in a position to disagree with me? Would that make it easier to avoid mentioning his name to Ethel, at least until the book is published? Gail is still stirring her coffee, and the action eases my discomfort. She isn't as blithely confident as she tries to appear. "I have the final say," I tell her. "The book is essentially mine."

And before she can query anything else, I deflect. "Who is the other person who'll be joining us?"

As I'm asking that question, the maître d' makes another appearance, this time escorting a frail, familiar figure with glistening white hair, the real Mrs. Smith. We both stand and greet Ethel. She gives each of us a quick kiss on the cheek, and we all sit down.

"Why didn't you say Ethel was coming? Why the subterfuge?" I ask Gail as lightly as possible. "I don't really know," she says and tips her head to Ethel, eyebrows raised.

"I wasn't sure you would want to meet with me," Ethel states. "And if you did agree to, I didn't want Charles to know. He'd have had a fit. And if he found out and thought we were meeting alone, oh, I'd never have heard the end of it! So I just told him I was having lunch with our dear Gail."

"So, this is a pretext?" I ask the younger woman.

"You aren't actually interested in handling my book?" I'm angry, and glad, and suddenly longing for a slug of whisky. Here I have the much-desired meeting with Ethel.

But the excitement about the book was for nothing. I feel very foolish.

I mutter something about going to the bathroom. The coatroom is in the same direction. If I take my bag with me, I can grab my coat and slip out, get away. Libby and her girls have gone to the Met to see the medieval Christmas display and browse the Impressionists. I could go find them there—or find a cozy pub first and have that drink.

Before I can stand, Gail holds up her hand to stall me. "Please don't be angry, Sally. Yes, it started as a pretext to please Ethel, but I meant everything I said about your book. I really am fascinated. And I have a publisher in mind who would probably jump at it. Ethel, you don't mind if we take a few more minutes for shoptalk. And then I think I will leave you two to chat. Sally, when you come back from the ladies', will you tell me how long you want the book to be and what kind of illustrations you have in mind? It would be immensely helpful too if you can send me the first few chapters, just to give me a feel for the style and structure."

~ ~ ~ ~

"Love" is a pathetically inadequate word. If Greek has seven different words, why doesn't English? I feel such tenderness for Ethel, I want to snuggle up to her, put my arm around her bird-bone shoulders, and make everything just as she wants it to be. And I want her to love me back, as she used to.

So, when Gail finishes with her questions and leaves, I turn to my ex-mother-in-law and can't utter a word. The restaurant's tapestry of sounds and smells fades into the background. I lay my hand over Ethel's, feeling the diamond of her wedding ring pressing into my palm, and finally manage to stammer, "Where shall we begin?"

Her lips tremble. Her eyes, the same blue as mine when we met, milkier now, are brimming with tears. That almost undoes me. Ethel was always so strong, it never dawned on me till this very moment that she might be overwhelmed too. That she might have suffered when her son forced us apart. A flicker of anger breaks through, loosening my tongue.

"I wrote to you. I desperately wanted to stay in touch. You hated me too much to even write back?"

"Not hate. I never hated you," she says, shaking her head. "Just very disappointed."

I don't want to feel this, but the defensiveness is there again, the despair at being ejected from this family where I thought I belonged, forced from our gracious, book-lined home, exiled to that little basement apartment on Clark Street. Persona non grata.

It is on the tip of my tongue to say, "You know, your precious Charles was a philanderer." He still is one, for all I know; he's handsome enough. Though something about his demeanor in the café suggested otherwise, that his wings have been clipped. But I don't care how he conducts himself these days. I just want her to know I didn't set out to hurt him, and that the breakup wasn't all my fault.

Ethel sniffs, fumbles for a tissue in her beaded pocketbook. She is wheezing, her breath rasping with each inhalation. She says to me, "I did write back to you—a dozen different letters. I put stamps on two or three of them, ready to mail, but then tore them up. I would have had to ask Charles for your new address. If I did that, he would want to know what I was saying to you. He'd think I was taking your side."

She clasps her hands on the table edge and squares her shoulders. She says, "I love my son. You know that. But he's a very self-centered person, always was, maybe because of the polio. I think we spoiled him. And I know he was a womanizer. I saw him flirt with women. I thought it was some kind of compensation, but still it was wrong. And you put up with it! I didn't understand that. You were just as indulgent with him as we were."

Our food has come and is getting cold. Neither of us lifts a fork. Ethel's words are dislodging forgotten fragments—Charles turning on the charm at a bar mitzvah, sweet-talking the hostess at a dinner, flirting with students at university functions. I hate that she saw it too. Kaleidoscope-style, the pieces are all familiar, but they are settling into a different pattern.

"Do you know why we broke up?" I ask. My throat feels papery. A gulp of water makes it worse. I start coughing. Ethel reaches over to pat me, and the gesture makes me choke more. This is my chance to tell her my side, to lay out exactly what happened.

And I can't do it. Can't describe how sleazy her son was, how unfair.

"Shush, catch your breath," she says. "He told us you'd had an affair and that you were still involved with the man. He said he couldn't trust you anymore. Ben was appalled. He had you up on such a high pedestal."

"And you?" I ask.

"I didn't know what to believe." Ethel turns her knife over and over, staring at the reflections. "You seemed so proper, but I know how these things happen. If Charles hurt you, made you jealous, you might have acted on impulse, had a little dalliance to get back at him. That I could have understood. But the idea that it was ongoing, a long-lasting affair—that was very upsetting.

"Was it a long affair?" She is staring at me now, her eyes narrowed, as if everything hangs on my reply.

"No!" I shake my head again and again. "No!" But a dalliance—?

"So, you weren't still seeing him?" Ethel demands. As I try to find an answer, all I can think of is Felix. No, it didn't continue—but yes, I did see him.

My silence seems to satisfy her. "I knew it; you weren't that kind of woman." She sighs, blows her nose, and continues. "For years afterwards, I'd ask Charles if you were still single, and he'd say, 'As far as I know.' That other business didn't come to anything? I had a feeling he was exaggerating, making a big deal about nothing. I told Ben you were a one-man woman. That's true, isn't it?" Ethel smiles tentatively at me. "I'm the same. There were some boys before Ben, you know— flirtations, little romances. But when I fell for Ben, that was it. I never looked at anyone else."

The furrows in her face have softened, though I can still see lines caked in her face powder and a sheen of perspiration. She looks a little flushed. I smile back at her and urge her to start eating.

Like a seed caught between my teeth, I feel the unvoiced remnants of my story. The ghost is at my shoulder, teasing me. *You can deny me, it's okay.*

But I can't do that either. As if in a slideshow, I picture Felix—as I first saw him at Rhodes, long-haired and eager—

years later as a father, so proud of his feisty, funny children—
and finally, my gray-haired beloved in Kalk Bay. No, not a
dalliance. But most clearly, I see him that blissful day in Los
Angeles, in the sunshine at the restaurant, on the rumpled bed
later, in the shared shower, both of us still flushed with
pleasure. And there is why I can't tell her my truth, or her son's.

Ethel is breathing more easily and enjoying her veal. We
don't talk about Charles again. Dorothea isn't mentioned once.
The grandchildren provide material enough to keep us busy
through an elaborate dessert.

Though she says her appetite isn't good, Ethel insists we
order the house special, apple sorbet encased in spun sugar.
Gleefully, she shows me how to tap the fragile cage with my
spoon, shattering the golden threads to reach the frosty globe
inside. It's tart and sweet, so intense I have to eat very slowly.

I want to tell Ethel how healing the LA encounter with
Felix was, how good it felt. I want to tell her how it came right
after her son woke me with that smarmy call from New York,
disregarding how early it was on the West Coast, my brilliant
husband, who had written so many erudite academic papers
glorifying the cultural power of monogamy, wanting to confess
that he had slept with one of his students. Contrite and
demanding forgiveness, indifferent that I had a huge
presentation to give the next day, intent only on easing his guilt.

None of that really matters. Perhaps I did fall into Felix's
arms out of revenge. Perhaps if my marriage had been happy,
I'd have had more self-control. But the truth is the desire was
overwhelming. I yielded to loving and being loved, however
briefly. It was more than I'd felt with Charles in years, or ever.

Of course, I tell Ethel none of that. She and I talk about the weather, and I tell her how hot it has been in Cape Town, and how Libby made me buy a new coat at Saks. The only awkward moment comes when she asks why I went back to South Africa.

I say to her, "Well, I did finally get together with someone else, a guy I knew from college." The words have produced themselves, and I brace for her reaction. But she exclaims approvingly. Apparently, the one-man woman thesis allows for new love after a respectably long interval.

She wants to know how we got together. I say, "He was living in this picturesque seaside community full of fascinating eccentrics. I visited and never left." She claps her hands in delight and laughs at my description of the ramshackle cottage and our efforts to create a garden in the salty air.

"I'm glad you found happiness. You deserve it. Did he come with you on this trip?" she asks.

Deep breath in and a hard swallow. "He died nine months ago, from a brain aneurysm."

"Oh, Sally, I'm so sorry. Another tragedy in your life." Her face fills with empathy. She asks for more details of how it happened and tells me how bereft she felt when Ben died. We compare notes on loss and how we are dealing with loneliness. She too sleeps on one side of the bed.

Nothing in my arsenal of good resolutions can bring the truth to my tongue. I cannot tell her that my college sweetheart is the one-nighter, that all through my marriage to her son, there was this man I loved more.

She brightens when I tell her that I'm flying to Portland tomorrow. I explain I'm going to see my sort-of stepdaughter and this first sort-of grandchild, but how sad I am that Joanie's father is missing all of this. We talk about Ben, what a doting grandfather he was, and I get to ask about her daughters and the other members of the family.

"You know, I'm ninety-two," Ethel tells me as we're saying our goodbyes out on the sidewalk. She has flagged down a cab, and the driver is watching us with the meter ticking. "I've lived a good life, and I'm grateful for all the blessings I've had. But there were bad parts, and one of the worst was this, losing you. It was like an open wound. And now it has healed. I am so glad! My dear Sally, you will stay in touch, won't you?" We enfold each other in a real hug then, long and loving.

As I turn to walk away, she grasps my coat. "Hurry up with that new book. Who knows how much time I have left. I want to see it finished. You come back to New York, and I will throw you the biggest launch party you could ever wish for. And if Charles disapproves that we're family again, screw him!"

I grin and put my hands together in a "thank you." But, of course, he would have greater cause for anger about the book. And I can't risk losing her approval again, can't let her know I am "that kind of woman."

~ 8 ~

Portland is gray but almost balmy compared to New York. I'm overdressed, and by the time I make it through the baggage pickup and out to the taxi rank, it feels positively tropical. I'm clutching my case and shoulder bag and coat, struggling to get my bearings, when I hear an imperious exclamation from a statuesque brunette in a beige pants suit.

"Sally Paddington, what took you so long? I've had to fend off half a dozen policemen." She towers over me.

"Deidre? You drove out to meet my flight? How kind of you!"

"No, I got a ride. He's over there in the double-parked Jeep, waiting to drive you back to Joanie's. I'm catching a flight—if I don't miss it. Fuck, look at the time! Weren't you a flaming redhead? Oh, well, I suppose we've all faded a bit. No time to get acquainted, so hello and goodbye. Good luck with everything." And away she strides, pulling her neat stack of matching suitcases.

I'm about to wrestle mine over to the Jeep when the driver hops out and jogs over to me, a tall guy with a mop of wild tawny curls and caramel skin. It's our beautiful Trevor, the former *skelm* himself. He has on my favorite jacket, the battered leather bomber his father wore for years.

"What are you doing here?"

He kisses me on both cheeks. "Arrived this morning. Joanie told me you were coming. I hadn't seen the baby yet, and the dragon was leaving. How could I not come?" I stretch up on tiptoes to hug him tight. He hugs me back and swings me around, just as his father used to. For a moment, I feel light as a bubble.

If Joanie is a female version of Felix, Trevor is more like Nellie. He has her slender build and thick hair. But he has his father's eyes, the topaz unlike anyone else's. They crinkle in delight, tickled by my astonishment that he's here. For the past few months, as far as I know, he has been working around the clock on a design project in San Francisco. "No big deal," he declares. "Took a couple of days off, and I drove up overnight. Not much sleep but I'm cool!"

The freeway is congested though it's only midday here, not all that much later than it was in New York when I left, though the trip felt endless. Trevor drives as fast as he can, the way Felix rode his motorcycle, dancing through the gaps. The last time I was in a car with this guy was in Cape Town, when he came for his father's memorial, and there he was mindful of being on the opposite side of the road. Here he is in his element, despite what has become a downpour, and after a few minutes I relax, the pleasure of his company outweighing all else. I haven't seen rain like this in so long, I reach out the window to feel the splatter on my hand.

There is no contradiction between that sensation and the song I hear coming from the sound system: "Here Comes the Sun." I know Trevor has put it on specially for me, and it plasters a smile across my face.

He glances across at me. "What's this I hear about Uncle Boet putting the moves on you?" I snort in surprise, drying my hand on my thigh, and he laughs. "Yeah, Joanie told me he paid you a visit—or a few visits."

"Just two." I am glad that he's looking out for his next lane change and can't see me blush. How ridiculous to get embarrassed—about one kiss? The faint question arises: Would the kids regard it as a betrayal of their father if I got involved with Humphrey? Not that it's a possibility.

Humphrey and I have exchanged a couple more emails, and a phone call last night. I told him I was coming to Portland and how worried Joanie and Eric are about Freddie. We've also shared more speculation about the mysterious Josie who was so very important to his dying mother. "You said there might be something in those journals?" he asked. "But it can wait until you get back. You are coming back, aren't you?"

I ask Trevor, "What makes you think he has designs on me. Strikes me as a happily married man."

"Ugh, not so happily," Trevor says. "We met his wife years ago when Dad brought us to visit Grandma. Magda? No, Helga. I can still remember how she nagged him. She was quite nice to Joanie, but she ignored me completely. A bit too brown for her liking."

"Really?" I tend to forget that he contends with racism the rest of this family is spared. But I understand better why Felix was so scathing about Humphrey and Helga as a couple.

To change the subject, I tell Trevor about giving his father's hat to his uncle. "It fitted him perfectly," I say. "Your dad put it on once, snagged his hair on the price tag, and never put it on again. But maybe you should have taken it."

"Nah, I'm not a hat person like Dad. I've got the jacket. And I can just imagine Uncle Boet in it, doing his thing. He's a smooth operator."

I'm inclined to defend Humphrey, but I know what Trevor means. Humphrey is definitely more debonair than Felix was. Now I'm flat-out embarrassed by my interest in him. The chemistry between us has buoyed me for days, but suddenly it feels delusional—the way Libby saw it.

All nonsense anyway. I'm here because of real relationships, built on solid love and years of attachment.

~ ~ ~ ~

Joanie and Eric's home is a handsome townhouse with a façade that sets it apart from the rest of the street. A fretwork of concrete stretches all the way up the three floors, each level defined by planters filled with trailing greenery. Eric designed it, and though I generally prefer a more traditional style, the image is full of vitality. It makes me feel hopeful about what I'll find inside.

The interior is similarly modern, with the ground-floor rooms merged into an organic open flow, all airy and bright.

After the layers of accumulation at Libby and Doug's, this place—even with the casual disarray Joanie always leaves in her wake—looks empty. The third-floor room I'm assigned is pretty and cozier, aside from the wide skylight that frames a view of scudding clouds. Trevor first brings me and my bags up there, then leads the way back downstairs to the nursery. The room is painted a soft yellow, with a mural of birds and animals. Joanie is curled up on a chaise longue, fast asleep, while a sturdy woman in a white uniform occupies a big bentwood chair, rocking herself and a tiny bundle with a round fuzzy head.

I tiptoe over and she opens her arms just enough to show me his face. It's wide, as I saw in the photos, with lips that curve like Cupid's bow. I'd thought he looked like Joanie, but he has a pugnacious little chin with a dent in the middle exactly like Eric's.

Just as I lean in, he opens his gray-brown eyes and stares up at me as if he's looking straight into my soul. A smile plays across his mouth. "Gas," the nurse says, lest I get any idea that he's showing approval. Sure enough, his expression is aloof once more. She lifts him now, offering him to me to hold, but I back away. What if I drop him? In any case, I should change into clean clothes and wash my hands first. He closes his eyes, the lids a translucent mauve, shutting out her and me.

As I turn away, Joanie stirs. She sits, sees me, leaps up, and hugs me.

"Oh, thank goodness you're here." Her hair is pulled up in a ponytail, but tendrils have escaped and she shoves them behind her ears. She is pale and looks wearier than I've ever seen her. She checks on Freddie, nods silently to the nurse, and signals to me to come with her.

We head downstairs to the living room-kitchen-dining area. Trevor is at the stove and grins over his shoulder. "Come sit. I've made you gals my specialty, chai tea. Sal, are you hungry? I make a mean grilled cheese. I picked up a great organic multigrain when I went out for my run this morning, and these guys have a pretty good soy Swiss."

I look at Joanie in querying astonishment. She laughs and says, "Yup, our dissolute wild boy has turned into a domesticated health nut! He's much stricter than I am. I think he's in love, but he hasn't told me any details yet."

"And neither will he," Trevor declares, handing us tall steaming mugs. "My love life is my business. And this health stuff is all my doing. I want to do the Boston Marathon next year. Part of my master plan. By the time your Freddie is ready for a role model, I'll be ready to show him the ropes. Start him early and we can grow a champion."

I'm delighted and relieved. Trevor has had his rough patches, and in Cape Town it worried me that he was drinking too much and had gone back to smoking. I put it down to grief about losing his father but wasn't sure. I turn to Joanie, knowing she has worried about him too and must be pleased to hear this, but she's looking woeful.

"If Freddie—" and she stops. Trevor and I both wait for her next words. "His legs, something isn't right. He's not kicking the way most babies do. I don't know if he's going to be able to run."

Silence envelops us. Felix should be here. There is a cruel

irony if this man who dedicated his life to helping disabled people now has a grandchild who might need him, and he isn't here to share his expertise. But actually, that doesn't feel true. Even as my rational mind dismisses the notion, I feel his presence in the air around us.

I go give Joanie another hug, rubbing her back. "From your dad." She doesn't query that, just leans into it.

Nurse Rawson withdraws to have her afternoon rest, and Joanie and I take Freddie for an excursion. She looks as if she could do with some sunlight. I ask if she has been getting out. She says her mother took her to lunch a few times and to a shopping mall. "She doesn't do walks. I could have gone on my own, but I've been too anxious. Whenever I'm away from Freddie, I worry about him all the time. It's like the umbilical cord is still attached. And Rawson wouldn't let me take him with me. She said it was too cold. Today's warm enough, I suppose, or she thinks you know what you're doing."

That's funny. I have had no experience with babies, but white hair seems to convey authority. Trevor helps us get the baby carriage down the front steps before going to take a nap himself, and the two of us—or three, rather—make our way to a park a few blocks from the house.

"Tell me about you," Joanie says. "I need to hear about something other than baby stuff or effing politics. Tell me, did you ever hear from your ex and his mother?"

That opens a wonderful door. She is the one person, other than Libby now, who knows my whole story—or at least most of it. She listens as she walks, dipping the carriage carefully off the sidewalk and across the street and up on the other side, not adept yet with the maneuver. Freddie, joggled in his cocoon of blankets, flails his minute, starfish hands but doesn't wake as we keep rolling. The streets are clean and pretty, with handsome houses and carefully tended trees, each with its protective circle of wrought iron, wrapped now in fairy lights. A little like my old neighborhood in Brooklyn Heights, but tidier and quieter, the scale of everything a bit smaller. People walking by nod in greeting. It feels like a safe place.

I tell her what Ethel said about Charles, and how she asked me if the "other man" was a dalliance. Joanie sniffs when I tell her how I held my tongue. "What about the fact that you ended up living with him?" she asks. I explain how I sidestepped the question by referring to my Kalk Bay companion as a friend from college.

"How could I tell her I'd been in love with him all along?"

"But Charles knows you and Dad were together as students, doesn't he?" she asks. "Wouldn't he guess who the old college buddy was?"

"Yes, but hopefully Ethel's not planning to tell him about our discussion."

We settle on a bench overlooking a pond. The scene looks like a Japanese painting, with little bridges and umbrella-shaped trees. Talking like this, keeping everything as light and entertaining as I can, it begins to seem less complicated than I thought.

"There was another episode involving your dad," I venture. I tell her about Gail Tennant, Ethel's agent friend, and her interest in *Next Steps.* And for the first time since yesterday's get-together, I have a chance to review the seesaw of excitement and hesitation. I have no idea what side Joanie will come down on, whether to mention Felix's participation.

"Whew, what a pickle!" she exclaims. She goes quiet for a while, gently rocking the carriage. "You say you told Gail you've been gathering material for more than a decade? If you tell her your coauthor is the man you were living with, the man who died, won't Ethel guess who it is? She'll realize you were communicating with him long before you landed up in Kalk Bay. She'll know you lied."

"I didn't lie, just didn't tell her the whole truth," I say. "But even if she doesn't click to that, the moment Charles hears his name, he'll tell his mother. Libby suggested I give him a pseudonym and just make out he was a friend or a colleague."

"And not mention the name Felix Barnard?" Joanie turns to me with her eyebrows arched high, her voice sharp with disbelief. The tiger gleam is there. For a moment she reminds me of her Uncle Humphrey.

Our bond is strong, but Joanie and I have had our misunderstandings. My heart sinks. The sun, which has been dipping in and out of the clouds, chooses that moment to half emerge, casting a yellowish glare over everything. I'd rather be in shadow.

I remember a chill just like this in Cape Town six months ago. I assumed Joanie and Trevor wanted their father's house sold, and though it was breaking my heart to move out, I was working diligently towards that goal. Suddenly, the easy warmth between us vanished. She skirted around me without looking at me and went out for walks without asking if I wanted to come too. The conversation over meals became stilted. Every muscle in my body started to ache, but asking what was wrong elicited "Nothing!" I became annoyed and stopped trying to reach her.

I wish Eric was with us now. In Cape Town, it was he who explained that it was my talk about real estate agents and property prices that had upset Joanie. She had taken my efforts to sell their father's house to mean I wanted to cut ties with them and start a new chapter. That was so far from the truth, I got angrier. But then I realized how hurt she was. Eric played go-between and the ice melted.

How can she think this poorly of me again? It has been a very intense few days—an intense few weeks. In every direction, my relationships seem as brittle as those flowers in my faraway garden. But I can't bear to be at odds with her, not now, not today. I grab her forearms and say, "Joanie, you know me better than that. I would never not credit him. Half my reason for plowing ahead with this benighted project is to create a lasting record of his work."

She glowers at me for another few beats, lips pursed. Then she scrunches her shoulders up around her ears and exclaims, "But then what happens? Charles will recognize the name and tell his mother—and that could wreck everything!" She becomes more kitten than tiger, wilting again.

"I want you to have your second book. I want Dad to be remembered. I want everything to be smooth and simple the way it used to be." She slumps over, her head against my shoulder. The movement jolts the carriage, and Freddie wakes up and starts bleating, a frantic staccato of discomfort.

"Let me," I say. Joanie sags back against the bench, as I

scoop Freddie up, half entangled with his blankets. I turn him the wrong way and switch sides, before working out how to lay him against my chest. Stiff and still afraid of dropping him, I pat his back, sway slowly, murmuring, "There, there, everything's fine."

"Is he hungry?" I mouth to Joanie.

She shakes her head, her face still shiny with tears. "I fed him just before we came out. If he feeds too often, he spits up. If he doesn't feed too often, he spits up."

My face rests on his warm crown, and I can feel it bob with each jerking sob. He sounds so desperate and goes on so long, I can't imagine where he gets the breath. It's gut-wrenching. People strolling past cast sympathetic glances our way. Does he have colic? Isn't that something lots of babies have? Is this what it sounds like? At last, his wails dwindle to gasps and finally regular breathing.

"That's what my mother couldn't do," Joanie says. "How did you know how to soothe him?"

"I don't. I just hung in," I reply, though proud of the achievement and trying to shift Freddie without upsetting him. The mottled red in his skin is fading back to satiny pink. Poor little fellow. My arm is aching from the unaccustomed position.

The sun has slipped behind a dark thunderhead. Joanie stands up and takes Freddie from me. She lays him in the carriage and tucks the blankets around him. I pull a bottle of juice from my shoulder bag and thrust it at her. "You need to drink too," I say.

She accepts it eagerly and sips as we walk home—with me

pushing the carriage.

"Is my baby going to be okay?" she asks.

"Yes," I state and smile at her. I know that might not be true. She does too, but for now a "yes" is what she needs. In any case, her father said he'll be all right.

~ ~ ~ ~

Three emails await me when I check later. I'm flat on my bed with my phone, drained by the day's ups and downs, and relieved that Nurse Rawson has taken over again. Joanie is in the kitchen, cooking supper with Trevor. Eric should be home any minute. I just need some catch-up time.

One message is from Libby, saying the house feels empty without me. It has a smiley face emoji after it, so we both know what a joke that "empty" is. She tells me the little kids are indignant that I have deserted them. She says: I promised that you'll be back, or we'll fly to South Africa to get you.

It's soothing to read her enthusiastic tone. I had been worrying about my increasing irritability and wasn't sure if she'd noticed. Libby is like the hub of a wheel; everything pivots around her, and she holds it all in place, but that leaves too little space for her at the center. I think my presence gave her a chance to be uncharacteristically needy. Hopefully, here I'll be less scratchy. The next email is from Ethel.

Dearest Sally,

I am so very happy to have you back in my life. A little under the weather today, sniffles and a touch of fever—nothing serious, but I am beyond glad we were able to meet up yesterday.

With love, Ethel (your mother-in-law forever)

Oh, I am so glad also. I hope she gets over the infection quickly.

The third is from Gail, the agent.

Thank you so much for meeting with me yesterday and being gracious about the "ambush." Just a reminder: Please send me two or three chapters as soon as possible. My partner Martin is going away in a few days to a book fair. I would like him to see a sample of *Next Steps* before he goes.

So much for resting. I haven't given those chapters a thought since she asked for them. I have less than a dozen completed, and those are rough, totally unedited. And I don't have access to my files. Other than the introduction I was trying to write at Libby's, everything is on my home computer, not stored in one of those fancy "cloud" programs. In fact, most of my work is on paper, notes divided into ring binders. She is going to think I'm from the Stone Age.

Roxie next door! A stroke of genius: I can ask her for help. Roxie is super-efficient, way more tech savvy than I am. But first I must give Jacob a heads-up.

I am about to phone Jacob when I register the time. Now I'm ten hours out of sync with Cape Town, not seven. The math is too complicated to work out, and they are surely still asleep. Instead, I write an email to Roxie that she can read when she gets up, with my request that she find the latest Word document on my computer and send it to me. But first I must check with Jacob when it will be okay for her to come over. If I don't do that, she is liable to go barging in on them.

~ ~ ~ ~

Of course, bedtime in this Portland household is three hours after mine would have been on the East Coast. I could excuse myself early, but I want to spend time with Eric, and Trevor might have to leave before the weekend. I rub my face and do deep breathing to perk up. Every hour here feels precious.

When Freddie is settled, Joanie joins us, keeping the baby monitor close by. For now, all we can hear is a faint whiffling breath and the slowly fading lyrics of a lullaby. She snuggles up next to me on the sofa and then pops upright. "Want your toenails painted? I'll do yours if you'll do mine." She scampers back upstairs and returns with a plastic silverware tray filled with bottles of polish. This is a ritual we have shared since she was a teenager visiting me in New York. She chooses a creamy pink for herself, and when I can't decide, pulls out an iridescent orange for me. It's not a shade I'd have selected, but it's pretty, like the geraniums growing in Kalk Bay—even on my bumpy dancer feet. We natter as we dab at each other's toes, catching up on news of friends and favorite places. For a blessed while, the stress ebbs from her face.

Finally, Trevor declares he's tired and wants us out so he can bed down on the sofa. Joanie says she will do one more feeding, or try to, before turning in, and she, Eric, and I head upstairs.

Fatigue swallows me the moment my head hits the pillow. I sleep like the dead until a mewling sound penetrates, puzzles, and then has me wide awake, listening for the sounds of movement on the second floor. I can hear Joanie and Eric speaking, a door opening and closing—the nurse offering her help? Her room is next to the baby's. Now lying here wondering if she has taken over, offering Freddie a bottle, or whether Joanie is trying to breastfeed him. Because his sucking is weak and erratic, she says, her milk supply has tapered down. Now she is afraid that even when he is sucking, he isn't getting enough from her.

The crying starts up again, more frantic this time. Then it grows quieter; they must have closed a door, possibly in an attempt not to disturb me. Joanie said she hoped I'd sleep through the nighttime dramas. I wish I could help but can't, so I try to bury my head in my pillow and focus on my tinnitus instead. It has its uses. Babies cry, I tell myself. But most don't throw up this often. And most can kick their feet. This little guy seems trapped in a body that doesn't match his impulses. Sleep is gone.

By now in South Africa, they must be awake and going about their day. Making a tent of the comforter and huddled underneath it, I call Jacob, who picks up on the second ring. I apologize for speaking quietly, and he insists he can hear me well. We go through our usual pleasantries, and I explain that I am now at Joanie's. He sends his regards to her and Eric. Then I tell him about needing Roxie's help with the computer. He says he just saw her working in her garden. "I will go over and tell Miss Roxie she can come now," he says and rings off. He is eager to help, especially knowing the book I am writing involves Felix's work.

Things have gone quiet on the second floor. I'm still hunched in the dark under the comforter, trying to picture what is happening in the Cape Town sunshine, when my phone rings. I answer as quickly as I can, praying it can't be heard downstairs. Roxie is on the line, brisk and curious as usual.

"Hello, Sally. Got your email. You weren't asleep, were you? I'm in the attic, and the computer's booting up. What is your password? And what exactly must I look for?" She sounds happy. Retirement hasn't suited her; she loves to feel useful, but this task is too quick and easy. To her disgust, I have no passwords. In two minutes, she has found the *Next Steps* file, opened an email to me, and is ready to send it.

"While I'm here, what else do you need?" she barks. Long-distance seems to elicit greater volume from her, and she's annoyed that I'm responding in a hushed voice, though I've explained that I don't want to wake anyone. I remember Deidre's call to me and how impatient I got with her for speaking this way.

I'm about to hang up when another thought arises, not involving the computer or anything in that room. I've been racking my brain trying to remember where in Felix's journals I might find a clue about Bob Halpert's question. Where did Felix go looking for a man he thought might be his father? That part is so vague, it probably must wait until I get back. Or I could start with what Felix said about the people he met in Spain, when he first met Maria, and I'm pretty sure I know where that part came.

"Roxie," I begin, "are you allergic to house dust?"

"Yes, you know what I'm like," she says. "Why? I can handle a couple of sneezes. You want me to check whether this Nomse is cleaning properly?"

"No! Heavens, Roxie, I never asked her to clean, especially

in places I don't." I tamp my voice down again. "But I have another big favor to ask. There are some books in a box under my bed. You know about Felix's journals, don't you? There's a section in one of them that might help me with my book. Would you mind going to look for them now, while we're talking?"

I hear her thump down the steps, and a minute later she exclaims, "Ha, I've found the box of books." I hear puffing and grunting as she pulls it out. "Actually, everything is perfectly clean. Not a dust bunny in sight! Your place looks better than when you're here if you want to know the truth."

Blessings on Nomse's head. Now I know Roxie will probably leave her and Jacob in peace. Regardless of what I said to the contrary, she is satisfied they are filling their appropriate roles.

"Look for the volume marked 'Spain,'" I tell her. Might as well begin there.

"Got it. Now what?"

"I'm looking for a mention of someone called Maria. This could take a while. Would you mind taking it home with you and skimming through it? If you could send me a copy of the pages with her name, that would be great."

"No problem," she chortles. "I always wondered what Felix got up to in his youth."

Sorry, Tiger Man! I tell his ghost. The presence is observing me, silent but not objecting. I know I'm doing the right thing.

~ 9 ~

With thoughts churning and sleep out of the question, I tiptoe downstairs to the kitchen, phone in hand. All is quiet on the second floor and on the first floor.

As quietly as possible, seeing my way with help just from the streetlight outside, I put on a pot of water for coffee and sit down at the kitchen counter, intending to open Roxie's email and start reading the first chapters of the attached manuscript. Eagerness to dip back into Felix's anecdotes mixes with dread about my rusty writing and even rustier punctuation. Those pages did not come easily. Working on them brought back how eagerly we began, hopes so high, sitting on the porch of the beautiful bed-and-breakfast in Greenport, our hands almost touching, our minds attuned—before we began arguing.

Turn away from that image. Remind myself yet again that things happen in their own time, can't be rushed. And now seems to be the time for our book, perhaps.

Wary of disturbing Trevor, I glance back at the sofa and register that the roll of blankets is empty. My heart lurches. Where is he? Please, not gone already, lured back to San Francisco by the secret girlfriend? Absence always does this to me, triggers despair. I know the root cause, but that doesn't prevent the reaction. I feel tearful, cast aside. Whatever he decided to do is his business. He always has been a fiercely independent soul. I try to turn my attention to the screen in my hand, waiting for the Word document to open.

A beam of light erupts from the bathroom, and I jump. Silhouetted in the doorway is Trevor, rubbing a towel back and forth. He sees me and jumps too. "Whoops! Sorry, Sal!" He wraps the towel around his hips. "Why are you awake so early?"

I explain what happened with Freddie and then my South African contacts (minus mention of Humphrey), and the need for coffee. "Turn that off," he whispers, pointing at the stove. "I just went for a run. Was planning to go get breakfast at this funky little twenty-four-hour place I saw a few streets over. Come with me? The others won't be up for hours."

Both dressed, still tiptoeing, we slip out a few minutes later and head around the corner and down the hill. I'm exhilarated, to have Trevor still here and to be out with him in the gray, sweet, dawn air. Other than the drive yesterday, we haven't had time alone in years. I remind him of our last outing, just us two—to a hip-hop festival in the Bronx when he was in his teens. We won a dance contest, to his huge embarrassment, because the judges thought I was his mother.

We're still laughing over that as a waitress seats us, tosses menus our way, and goes back to the book she's reading behind the counter. Every spare inch is adorned with a mess of Christmas décor—tangled strands of lights, shiny paper cutouts, Santas of various sizes, some static, some swaying, and pots of scarlet poinsettias. As always, it tickles me to see the flowers displayed like this. They are blooming in gardens all over Cape Town, pretty much ignored as people put up fake snow and plastic mistletoe.

It takes a while before the waitress strolls back to get our orders. Trevor says to her, "This woman is starving. Can't you see how skinny she is?!" She shoots him a look of annoyance, registers his grin, and smiles back. It's exactly how his father would have behaved, and exactly the effect he always had.

Ravenous, hungrier than I remember being in ages, I order the "Big Man's Breakfast." The menu says it comes with eggs, mushrooms, sausage, fries, and a muffin. Trevor's eyebrows shoot up and he says, "Oh, screw good resolutions—for today anyway. I'll have the same."

As we wait for the food, I tell him how much he reminds me of Felix. To my surprise, he frowns. He looks at me from under his brows, and I see the glints of green and gold in his eyes. "I don't want to be like him," he grunts. The butter he has slathered on his muffin melts, and he takes a big bite.

"But you guys were such buddies, no?" I ask. "You had your rocky patches when you were younger, but I thought that all smoothed out. You seemed so close. He doted on you."

"That was the problem." Trevor lets out something between a huff and a snort. "It's like he was set on staying close to me, I don't know—maybe to make up for the divorce and going back to South Africa. He was on my case all the time. He phoned or emailed like every other day. Was I studying? Was I getting a job? Was I dating someone nice? I get that he cared, and I was lucky. So many of my friends had deadbeat dads or didn't know them at all. But it was too much."

He tips his face down, and all I can see is the dense mat of brown curls. "And now I feel fucking guilty for pushing him away."

I have no idea what else to say. "You looked so happy when you were together."

"You saw us at our best, on the trips to New York or the holidays in Kalk Bay. It helped to have you around, like you diluted the intensity. He relaxed a bit. Look, don't get me wrong—I did love him. But why did he have to be so over-the-top? It was nuts."

This hurts. As the only child of a couple with no other relatives, I remember feeling burdened by my parents' concern—but not resentful ever. I just wished I could give them enough love to make up for all they had lost. Going away to college and then coming to the U.S. to study felt unbearably callous, but they insisted I do it. More than anything in the world, they wanted to see me safe and happy, and I was grateful for that.

Felix's devotion was "nuts"? I want to weep for him.

"You know about his father, don't you?" I ask Trevor.

"Yeah, I get that," he says. My appetite has disappeared, but he is wolfing down his food. I pass him my sausage and fries. The resilience of youth, I think. "I know he had a shitty time with Grandpa, and he wanted to be a better father. But there was something that didn't add up, something weird about his determination."

"Did you ever ask your mother what she thought?" I've been so jealous of the other women in Felix's life, Nellie included, but I respect her judgment. And much as I dislike the idea, she lived with him longer than I did. Perhaps she understood dynamics I missed.

"Her father had two other families," Trevor says with a shrug. "She nagged me to be more appreciative with Dad. But I reckon she understood. She'd have gone ballistic if anyone tried to control her the way he controlled me. She said he was haunted, that some spirit made him act like that."

Oh, wow! Skepticism jumps to the fore. Is this a family belief? I want to dismiss it; how else can you take a comment like that? "Some spirit?" "Haunted?" I clamp my lips to stifle any further exclamation.

"Not by a ghost-ghost," Trevor says earnestly and goes silent. His Jamaican relatives are very dear to him. Other than his mother, I've never met any of them and know very little about that side of his life, and only a bit more about his stepfather Bertrand (yes, the Ebony Adonis), who comes from New Orleans. But he's just searching for the right words. "Like Dad was driven by something else, old demons, not by what went on between him and me. I wish I knew how to make him see how ridiculous it was."

Humble pie. Of course, his mother is too smart to believe in superstitions. And then—whap! —I get taken down another step with a reminder of the spirit/ghost/dead guy doing his thing in my own life.

Tell him, Felix says.

Tell him what?

Don't be silly. You can tell him only what you know. But tell him.

What else can I tell him? Sure as hell I'm not going to let on that I'm still listening to his father nine months after his death.

Trevor's misery rakes at me. His mouth is hooked down in an effort to hold back tears. Even his curls seem to droop. And now he's stuck with this ugly, ragged feeling that can't be put right. What can I say that might help?

I blurt out, "It's possible, just possible—I'm not sure at all—that his father wasn't his father, and he knew it—or he suspected it." Was that what Felix meant?

Trevor sits bolt upright and stares at me. "Huh? What d'you mean? You sure that wasn't just wishful thinking?" He gives me a querying look, one eyebrow peaked. "Is this some bullshit story Uncle Boet told you?"

I burst out laughing, partly at how fast he has switched from despair to mockery, and partly because he has a way of turning my fixation with Humphrey into a puffball.

"No," I say. "Actually, I heard about it from a priest—you know, Reverend Halpert, the guy who helped us do the memorial party? He said your dad mentioned something to him."

"Holy shit! Then who the hell was his real father? Was the other dude Humphrey's father too?"

Hearing him say that name instead of "Uncle Boet" feels

odd. As that thought enters my mind, another does too. I puncture the egg and the yellow trickles between the toast and mushrooms, linking it all. I push the toast to the side.

"This is such a jumble. I don't know, but I think your grandfather was Humphrey's real father, just not your dad's."

"And my grandmother? Was she Dad's real mother? He wasn't adopted, was he? You know, my girlfriend was adopted. It's a huge deal in her life. She is desperate to find her birth parents. She says not knowing who made you can really screw people up."

"Yes, it's a tough thing to handle," I say, glad he's divulged something about her. "No, he wasn't adopted. You can tell; he looked so much like his mother, and Humphrey does too. Though Humphrey says she had a mystery of her own of some kind, some person called Josie—or José, I think—who was sending her money." Trevor's eyes open wide and he does a "Wow!" but he's distracted. The waitress has just slipped him a note—with her phone number, I gather.

The sky has brightened, casting a hazy glow over the view stretching below us. As we trudge back up the long hill to the house, I remember how the whole discussion got started. I stop—also to catch my breath—and say, "Trev, this might all be nonsense, just a bunch of questions with us jumping to the wrong conclusions. But it seems your dad had the same questions. Can you imagine how he felt, maybe having a father he never met, a father he missed out on altogether?"

Trevor nods slowly. "Yeah, shit. That could really fuck things up." As we start walking again, he shoves his hands deep in his pockets and he's silent all the way home, till he realizes that neither of us has a key. We can't get in unless we ring the doorbell.

"I hope they're up," I say.

"Oh, boy, if Joanie's awake," Trevor exclaims, bright as a button again. "I cannot wait to tell her creepy old Grandpa might not have been our grandpa after all."

As we turn the corner and approach the waterfall of greenery, we notice the front door is open, and an ambulance is parked in front of the house.

~ *10* ~

The waiting has gone on forever, with the phone silent and my nerves jangling. My tinnitus has grown louder as the tension in my muscles has tightened. Muttering prayers to any and all deities.

Trevor and I asked Joanie and Eric if we could go with them to the hospital, drive them, give moral support. But they insisted they were all right and would rather go alone. The routine is familiar now, marching from section to section, doctor to doctor, waiting for their verdicts.

We didn't get a chance to ask what had happened, but Nurse Rawson, cornered in the hallway, still in her fuzzy mauve bathrobe, agreed to sit down with us and explain. Her condescending tone set my teeth on edge. Trevor didn't appear to have any problem with her, so perhaps it was just me being ratty. He peppered her with questions, and she began to open up.

It seems that after the weeping I heard during the night, Joanie breastfed Freddie and dozed off on the chaise longue with him in her arms. She woke early in the morning, still holding him—it must have been just after Trevor and I went out—and assumed he was fast asleep. When she laid him down in his crib, she noticed he felt even more limp than usual, turned on the light, and saw his color.

"He was blue," the nurse said. I don't know how literally to take that, but when Joanie screamed for her, she came running and started doing CPR on him. "They called for an ambulance while I was working on Freddie," she stated. "I got him pink again before they were off the phone, but you must understand we don't know how long he had stopped breathing." Her rigid calm cracked a bit then. Her chest was heaving. "It can't have been more than a few moments, but any time is too long. Poor little sweetheart."

It was reassuring to see how fiercely she cares about him. I found myself calling her by her first name, Nancy, dropping the formality of her title and my irritation.

"I wish they would call," Trevor said. He turned to Nancy and asked, "You've looked after many babies, yes? Have you seen one with problems like his?"

She shrugged. "I've seen everything. But I don't know what to make of this one. I told them right at the start that I thought he should be in the hospital, where they can keep an eye on his vitals, but they wanted him here with them."

She pulled her robe tighter and laid her hands flat on the counter. "But the vast majority do just fine." There was a hollow ring to her words. This was a spiel she must have delivered in lots of other homes. But I understood her need to sound positive. It's her job to help parents stay sane, not to elevate their anxiety. I did the same thing yesterday when Joanie asked her question.

"They come through, and they thrive," Nancy said. "You see them a few years later, when the mother has another baby, and you wouldn't know there'd been anything amiss. Some are small for their age, but they look as lively as any other child. I'm quite sure Frederick will be the same."

She excused herself to go upstairs and get dressed. Trevor slouched on the sofa and turned on the television. He patted the seat next to him, inviting me to come watch with him, but I was too antsy. I climbed the two flights back to my room. Put away my coat, showered, brushed my hair, and tried to settle into working on the book, reviewing my notes from the meeting with Gail Tennant.

But it was too quiet up there to concentrate; the silence filled with my fears. I began writing in my diary instead, so as not to get too far behind, but all I got down was: *Here in pretty Portland with my beloveds, Trevor included. Heart very full.*

With diary and phone in hand, I descended again. Trevor offered me the use of his laptop, and finally I got down to polishing the opening pages of the manuscript, Americanizing the spelling, and double-checking some dates. The mundane mental exercise helped still the drumbeat of fear.

~ ~ ~ ~

I've been typing all afternoon, and my shoulders are sore from hunching over the screen. Eric called an hour ago and said things were going well, but they would still be while. "We're waiting for a few more test results," he said. Deep breaths of relief.

I get up and prowl the length of the room, wondering about Joanie's state of mind. She asked yesterday if I think her age was an issue, if it could have caused Freddie's problems. "The obstetrician wrote in his report that I was a late *primigravida*," she'd said, scowling, "though my doctor insists that had nothing to do with anything. Why did we wait so long to get pregnant, as if we had all the time in the world?"

I tried to reassure her, in my ignorance. She is 36, older than usual to have a first child, but surely not all that old. It's roughly the age I was when I had my pregnancy. But that, of course, didn't go well. I lost my baby very early, just a few months in. But that was hellish enough. And thinking back now, I remember also wondering if I'd been too old—just over half the age I am now.

Leila—that was her name. No idea really if it was a girl or boy, but I felt I was having a girl. There were nights afterwards, lying next to Charles, hoping he wouldn't wake up and want to talk, when I'd picture her face—as a fully formed baby, as a little girl, as an adolescent, all the selves I'd never get to know and nurture. Imagined she'd have looked something like Joanie, whom I'd only seen in a photo—if in fact my Leila was Felix's child.

But could it have been a family flaw, not my age, that doomed her? Trevor doesn't know about that ill-fated pregnancy, so I restrain the desire to blurt out the question. Consider how to phrase it. And I could be grasping for leads where none exist. Joanie and Trevor are strong and beautiful.

As far as I know, Felix and his brothers and sisters were healthy. They still seem to be doing okay, aside from Joanne, who died in the motorcycle accident, and Felix, who had the aneurysm. What about their kids, Joanie's cousins? Have any of them had problems?

Without any more second-guessing, I pick up my phone and call Humphrey. He exclaims with unmistakable pleasure when he hears my voice. "Can we do the video thing again?" he asks. I tell him no, that this is just a very quick call. I explain about Freddie being back in the hospital, how Joanie and Eric are having blood tests, and how they are trying to narrow down the likely factors.

Trevor has pricked up his ears and is listening to my questions, eyebrows raised in puzzlement. I ask Humphrey about his children and his other nieces and nephews, if any of them had problems as infants or have issues now that could be related. "Nothing comes to mind. We're a pretty healthy bunch," he says. "I don't remember anything except the usual baby stuff—ear infections, stomach upsets, that kind of thing. I'm sorry. I mean, not sorry—I'm grateful they're all fine—but I wish I could help." His voice is low and intense, and I can feel the rumble in my solar plexus. This is the side of him that feels dear and familiar.

"I wish my brother was alive, to get tested," he says. "Would it help if I had it done? Presumably, I've got the same genes."

I say yes eagerly, and then I hesitate, remembering what Reverend Halpert said in his email last Saturday at Libby's. Do they in fact have the same genes? But again, I can't drop a topic that heavy into a chat like this. It's pure speculation anyway "I have to go," I tell him. "Call or text as soon as you know anything. Or send the results directly to Joanie and let her compare yours to theirs."

~ ~ ~ ~

Back to working on the chapters for Gail. The first one opens with a series of vignettes of people helped by dance. They have all faced injuries or illness, and all—with special equipment or physiotherapy or both—have discovered the joy of rhythmic movement. It's true even of those, like Felix's Maria, who have long-term disabilities. Seated in her wheelchair, she has taught dance with great success.

She taught Felix way back. I didn't know that until after he was gone, when I discovered a dusty pair of black dance shoes, deep at the back of his closet, the kind used for flamenco. He knew I loved that whole tradition, but he'd said nothing about having done it himself.

That was the first time I sensed his continuing presence. Clear as can be, cutting through the chatter in my brain, I heard, *Silly girl, let me show you.* I'd begun to browse his travel journals just days before, and on the very first page that I turned to after finding the shoes, there was the word "flamenco." Felix wrote that he was working in a bar with this marvelous girl, Maria, and studying dance with her each morning. He added that a friend of hers was teaching with her, though he didn't explain why she needed an assistant.

Often through the years, he mentioned Maria, always with glowing affection, but he didn't go into detail about her. In fact, it still puzzles me why he explained so little. When I probed, all he'd say was that she inspired him to study and encouraged him throughout his career.

It wasn't until we started work on the book, on what should have been that blissful weekend tryst out in Greenport, that I learned that she was a dance teacher. He simply announced that he wanted to include her. I was taken aback: What handicap qualified Maria to be in this lineup? That would have been the moment to ask, but we got sidetracked by our stupid argument. My question about Maria was forgotten along with our wonderful plans for the book.

I didn't get my answer about her until this year, a couple of weeks after finding the flamenco shoes and Felix's journal entry about meeting her in Spain. Sifting through his photographs, I came across a picture of Maria I'd never seen before. There she was with her elfin haircut and big smile, beaming up at him—from a wheelchair. He hadn't said a word to me about her being paraplegic.

I was stunned but not surprised by Felix's omission. Just as he found race irrelevant, he regarded disability as a minor part of a person's life—even as he dedicated his career to counteracting it. I disagreed and still do.

In a world shaped for the able-bodied, how can the daily barrage of challenges not affect one's personality? I think it can build strength, or erode it, or grow emotional calluses thicker than those on a dancer's feet.

In Maria, I suspect, it has done all of that. On the phone and in our email exchanges, she has been wonderfully warm, but it's clear she has no patience with dithering or over-analyzing. And she never brings up her own disability.

Trevor has gone back to watching television. I curl up on the couch with the laptop, lost in my thoughts. Maria was emphatic that I helped Felix recover from the first aneurysm, but I still want to know: Why couldn't my presence save him from the second one? Hovering by me here in this home in Portland, he is impatient.

Sal, this isn't what matters now.

But I was right there next to him in the bed, fast asleep. Were there signs I should have recognized that prior evening? Did he voice any distress? If I'd woken, could I have summoned help in time?

This is what haunts me. I can feel the stillness I registered as I woke in the semidarkness of our room. None of the usual soft snoring or twitches of the shared blankets. Dozy and not even sure if Felix was beside me in the bed, I turned on the bedside lamp and saw him, saw that beloved face, utterly serene and the color of clay.

That image disappeared for a long time. I recalled nothing after switching on the lamp, just a void. But it's different now. In the past few months, since his ghost has eased the trauma, fragments of memory have gradually coalesced.

Now they are pulling at me like the undertow of a tide. Try to push them away, to block the association. I don't know if it's Freddie's crisis this morning that has brought them to mind. This time, please let things be different. Please let us recognize the facts, see the patterns in time, in time to take action. Please.

~ ~ ~ ~

Early afternoon, Trevor and I are having yet another mug

of tea when Eric arrives home from the hospital alone, carrying a shopping bag. He looks haggard. "They've tested Freddie and say he is doing all right, that it was just one of those things that happens. But they still wanted to monitor him for a while longer. They tried to persuade Joanie to take a break, but she won't leave his side. He's asleep, but she says if he opens his eyes, she wants him to see a familiar face. I'll go back later and make her trade places with me."

From the bag he removes a white, quilted pad with an electric cord. "It's to put in his crib. This way an alarm will sound if his breathing halts again. We have to have this; otherwise, neither of us is ever going to get any rest."

I don't say it aloud, but that pad will work only if Freddie is lying on it, not if his mother falls asleep with him in her arms.

Trevor makes tea for Eric, and the three of us sit together, mostly silent. After a while, Eric asks me how I'm doing with the book. He knows how important it is to me. He was with me in Cape Town, in one of the best bookstores in the city, when the manager asked if it was true that there was a sequel in the works.

"Joanie told me you've got a hotshot young agent in New York," he says.

"Yes, bizarrely enough. I'm polishing the first section so I can send it to her."

He asks what that part deals with, and I mention the various profiles, including the one of Maria.

"Felix's Spanish friend? You know we visited her when we went to Europe last year?" he tells me. "We met José too." I do a double-take, and Trevor gives me a querying look. "He was very old but quite sharp. He wanted to know all about Felix. He asked how he was doing, what he was doing, where he was living. Maria said she'd told him all that, but he forgets."

I pick up my phone again on impulse, and without telling them what I'm doing or checking the time, I call Roxie. Her partner Edith answers, sounding groggy and suspicious. When she hears my voice, she softens and hands the phone to Roxie.

"Yes, what's up?" Roxie demands. "You do know it's almost midnight here?"

I apologize but push on. "Have you had any luck finding those Spain pages in Felix's journal?"

"Yes, I think so," she says. "But there was some other material, a greeting card and a photograph that seemed to have been glued to the same page. I was going to get a proper scan at the copy store in the morning. Do you want to see them too?"

I flick through my mental Rolodex, searching for a memory. I dipped into that journal in the first days after Felix's death when my mind was a mush. Very vaguely, I recall seeing a photo of Maria and a man in a bar, I think, and there was a card, some kind of religious image. "Yes, please!" I yell, as loud as Roxie. Trevor and Eric both swivel to stare at me. "And don't worry about getting a perfect copy; just use your phone and photograph everything, and send it now, please." I apologize again for being demanding at this ungodly hour.

"No problem," Roxie grunts, "but don't do it again."

We three sit chatting for the next ten minutes, casting

glances at my phone. I tell them about the card, which I assumed was from Felix's mother. He'd been estranged from the family for a few years by then, and it puzzled me that she would have known where to reach him on his travels.

It surely doesn't take that long to photograph an image and send it with an email. Ha, this from me, the high-tech expert. But at last, there's a ping, and I see Roxie's name pop up, with the paper clip showing there are attachments. Trevor suggests I open my email on the laptop, with the bigger screen, so I can more easily see the images.

That works; they are perfectly clear. The journal text, written in Felix's awful scrawl, talks about working in a bar in a quaint seaside town—Moraira, I think—with these people, enchanting Maria and this fantastic man, José. I punch the air in a private moment of jubilation. Yes, the tickle of memory was right! He goes on to describe long conversations with José, and about Maria giving him dancing lessons. The photograph is of the three of them. I remember being shocked that Maria is as fair as he is, not dark-haired as I had always imagined. She seemed either very short or was sitting. Now I know she was in a wheelchair.

Eric enlarges the photo image, and he nods. "Yes, that's them, Maria and her papa, though obviously much younger than when we met them." He turns to me and asks, "It's interesting to see, but why is this such a big deal?"

"Her papa? You met her father too?" I ask.

He gives me a funny look. "I just told you we met Maria's father, and how he asked about Felix."

Trevor wrinkles his forehead. "Didn't you say Uncle Boet

talked about a José or was that a Josie?" He sounds disappointed. "So, José is Maria's father, not Dad's?" Eric and I both give him a "Huh?" look. "I thought that's what all your excitement was about, that this José was Dad's real father. Sorry. My bad. I was off on the wrong track, twisting up stories."

"You smoke too much weed," Eric says.

Trevor ignores him. "But how did my grandmother know Maria's father?"

"The Josie she mentioned might have been a totally different person," I say. "Or maybe he is this José."

"José is a really common name," Eric puts in. "I don't know what you two are talking about, but I personally know about three Josés here in Portland."

Trevor is glued to the laptop screen. He says, "Doesn't that old guy look like my dad?" He's almost levitating off his chair now, examining the photo as if it holds a secret code, the clue to where treasure is buried.

"Wishful thinking," I tell him. The guy is hawk-faced and totally bald—but who knows?

Eric peers at the image and shrugs. "I don't remember seeing any resemblance when we met him—but then I wasn't looking for it. I don't understand what you're talking about. I thought this was just to help you edit your book material, Sally. And I'm too tired to make sense of anything right now. If you two will excuse me, I'm going upstairs to get some shut-eye." He pushes back his chair and stands up.

"Poor guy, you must be exhausted," I say. "But wait. Never mind my book. The father talk isn't just idle curiosity. It might help us with Freddie."

"Freddie?" Eric turns back to us.

"Freddie?" Trevor asks me. "I thought this was about Dad or Maria or José."

Eric says, "Jesus, Sally, no more riddles. What the hell is going on here?"

"Can you give me a paper and pen?" Eric finds me a wire-bound notebook and passes me a jar filled with writing implements. My preferred mode—maybe from all the years of plotting choreography. "Going old style, if you two don't mind," I say.

Not as elegantly as Eric would have drawn it, but reasonably clearly, I jot down my chain image and extend it into a reverse family tree. It spreads out from Freddie to Joanie and Eric, who gets a big blank balloon, and from Joanie to Felix and Deidre, and from Felix to his mother and ostensible father, and then a side arrow with a large question mark.

"If what's wrong with Freddie is connected to genes, then it could come from Felix via one of his parents—or from some person we didn't know about before, who might be his real father."

That sounds so flimsy. I take a deep breath and add, because this is no time for discretion, "I had a baby that didn't make it to term, and it was Felix's. There might be a gene in his line that causes complications."

"You—? Wow, Sal, a kid with Dad?" Trevor's eyes tilt with surprise and sympathy. I can see how hard he is trying to weigh everything. "But I'm fine, and Joanie's fine. Could it have skipped us?"

Eric nods, doing his own processing. "Not skip, but not show up. Some things are recessive unless the genes come from both parents."

He isn't shocked the way Trevor was. I assume Joanie told him what she found out about me in Cape Town. That's all right; I regard them as a unit. He's trying to fit this new piece into the puzzle that is his son. And then his head shoots around and he says, "If José. . . If Maria . . . Do you have any idea what's wrong with her, why she can't walk?" His face is a crosshatch of excitement and wariness.

Trevor jumps up. "I told you they look alike!" He starts pacing. "But how could Grandma Elsabet ever have met José? So many X factors. My head feels like a fucking pinball machine."

Too tired to think clearly. Life takes such confusing forms. I picture my breakfast—the last thing I ate, come to think of it—with that yellow yolk encircling the different items on my plate, so it looked like an amoeba. Maybe this whole genetic thing is nonsense.

Nancy Rawson is sitting behind us in a chair in the living room area. I'm startled when I notice her. I have no idea how long she has been sitting there, listening to us. She gets up slowly and walks over.

"You asked before if I've seen other babies with problems like Freddie's. I've been thinking back. A few years ago, I looked after a newborn with limbs that didn't seem as strong as they should be." Her usually brusque tone is a little more hesitant. "The mother's brother came to visit, and he was using crutches. I just thought it was a coincidence, but maybe it was something they shared, one of these threads that run through families. These days they can test very early, even in utero, can't they?"

"A bit late for us," Eric says, cutting her short. "And they need to know what they're looking for. What happened to that baby?"

She stares at us, silent for a few beats. "Well, it was a long time ago, and I'm sure that the doctors know much more nowadays." The doorbell rings, and before he can ask her anything more, she bustles off to answer it.

The three of us watch her exit into the hallway. She speaks to someone on the front step, and then comes staggering back inside, dragging a knee-high parcel by the string that surrounds it. Trevor, who's nearest, goes over to inspect the labels. "Ugh," he says, "It's from the dragon. Shall we open it?"

"Leave it for Joanie," Eric says. "It's probably for her."

"It's addressed to Freddie," Trevor says.

The four of us look at each other. Were it from anyone else, I would still suggest leaving it for Joanie. Perhaps a gift will cheer her up when she comes home. But this is Deidre we're dealing with.

"I think I'd better open it," Eric says. He takes out a pocketknife and slices through the string and then the layers of brown paper and green Christmas wrapping, and rips open the big white box. He draws out a gaily painted wooden horse, with a shaggy woolen mane and gleaming gold rockers. "CAUTION," the label on the front says. "Not for children under two."

"She's an idiot," Trevor says.

"I'm sure she meant well," I venture. But I agree. It's making assumptions about the future when these new parents are so fiercely focused on now, taking one day at a time. Looking that far ahead is tempting fate.

"I think I'll stash it in the basement for now," Eric says.

Trevor gets up to help him and they're about to start moving the horse when Eric's phone buzzes. He walks into the kitchen area as he's talking and then hangs up. He takes a container out of the freezer, saying to us, "Joanie. She asked if I'd bring her some soup. She hasn't eaten the whole day." He gathers his car keys off the counter, ready to walk out.

I say, "You didn't get that nap. And you probably haven't eaten."

He nods and turns to Trevor. "Would you mind driving me? I'm not sure I can steer straight."

"Then I'm coming too." I scurry after them.

~ ~ ~ ~

We find Joanie in the lounge area outside the infant intensive care unit. There are other people—some women on their own and some couples, sitting far removed from each other, as if to avoid infecting one another with their anxiety. Some are staring at the television suspended from the ceiling, with lyrics of jolly Christmas staples scrolling over a Yule log image.

Eric gives me the soup and heads off to see Freddie. Joanie smiles wanly and reaches for the container, but then grimaces as she registers how cold it is. I take it from her and double back the way we came, to a room with vending machines, a microwave and a tall coffee urn.

"How come I didn't notice this?" she asks. "You're so efficient. My brain isn't functioning."

"You were kind of distracted? I smelled food," I tell her. "My stomach is growling. Let's go get a snack."

"There'll be chocolate," she says. "After this soup I need chocolate. And coffee."

Maybe this was a dumb move. If she breastfeeds Freddie, won't the chocolate and caffeine make him jumpy? It could also make it harder for her to sleep tonight. I don't say anything, just think I'll try to divert her to something more nutritious. We get Trevor from the lounge, and the three of us go in search of the vending machines.

The room is furnished with plastic tables and chairs that are unnervingly wobbly, as if to guarantee that no one stays there too long. Trevor and I get sandwiches sealed in impenetrable celluloid boxes. When I finally get mine open, the smell of salami douses my hunger. I nibble the crusts, trying to avoid the congealed mayo. Joanie gives up on the chocolate but reaches for a cup of bright pink strawberry pudding. "I need sweet stuff," she says, looking at me defiantly as if I've voiced my disapproval. "I know, I know, I look like a whale."

"You look fine. Have whatever helps you keep going," I say. "The weight will come off when you're ready."

Two mouthfuls in, Joanie shoves aside her pudding and puts her face in her hands. "I'm such an idiot," she says. "They keep telling me this thing happens with babies, that their breathing can pause for no reason. But he was in my arms. If I can't keep him safe when he's in my arms, how can I ever keep him safe? There is something wrong, and the flipping doctors are no help."

I reach across the table to stroke her arm. What is there to say?

"Can I tell her?" Trevor demands.

"Only if it's good news," Joanie says. "Can he tell me what?"

"Creepy Grandpa Barnard might not be our grandfather after all." He makes a duckbill mouth, watching for her reaction. Joanie frowns at him just as she used to when he was a kid trying to convince her of some wild story. She turns to me with eyebrows raised. He goes on: "And we think maybe that's why Dad was so neurotic with us, me especially."

"How do you know this?" she asks.

"Remember Reverend Halibut?" he demands.

"Halpert," I say. She nods.

"He says Dad told him something."

"Then who was his real father?" She wrinkles her nose, clearly skeptical.

Now Trevor is the one looking at me questioningly. I know what he's asking, but I shrug. It's all too tangled to simplify.

"Maybe. We don't know," he tells her. "But there's a chance it was his friend Maria's dad. His name is José."

"You mean Dad and Maria were brother and sister?"

The words are so blunt, I gasp. Goodness knows why, but I hadn't fully registered that idea till now. "Halfs," I say. "Half-siblings at most, like you two. They had a special bond from the moment they met."

"You think he knew?" Joanie gets up, circles the table, and

returns to her seat.

"I haven't a clue."

"But how? How did this guy—a Spaniard…?" And then she sits up straighter and answers herself—or begins to. "You know, Grandma Elsabet might have been in Europe as a girl. Do you remember how musical she was? Aunt Helga told me Grandma could have been a concert pianist. She won some big scholarship to study music—I don't know where—but apparently decided she wanted to get married and have a family. Helga, of course, thought that was the correct decision. Maybe she did go abroad to study."

Eric comes looking for us. "They say Freddie is stable and we can take him home," he says. We all rise, welcoming the news. The word "stable" has let breath enter my lungs properly for the first time since this morning.

"These two have been telling me a wild story," Joanie tells him. "Did you know about my father?" and she stops. "No, this is soap opera stuff. It's nonsense. Grandma and Grandpa were the most uptight, conventional people I ever met."

"What you know of them," Eric says. He grasps her hands in his. "If that José we met is your dad's father, then with Freddie there might be some link to whatever is wrong with Maria."

Joanie's jaw drops. "Oh, my God!" Her bloodshot eyes focus on his, as if trying to push back the implication.

He carries on. "We need to find out if she and your father were related, and if they were, what is wrong with her. You know, we told the doctors our relatives on both sides were from northern European stock, but maybe that's not true. My mother says some of her information might also be faulty."

Joanie rounds on me, her face flushed and agitated. "How do we find out now? Dad was always so tight-lipped about his family. And now it's too late to get his effing DNA. For someone who was interested in science and the body, he was pretty useless when it came to the stuff that matters most."

I really don't want to confess my wrongdoing, but I hate to hear her also judging Felix unfairly. Glumly, I tell them about the genetic history chart he ordered that I threw away. "I thought it was some scam," I groan.

Joanie doesn't react, just says, "So what do we do now?" Her tone has gone flat, buttoned down. Her only show of emotion is a deep sigh as we head back to the ward to get Freddie.

Humming from the air-conditioning and the incessant beeping and intercom messaging merge with the ringing in my ears. The cold smell of antiseptic gets sandwiched with a cabbage aroma from a cart laden with half-empty food trays. I can't wait to get outside into the fresh air.

You've got this, Copper Girl. Time to dance.

It sure doesn't feel that way. My feet are leaden.

~ 11 ~

So much for having Christmas Day with dear ones. The only good thing about the date is that most people are already where they want to be or have no choice. The plane is half empty, and I have a row of three seats to myself. I can be as antisocial as I want. But ridiculously, after the incessant companionship of these past two weeks, I feel isolated and adrift. I have to remind myself that I made this choice, that I am on a mission.

When it comes time to serve snacks, they offer us a special treat, a creamy eggnog with a sprinkle of cinnamon. I'm not the least bit hungry, but I'm hoping it has alcohol in it. Early as it is, a drink might soothe the roiling inside. Each food tray, laid with a red and green paper cloth, comes bearing a cellophane-wrapped gingerbread man. I see the woman across the aisle slip hers into her bag. She sees me looking and says, "For my grandkids. They'll have to share it." I offer her mine as well, and she accepts it gratefully, after asking twice if I really mean it.

The flight attendants, also missing out on family celebration time, share commiserations with the passengers. They are doing their best to make things feel a little festive. We even get a duet from the pilot and copilot, singing a verse from "Holly Jolly Christmas." The attendants wave their arms, trying to get us all to join in.

I don't want to sing. Trying to focus on practicalities, replaying the events of the past week, so I won't dwell on what happened this morning. Out comes my diary, and I begin recording the bare-bones facts.

Misery hovers like a shadow. Pricewise, the flight has worked out well, thanks to Deidre and her contacts in the travel netherworld. I have been able to exchange a Portland–New York–Cape Town ticket for one from Portland via O'Hare to Spain, and from there to Cape Town. That doesn't give me much time in Barcelona— basically from dawn when I arrive tomorrow to dusk the same day. In total, by the time I arrive home, I will have been traveling for two days.

"Home"—after all Libby's efforts to talk me into staying? It has felt good being back in the States, but I'm beginning to long for my quiet little cottage. And Humphrey wrote that he is going to be in Cape Town next week. He asked if I have plans for New Year's Eve.

It made my mind flutter when I read that, hard as I try to dismiss the idea now. And he urged me not to undertake such a tiring detour.

I'd emailed him about Maria's José and all our speculation that he might be their mother Elsabet's secret benefactor. I still haven't mentioned the father idea, simply said I wanted to meet Maria in person because of the book, and incidentally to see if she knew anything about the connection to Elsabet. Humphrey wrote back:

This is nuts. Why couldn't you ask your questions on the phone? Or if you're going there, stay for a few days. You'll be exhausted.

Libby said the same, almost word for word. I took her concern for granted, but reveled in the message from him, touched that he cares. I didn't explain that a longer stay would push up the ticket cost and involve a hotel room.

Maybe—eventually—the book will generate income. I sent the opening pages to Gail Tennant, with a note that I am on my way to meet the woman mentioned in the first chapter. Also told her, by the way, that Ethel has offered to host a grand launch party if we get that far. But how much longer can I stall on the coauthor question?

Reclining across my row of seats, I flip open the in-flight magazine. It's packed with lush descriptions of exotic cultural sites, some of which I've visited, and luxury holiday resorts I never expect to go near. There is a section on books, most of them nonfiction and related to culture. I try to imagine *Next Steps* featured there. It could happen. I just need to set goals and believe—like Deidre said.

But more important than that, we need to find a way to help Freddie. I might have just made everything even worse.

~ ~ ~ ~

At Joanie's urging the morning after the hospital visit, I put through a call to Maria in Barcelona. I told her I had a range of questions related to the book and "some other subjects" and wanted to come visit. She squealed with delight. Her accent is heavy and the line wasn't good. It took a while to clarify that I wasn't coming on vacation but wanted to meet briefly if it could be arranged. She adjusted at once. "I am happy we meet at last, long or short. We will talk fast," she exclaimed.

With that established, Joanie insisted I call Deidre to get help changing my booking. "She wants to be useful? Then let her be," she said. She was still seething from the gift received the day before.

The trouble had erupted the moment we walked in from the hospital. Trevor and I tried to block the rocking horse from Joanie's view while Eric hustled her through to the stairs. But she caught a glimpse of it, and her face contorted. She yelled, "What the hell is that?" She saw the "from" address and ripped the wrapping paper. The baby, in Eric's arms, woke and began to cry. Joanie lowered her voice. She hissed, "I told her a thousand times that we just want to take one day at a time. No tempting fate. Why can't she understand that?"

Evidently, daughter sent mother a scathing text to that effect. First thing on Friday, Deidre called the house phone. She got Trevor on the line and asked for me. "You're a grandmother too, sort of," she said. "Do you understand why I sent that horse? Can't you explain it to that brat of mine?"

I was stumped. I'd joined Eric and Trevor in condemning the gift. "What would you like me to get across?" I asked.

"Look, Sally, I'm as scared as they are," she said. "I've talked to their doctors more than they have. But I was brought up to look ahead. If I worried about failing, my mother would launch into one of her Positive Thinking lectures. She taught me to set goals and assume success until I achieved it. I thought I was doing the kids a favor by focusing on the future. I want them to believe Freddie will survive, that he will be a healthy toddler, and then a big kid, that one day he'll be galloping on a real horse."

It was a joyful vision. She actually made me smile. I sought out Joanie upstairs, and while she was pinned down, feeding Freddie, I made her listen. There was no point asking her to believe in the future; that's still too much of a stretch. But I urged her to remember who her mother is and how she has functioned all her life. It's not entirely a bad way to be.

"You know, I plan to become more that way myself," I told Joanie. "Enough with being a little mouse. Like your dad used to say, it's time to dance!"

"I never heard him say that—and you've never been a mouse," she said. She drew in a deep breath and exhaled slowly. "But I suppose it's the way he lived too. Maybe he and my mom weren't so incompatible after all."

Within an hour of my calling her, Deidre had my flight organized. Once again, I was indebted to her, but she didn't see it that way. She kept thanking me for smoothing over the rocking horse row. "Apart from the fact that you fucked my husband, you and I could become friends," she said, and rang off before I could respond.

I told the buzzing static, "You might be right."

With travel plans settled, that day and the next were good or as good as possible under the circumstances. When she could, Joanie hung out with Trevor and me, and we did our best to divert her. We walked with her to the park and went back to our funky café for lunch. On Friday evening, we all cooked dinner together, each taking the lead on a different course.

On Saturday—yesterday—Freddie was fussing, and Joanie asked me to hold him while she showered and dressed. I wanted to pull back, but she plopped him into my arms and walked away.

I sat down in the big rocker and laid him lengthwise on my lap, cradling him between my thighs. He stared up at me as I softly, softly massaged the soles of his feet, hardly bigger than the pad of my thumb. The pink toes stretched and flexed—a good sign, I'm sure.

When I stopped, he began to cry, so I lifted him to my shoulder and began to sing the most soothing songs I could think of, *Twinkle Twinkle Little Star* and *Silent Night* and *Frère Jacques*, and then hummed a Polish tune I don't know the name of that my mother used to sing to me. Gradually, I felt him relax and grow heavier in my arms, and his eyes slowly closed.

I could have stayed like that all day, just studying those mauve eyelids and the perfection of his round-button nose and the delicate swoop of his lips. "I'm your other grandmother, sort of," I whispered to him, tears dripping onto his onesie and leaving dark spots, "and I'm not always this weepy."

When Joanie came back in, she just smiled and nodded as she took him from me. "This is the part that makes it all bearable," she said.

Trevor wanted to explore the city to see some of the innovative new buildings Eric had described to him. Leaving Nurse Rawson in charge of Freddie, we headed out in his jeep and did a quick spin around the downtown area. He had folded back the roof, all the better to crane our necks and see—but disastrous for my hair. That didn't matter; it was worth it to hear Trevor wax professorial about the influence of I.M. Pei or Frank Lloyd Wright. Joanie teased him about it, but even she sounded impressed.

We found parking near the flea market at the waterfront. By agreement, we bought little gifts for each other—for Hanukkah or Christmas or both. "No spending over $10 an item," Joanie declared. "That way, we have to get creative."

"And for Kwanzaa," Trevor added, grinning. "I should get for all three."

Joanie gave a snort, but he turned serious. "I'm spending all next week with my mom and Bertrand, and they're very into it, with all the themes and celebration—and lots of gift-giving. Joanie, remember how they used to invite Dad to come on the last day, for Imani? He loved it. You know how he was about exploring other people's traditions." He looked down and I saw him swallow hard. It was as if a cloud had moved over the sun. "It's still so weird that he's not around." I gave him a hug, pleased to hear the softened tone towards Felix.

Silly, but I agonized over the choices. I wanted to find things that would last, that would keep reminding these two of my love. That ruled out food or fancy soaps or candles. At last, in a jammed-to-the-ceiling old bookstore, I found Trevor a nearly pristine, second-hand copy of Frank Lloyd Wright's autobiography. To boost Joanie's resolution to get healthy, I bought her a wooden juicer based on a design from the British Museum.

The kids were far blither in their choosing. Joanie bought me a fabulous vintage scarf with Fifties-style biker chicks—including a redhead she said looked like me. Trevor got us both pink knitted "pussycat" hats, charmed by the passionate patter from a solo protester who said they were going to be the badge of women for the next decade, "till we overturn the patriarchy!" Joanie gleefully donned hers. It was the first time all week that I'd seen her tiger-girl grin.

We had to rush in the end, because Trevor needed to pack and get on the road if he was to spend Christmas Day with his girlfriend. But I found gifts for Eric and for Nancy too, and a little wind-up musical mobile to hang over Freddie's crib. I looked without success for something appropriate for Maria, but did find a small lapel-pin print for her husband, Diego. It's of a painting by Diego Rivera, whom I remember her saying is his idol. She didn't mention that he also had a brilliant, disabled wife.

Saying goodbye to Trevor was hard. I wrapped my arms around his waist, and as I pressed my face against his leather jacket, I heard him say, "Hear my heart? That's where I hold you, Sally." Of course, I cried. I promised I'd be in touch as soon as I learned anything more about his father's story.

~ ~ ~ ~

I thought the parting would all be like that, sore but the good sore of loving so much. I felt I was gradually learning again to let such feelings flow, without freezing at the thought of what can go wrong. But it has gone wrong.

My alarm went off at five this morning. I woke with a jolt from a restless sleep, feeling faintly nauseous, with a throbbing head. It took about three seconds for stark dread to strike: Am I sick? It might be nothing, just fatigue—or I could have caught whatever Ethel appears to have. She says she's sick as a dog, coughing and running a fever. How many days has it been since our lunch date when, apparently, she was coming down with whatever? Wouldn't be a big problem—I'm still overjoyed that she and I reconnected—if it weren't for the Portland family. My throat, as I sit here in the air-conditioned plane, feels like tissue paper.

I had booked a taxi to the airport and hoped to creep out before dawn to catch my flight, without waking anyone. But as I tiptoed down the stairs with my luggage, I heard Joanie moving around in the nursery, and I went in to tell her I might be sick. Freddie was deep asleep, breathing with soft, quick little whiffles. I started to smile, and then remembered why I'd gone in. I seem to spend my time confessing terrible things I want Joanie to forgive.

She stared at me with her eyes round and dark in that dim light, and then shout-whispered, "Damn it, Sally, I wish you hadn't told me! Shit. Now I'm going to be watching for symptoms and scared every time he burps. Step away from me, and please don't go near him."

I recoiled. It was too early to absorb such harshness. For Once, I didn't weigh my words with her. I hissed back, "I haven't done this deliberately! I love you, you know that, but you can be a real bitch!"

I heaved my bag back on my shoulder and headed down to the first floor. The sofa looked horribly neat without Trevor's sleeping bag. I poured myself a glass of water and sipped it between deep breaths, trying to calm down. The taxi was due in ten minutes—not soon enough. I washed the glass twice, put it in the drying rack, and picked up my stuff, intending to wait outside on the sidewalk.

As I turned to go, I heard the creak of footsteps on the stairs. Joanie came in and planted herself in front of me, pigeon-toed like a kid, in her socks and flannel nightgown. "I am a bitch, you're right. If I hurt your feelings, I'm sorry."

She made a half-hearted move to hug me, but I waved her off. Of course, I had already held Freddie often—and held him for a long time yesterday. Had I been exhaling germs? Typhoid Grandma, that's me.

I said, "I have to go. Merry Christmas." She just nodded.

Joanie walked with me to the front door, and we stood in silence looking out into the gray light. I walked down the steps. "Aside from the scare the other day, his lungs seem pretty strong," she said finally, as if trying to reassure herself, or me. "You can tell from his crying. I think his metabolism is all right. It's his leg muscles that are weak, not his organs."

I appreciated her effort, but that didn't really make sense. I looked back up at her from the sidewalk and said, "I'm really sorry if I've made Freddie, or you, or anyone sick."

As the taxi drew up, I made a ballet curve with my arms, in lieu of an embrace, and tried to smile. She did too. I climbed in and collapsed like an empty coat on the back seat. At the last moment, Eric appeared on the top step. He put his arm around Joanie, and they both waved to me.

This is what I feared from that moment on the phone when Joanie told me there was something wrong with Freddie and asked me to come—this intolerable ache, with fresh wounds deepening unhealed wounds, loss resonating with loss, cracking my shell. I tried to be quiet, but my sobbing caught the attention of the taxi driver. He said nothing, simply reached back with a box of tissues.

~ ~ ~ ~

Now, on the plane, as the second cup of tasteless, searing hot coffee has gone down, my shivers are subsiding. The flight attendants are leading the passengers in a jaunty rendition of "Jingle Bells." Perhaps I scared Joanie for nothing. The headache has dissolved, might have been nothing but too many nights of broken sleep. Perhaps I could have had that final— no, not final—just a last hug for now. They will come see me in Cape Town, all three of them, soon, and Trevor. I sit up straighter, clutching onto that hope.

We are crossing the Rockies, massive even from this great elevation. Etched by the light of a clear winter day, they look hand-drawn, like the illustrations in a geography textbook. I almost expect to see the parallel lines tracing their contours, swooping out and back and around.

Very deliberately thinking ahead, but with no idea of the steps needed or the pace, or even the theme.

So, I ask my peripatetic ghost lover, what did you mean by dancing? Is it going to take fancy footwork? I want a choreographer I can trust, but there's only me making the decisions.

You'll know what to do. Just get out of your own way.

Ugh, it's so annoying when he talks that way! Do I tell Maria we think her father might also have fathered her best friend? Or does she know? Is José still alive? Do I ask him in front of his daughter whether he sent money to Felix's mother for many years? When last I heard of him, in Felix's journal, José was working behind the counter in a bar. How much help could he afford to send a woman he hadn't seen since his youth? Is any of that going to be relevant to Freddie?

Exhausted again, I try to lie down along the row of seats, but the armrest hinges poke into my ribs. My knee aches, and my spine is stiff, and I feel hollow inside and very much alone. The image of Joanie and Eric collages with one of Libby and Doug, and even Roxie and Edith, and Jacob and Nomse. Everyone I think of is paired in a cozy partnership—except me.

What has happened to the resilient woman Felix felt free to love? When I asked him why, after the many years of our long-distance dance, he finally asked me to come live with him, he said, "You're stronger now. I'm not afraid of wounding you."

I did feel strong then, but I don't feel strong now. I try to push myself into the pleasure of that memory. I had a cozy partnership too, even if it took us forever to reclaim it. Ironically, I have to admit, his brush with death worked in my favor too; he no longer saw time as a luxury, and he wanted to grasp all the happiness life could still offer.

He trusted himself more too, thanks to his diminished libido. Never thought that could be an asset. Though he still adored women of all shapes and ages, the drive to lay them was gone. That suited me just fine. My own sap was slower to rise, and snuggling felt good. I was contented in his arms, a glass bead embraced by his abalone shell.

So, what the hell happened with Humphrey? What began with a craving to have his brother back has turned into an obsession with the younger sibling. When I think of him, I go from soulful to buzzing in one lurch. Mmm, the crisp white linen of his shirt, the narrow hips in those khaki trousers. I see his hands, imagine the heat of his touch, and my skin tingles. I have daydreamed about lying in bed with him, my body light enough to float, needing his weight against me, desire meeting desire.

Enough of that! Not sure what is more ridiculous, the self-pity or the lust that has just replaced it. Change directions, steer my thoughts to the questions I want to address with Maria. As the plane begins its descent to Chicago, other thoughts rise. While I'm waiting for my connecting flight, I want to stock up on some of that delicious chocolate the tie-dyed accountant on my first flight shared with me. It will make a nice gift for Maria.

I pull out his card with the brand noted on it. Of course, on the other side is his name. I notice for the first time that he has the same initials as me: He's Sam Parker. And for the first time, I remember that he asked if I'd like to get together in Portland. But that was before I canceled my flight and went home with Libby. I'm kind of sorry I forgot. He was rather sweet, and Joanie and Eric could do with a good accountant, if he's the kind who does taxes. The card doesn't say.

On the back, under the chocolate name, he has printed in

small, neat letters, "Please stay in touch. I come to SA often. I'd love to take you to dinner." Libby would be pleased. She seems to think anyone would be preferable to the second Barnard brother. As for me, not sure about dinner, but I could also do with a friend who understands finances.

In my diary I write:

Merry Christmas. Next year in Jerusalem. Muddled in every way. If Freddie has caught an infection from me, will Joanie ever let me come near him again?

~ *12* ~

H ow do you know I love this stuff very much?" Maria demands. If I didn't already like her from the contacts we've had this past year, I'd warm to her now. She rips the holiday wrapping off the box of chocolates as eagerly as a child and insists we both have one immediately. They are just as good as those Sam Parker shared on the plane from South Africa, and perfect with the Turkish coffee she has brewed for us.

Losing track of the days. This is Monday? She met me at the metro station near her home. It was a quick, easy ride from the airport, as she promised, into a welcoming city with some strange and wonderful buildings. And there at the station entrance was Maria, still as gamine cute as in the first photo I saw of her, though gray-haired now, in a motorized wheelchair. A fluffy brown poodle, her beloved Gugli, was standing by the wheel, bottom waggling. Maria reached up to hug me, and we

177

clung to each other for a long moment, Felix present in our embrace.

Then with the whirr of her motor and the rattle of my suitcase wheels, we trundled the two blocks to her apartment building, nattering like long-separated pals.

Now, one of the first things I see when we enter her home is a framed picture of Felix. I almost don't recognize him, my Tiger Man camping it up in a blond wig and a fabulous, dotted flamenco dress. The curling lips give him away, even through smudged red lipstick. Next to that is a picture of Maria in tall bunny ears and fuzzy white suit. "It was for somebody's fancy dress dance party. We had very much fun together, he and I," she sighs. "You should have seen, I could make those rabbit ears flap, flap. We made each other laugh till we cried."

That's not what I shared with him at all. I tell her, fighting back a twinge of envy, that I loved his sense of humor, but I tend to be much more serious.

"I know," Maria replies. "And he loved that about you. He said you put your heart into everything."

I want a moment to savor that, but she fixes me with her round, dark eyes. "So, we have little time, and you are a woman with a purpose, no?" We're seated side by side out on her pretty tiled balcony, enjoying our coffee in the bright morning sunshine. The blue and yellow pattern on the floor looks like garlands of flowers. Gugli comes out to join us and hops up on her lap, looking from one to the other as we talk. Everything about this apartment feels expansive and open. It's a special building, Maria has told me, designed for wheelchair accessibility, but the only thing that feels different are the wide doorways and lower kitchen and bathroom counters.

"You tell me what you want to know," she says. She is as vivacious as I've always imagined, her mind bouncing from one topic to another, gesturing excitedly. "But first, tell me about the young ones. How are Joanie and Eric? They are wonderful, aren't they? And tell me, how is their baby?"

The mention of Joanie brings a prickle of tears, and a surge of urgency. I start to say, "Actually, that's why—" but she interrupts, both hands up.

"Wait. Before that, I must get this big, bad thing out of the way. I have a confession, Sally." What on earth could she have done wrong? I put my coffee down on the glass table between us, and smile invitingly, quite sure it's nothing.

"You remember when you started work on the book, you and Felix were meeting at a hotel near a beach somewhere?" I certainly do. The dream that turned into a nightmare, in that beautiful place out on Long Island. I'm surprised she knows about it, though I shouldn't be. Felix seemed to consult her on everything.

"He was happy about this wonderful idea you were having for a book together—but also to be with you. I had not heard him so . . . so *jubiloso* for a very long time. I told him, 'Wait!'"

My smile drops. Aside from the book, we were like horny teenagers, excited about being alone together. On the first night, in his rental car in a deserted parking lot, I thought we were going to make love. It would have been the first time since the night in Hollywood almost twenty years before. Instead, he drew away, glum and resolute.

"You know that he was three years older than me," Maria

continues, "so he was the big brother, but I am bossy like a big sister. I told him you are not someone for him to take to bed and then leave, to go back to his California life like nothing has happened. I told him if he hurts you again, he will lose you forever."

The prickling heat of the sun bakes my chest, adding to the burning indignation. I want to shout into her heart-shaped, anxious face that she had no right to interfere.

I take a deep breath and another and another, to still the clashing emotions. At last, I reach over the caramel fluff of the dog and squeeze Maria's hand. "It's all right. You were right. The timing was wrong. It would have been a disaster."

I've fought this fact since that weekend, but deep down I know it's true. If he had gone home and begun dating other people, rather than staying faithful to me until we could live together, I would have been terribly disappointed. It would have brought up all our old history. This past year I have begun to understand more of our history, and my own culpability— the distrust that helped drive him away in our youth—but I understood none of it at that point. And there would have been no reconciliation if he hurt me again.

"When we did get together, that was when everything fell into place," I tell Maria. "I will be grateful to you all my life for finding me when he was sick and telling me to come be with him."

We're both sniffing and smiling now. Gugli gets up and licks her cheek. Maria pushes him away with a laugh. She says, "Thank you, my dear Sally. Ah, I feel like a balloon, so glad, so light! For too long I have wanted to say that sorry. Now, why did you come?"

I take a gulp of coffee and begin: "I want to know more about you to fill out the description Felix wrote for our book."

She interrupts: "Nonsense! That you can be doing on the phone, or with email. Something else brings you to speak like this, mano a mano, or rather friend to friend."

She maneuvers the chair till we are facing each other. "Whatever you want to know, it is fine. Felix and I had no secrets, and now you and I have no secrets."

In that moment, I also feel like a helium balloon. The weight of caution and double-guessing falls away. I take a deep breath and say, "You asked me about Joanie's baby. That is really why I came." She tilts her head, surprised, and I forge ahead. "We want to know if your father was Felix's father too—if there could be a genetic connection."

The rosy tone of her skin drains to sallow. "My father and Felix? What are you talking about? I thought maybe you want to ask me were Felix and I lovers, if we were ever having an affair, something like that."

"I did always want to know that," I reply, trying to regroup. "I know he loved you, that he regarded you as his best friend. But I don't really care if you were ever lovers in the past. I know it wasn't when he and I were together."

"We were not lovers," she says, evidently determined to clear this up too, or simply not wanting to absorb what I've said.

"I would have been happy to be his girlfriend, and he was always saying I was sexy, that to be like this is not a problem. But he was telling me he did not want to spoil our friendship.

I accepted that."

She shakes herself and stares at me. "But what are you saying about my father?"

The feeling of freedom was so brief. Back to calculating. Back to worrying about whom I might hurt. The tile pattern that looked like floral wreaths now looks like intersecting handcuffs.

"I'm sorry I spoke too bluntly, without warning. It might be quite wrong," I stammer. "All we know is that there was a man called José—or Josie—who had a connection to Felix's mother, Elsabet. Felix believed the man he grew up with in South Africa was not his father. When he came to Europe, he looked for the person who might be the real one. You and he were so close, and your father is José, I thought—we thought—maybe . . ."

"Why now?" Maria demands, her forehead puckered in distress. "My father is very old. He could die today, tomorrow, who knows? After all our wars, we have made peace, he and me. I was thinking it would be a peaceful parting. And now all the old questions about affairs, all the suspicions, you bring back. But Felix . . .? How?"

"Did you never wonder why he came to the bar in Moraira, and asked to work with you and your father?"

She dips her chin down, thinking. "We always had travelers coming. He was not the first South African. I think he said his mother was telling him Moraira was very nice. It was wonderful, with the boats and the sea." Maria looks right at me then, her eyes a light brown not unlike Felix and Trevor's topaz, but not identical. "His mother was there, in Moraira—

with my father?"

Maria is trembling. She phones her husband, who has his art studio not far away, and tells him we need his help, that we need to go see her father.

I know almost nothing about Diego except that they have been together a long time and he helped her find me when Felix fell ill. From photos, I know he has a round face, a bit like his hero. I've imagined a short man, so I'm startled when he walks in and is a towering figure, taller than Trevor, with a broad barrel chest. He greets me with a nod and turns in concern to her and asks in Spanish what is wrong. She answers with a torrent of words, then turns to me apologetically to translate, but I understand the gist.

Assuming Diego can follow English, I answer Maria's "Why now?" telling them how Joanie's baby is struggling and about our efforts to find out what is wrong with him. I wish Diego would sit down instead of looming over us, but I keep going. I tell them what Humphrey told me about his mother's end-of-life desire to see "Josie," and what Reverend Halpert revealed about Felix's search for his real father.

Finally, I say, "We need to know if Freddie has inherited a genetic problem—" and I gesture vaguely towards Maria's knees.

~ ~ ~ ~

Effortlessly, Diego lifts Maria and places her in the front seat of his station wagon and stashes her chair in the back. Sitting behind them, I hear him ask if she wants to drive. The vehicle apparently has dual controls. She shakes her head, and he turns the key. All through the twenty-minute drive along leafy avenues and a brief stretch of highway to the nursing home where her father lives, she keeps up a monotone commentary. It is as if she had planned to show me her city and is still determined to follow through with the guided tour. I say, "Aha," and try to take it in, but the world outside looks no more real than the travel photos in the airline magazine. All I can think of is this daughter strapped into the seat in front of me, and the old man perhaps about to have a secret ripped open that he has guarded for a lifetime.

If someone came to me with a story like this about my father, I would reject it out of hand. But then my sweet, history-teacher Pops was the most open and honorable person I've ever known. Clearly, Maria has had a much rockier journey.

Diego, apart from checking a couple of times that Maria is all right, says nothing. When he parks near the entrance of the facility, he waves to me to stay put as he gets Maria into her chair. They disappear into the shadow of the porticoed entrance.

Alone in the car, I check the time—six hours before I need to be back at the airport—and turn on my phone for the first time since arriving this morning. My head is pounding, and my throat feels sore again. And again, I can't make out whether it's stress and thirst, or infection. Messages come skittering down the screen. There is an email from "Professor C. Smith." I don't want to know what Charles has to say, can't deal with him right now. Instead, I scroll to the name I seem to be looking for all the time these days, "HBarnard." It's like a life preserver in a sea that's threatening to swamp me.

Humphrey writes—or probably dictates:

I got back the results of the test. Sent them straight to Eric and Joanie. They sent them to their pediatrician pal.

All this since I left yesterday and with it being Christmas! Good to have friends who don't mind taking a break from celebrating with their families.

They just emailed me. Said their friend couldn't find anything significant, said that it wasn't a close enough match. Not sure why. Of course, there would be a better chance with her father's DNA. How are you? Are you in Spain? Have you asked your friend Maria about the mysterious Josie? Hard question to ask. Hard everything. I wish I could be with you to help.

I type back: You are helping me just by saying this.

I'm about to write more, but I see the giant figure heading towards the car, curling his fingers in a summons. I hit SEND.

"Maria says you should come now."

I have to scurry to keep up with his long strides. The floors are marble, edged with elegant cream molding, still evoking the luxury of the palatial home this must once have been. But instead of gold-framed Old Masters, the dark gray walls are adorned with bright, naive paintings, presumably done by the residents. As we head down the long corridor, I ask, hoping that we have enough time for him to answer, "What is wrong with Maria's legs?"

"She has no legs."

The man is so deadpan, I have no idea if he plans to expand on that statement or not. I want to ask another question, but there is no chance before he turns into a room with two chairs and two beds, each with curtains drawn back along a curtain rail. Maria is standing next to the bed at the far end, supporting herself with her hands on the back of her wheelchair. The bed is empty. Her head is bent down. My heart drops. "He could die today," she'd said.

Please not today.

~ ~ ~ ~

Age is strange. Around Trevor, in Portland, I felt young, hardly older than when we first grew close when he was an adolescent. I was in my fifties then, but he and I could always joke and play. Whenever we met, we shared our latest music finds, usually screeching in horror at each other's choices.

With Joanie, sometimes I feel young because she can be so assertive, I let her take over; at other times, when she lets her vulnerability show, I feel maternal and way older.

With Humphrey, though I keep trying to remind myself I'm almost seventy, the years seem to peel away. Even emailing with him, I feel girlish and coy.

With Felix? In those last five years, there was no age. Oh, there were aches and ailments to remind us of time, but it felt irrelevant. We were just Felix and Sally.

Maria is a couple of years older than me and felt much very much my senior this morning. But right now, she looks like a little girl. This dynamic woman who does such amazing work is afraid of losing her papa and that has melted away her sophistication.

Do what I can't.

The presence at my shoulder is just beyond my peripheral vision. I can almost hear him breathing along with me.

Apparently, her father has been taken to physiotherapy. Diego has left the room, gone in search of José's doctor. I walk towards the empty bed and go wrap my arm around Maria's shoulders. With her standing—on straightened-up artificial legs, I assume—we're almost the same height. For a moment, I'm afraid she might recoil, but she leans her head against me, and I stroke her back.

"What do I ask him?" She lets out a long sigh. "He will be back any minute. What do I say?"

"You don't have to say anything if you don't want to."

"No, I must. If he dies and I did not ask, I will always be wondering. Even if we can get the science facts, they will not give me his answer."

"Does your father speak English?"

"Yes, better than I do. Long ago, before I am born, he was a music professor with many foreign students. But something went wrong. No more teaching. That is why he was starting the bar in Moraira. Always he has had many friends from other countries. Why do you ask?"

"Let me ask him the question," I suggest.

I think, you better guide me, Felix. I have no idea what to ask, but there might be a way to find answers without shattering the fragile peace she has forged with José.

"What is he like?" I ask her. "Or what was he like when he was younger?"

"Charming." She gives a little laugh. "He can talk to anyone. And protecting, especially with me, like always he knows best. I have to get away from him, to make my own life, to prove that I can be independent." Ha! I hear Trevor with the same complaint about Felix. "He was blaming himself for how I am. I blamed God, not my father. What could he do about it—except to make me happy? And he did. He gave me his love of music, and of dancing. In his youth he was a champion dancer."

She looks up at me with pride. "You know, I am one of few, few paraplegic teachers of dance in the world? We are a very small group."

"I know," I say, nodding. "That's why I want you to be a star in our book."

Her expression darkens. "But my father was a man with many secrets. I would ask my mother, 'Where is Papa getting his money?' It was not from the bar; I can tell you. She—she died many years ago—she said better not to know, so long as we have food on the table, a home. When I asked him, he ignored me, refused to talk about it. He was going away often, for a few days or a few weeks. In the end, I learned that he was gambling. I do not know if it was legal or not legal. Not a surprise, you understand. He wasn't a man to respect rules. But I learned also that he gave away a lot of money. He helped many people."

That gives me pause. What if the money Elsabet got from him was simply part of that widespread benevolence? What if we have jumped to a totally wrong conclusion?

"Is your father's mind clear?" I ask.

"Usually yes," she says. "But some days when he comes back from the physiotherapy, if he is tired, for a few minutes he is very confused. I think the massage and the exercises are shaking up his brain. But then, if you speak about the past, he will tell you details like from a newspaper. You will see."

As if on cue, Diego pushes open the door and enters with a nurse who has her hand under the elbow of a hunched old man. At first all I can see is the glossy dome of his head, dotted with liver spots. He lifts his face, sees Maria, and scowls. Then he breaks into a stream of complaints.

I gather that he is giving her hell for not coming to see him in months. She answers in English, "That is not true, Papa. I was here a few days ago." She waves to me. "I have brought you a special visitor from South Africa."

"South Africa!" he exclaims. He switches from sulking to beaming and gives me a semi-toothless grin. "So, it is true that all South African women are beautiful! What is your name?"

"Sally Paddington," I tell him.

"Felix's Sally," Maria puts in.

His milky eyes widen in astonishment. "You are Felix's Sally, the one he always calls his Copper Girl? But you are not a copper girl, more a snow queen. Is he with you? Where is my boy Felix? I want to see him."

I would like to sidestep that question, let him think Felix has stayed at home. If he has little time left, why tell him? But Maria has a dogged look on her face. She says, "I have told you, Papa, Felix died."

He recoils. "Felix is dead?" And then he shakes his head as if to clear it.

Maria gives me a look, and then props herself against the bed. She puts her hands on his shoulders. "You always call him 'my boy.' Do you mean that? Papa, was Felix your son? Were you with his mother, with Elsabet?" The abruptness stuns me.

Couldn't she have eased into the subject?

"Elsabet?" His voice swells on that name. He looks around at us, all staring at him, and he goes from grief to joy. "She is here? My sweet Elsa. She called me always 'Josie.' Where is she? I will sing for her 'Marching to Pretoria,' like she taught me." And he laughs.

Then he tucks in his chin and in his raspy old baritone begins to sing, but it makes him cough and he has to stop. He collapses onto the bed, and the nurse helps him lie back and lifts his legs up. My eyes are riveted on his feet, all sinew and bone with a tracing of gray veins, the final vestige of life force. I consider various ways to ask him our questions, but each opening seems wrong.

"Felix is dead," he states. "And Elsabet?" I nod. He is back in the present, but surprisingly undistressed. "It is all right. I will join them soon."

Maria, with Diego's help, swivels back down into her chair. He bends her knees and places her feet on the footrests. She leans forward, her face at the same level as José's. "Papa, are you Felix's father?"

The old man manages to hoist himself up on his elbow, the better to face her straight on. He looks like a wolf, his rheumy eyes fierce and focused.

"I don't know. Maybe. Elsabet would never tell me. She said she did not know."

~ ~ ~ ~

Back at their apartment, Diego announces that Maria needs to take a rest. She agrees and suggests I have a siesta too. He goes back to his studio for a while, and I lie down on the couch, apologetically pushing Gugli to one side. I should be tired, but adrenaline is still pumping.

Without sorting out what to say or how, I start typing a message to Humphrey on my phone. It is such heavy stuff to discuss, I consider calling him so we can see each other on the screen. But I don't want to disturb Maria, and if I don't write now, will I remember all that happened? Maria's bluntness seems to have stiffened my spine. Or it's the fatigue.

H - Through all our talk about Josie/José I have wondered if you jumped to the same conclusion that I did, that perhaps he was your mother's lover. Forgive me if you find the idea offensive. But what other reason could there be for such a connection?

Because I was afraid before, I also didn't tell you something that might come as a shock—that Felix suspected that your dad was not his actual father. I wish we could be doing this face-to-face, but I want you to know everything I know. Rev Halpert wrote to me last week that Felix told him this.

It's why I really came to Spain. If this José was Felix's father, as he is Maria's, could there perhaps be a hereditary problem that is affecting our precious Freddie? It might also explain why your DNA was not a close match to Joanie's.

I asked Maria's father if he knew Elsabet and if he sent money to her, if it was for his own child. All those questions were asked today to this shaky, dying man. Miraculously, when it mattered most, he was sharp, able to recall what happened so long ago. He answered as well as he could. But after all this, we only have half-answers.

The voices are still clear in my head, but the image that lingers, of fluorescent lights overhead casting dark shadows across José's gaunt face, is like a scene from an El Greco painting. Did I dream it?

Staring into space, he said, "Elsabet was one of my music students, a little older than the others, a young woman. She was special—talented, passionate. We fell in love, me with her, she also with me. I wanted her to stay here in Spain, to marry me." His voice turned to breath on those words. Maria and Diego and I listened in total silence. "But she said her parents would never give permission, that they would not let her marry a Catholic. There was a boy in South Africa they wanted her to marry. And she would not go against them."

I tell Humphrey:

That boy was your dad, I presume. José said she was torn, that he believes she loved him, but she had known the boy at home all her life. She left very suddenly, and he never saw her again.

José reached out then and grasped Maria's hand. He said, "Two years later I met your mother and we got married. We were happy, as happy as people are. And we had this daughter we both loved very much, a child with the spirit of a lioness."

I saw Maria suck in a deep breath. She said, "What about Felix?"

"Elsabet and I wrote letters all through the years," he said. I wonder how she received them, if she had a secret post office box. "I knew she did marry that boyfriend—right after she came home, and that she had a baby very soon. I asked her if the baby was mine or from her husband, but she would never answer that question. All I knew was that her child was healthy, and I was glad."

To Humphrey I say:

I asked José why Felix came to visit him on his travels. He said Elsabet urged him to go to Moraira, to look up her old singing teacher, but without telling him about their connection. José says he promised not to reveal anything to Felix. To us today he just said, "What was there to say? All I know is that he was a wonderful boy, and a great man. I am proud of him, and I was glad to help him any way I could, if he was my son or not."

And there you have it. This was your mother's "Josie." As far as Freddie is concerned, we are still at square one. The only step forward is attached to this big IF.

When the old man finished speaking, the words lingered in the air. I waited for Maria to react. She looked down for a long time, and then she lifted her head and yelled at her father in English: "How could you hide it from me? You let me fall in love with Felix, that boy who might be my brother! And for all my life you have kept this secret. He was my best friend—and now I don't know what to think. Who are you?" She began to weep. Diego crouched by her side and shot me a look. It was clear whom he blamed for her distress.

José reared up against his pillows. "I am José, a man of my word," he roared back at her. Maria waved her hand in dismissal. "It was not my secret to share. Don't you understand? Elsa made me promise, if I wanted to see Felix, I could not say anything." His face crumpled, but then brightened. "I did tell him he must not touch my daughter. I threatened him, like any good Spanish father, with talk of a gun—and he took me seriously."

They turned to me then, another gullible Anglo. I didn't know whether to laugh or cringe. This much yelling in my family would have led to days of hurt silence. These two calmed down as if they'd drained their fury and were glad they had. Maria asked me to tell her father about Freddie.

He listened with frowning intensity as I described the baby's symptoms and the questions Joanie and Eric were facing. "That little boy might be your great-grandchild," Maria said to him.

"I know, I know," he responded. "He might be family. And you are asking if he has this same curse from our ancestors that I passed to you?" She nodded.

When I said goodbye, he grasped my face between his rough palms. "Felix loved you, so I love you, Copper Girl. Even though you made trouble, I am glad that you came to see me."

~ ~ ~ ~

What about Elsabet?

As we drove back through the streets of Barcelona, something shifted deep inside me. I've always resented her for letting her husband push Felix away; and I've given little thought to what she was like as a person. Quite unexpectedly, a channel of understanding has opened between us.

She chose deliberately to obscure the truth—I am sure of that—but what else was she to do? Every time she looked at her firstborn, and each time he clashed with her husband, that huge question must have flared up: Who was his father?

In my marrow, I remember what it means to carry a child you can't identify. My child was only with me briefly, and I finally did get an answer; Elsabet never had a definite one, and she had to face Felix every day of his childhood. But in the way she steered Felix to go meet José; it's clear she'd never stopped wondering and caring.

I send the email to Humphrey and then distill the relevant parts for Joanie. Without knowing if José and Felix are related, I'm not sure what their next steps should be. Maria just kept saying to me, "They must find the answers soon. I have a good life, but I don't want this—" and she gestured down, "for this precious child. If they were knowing what they know now, maybe they could have saved my legs."

There is a new therapy which the doctors are exploring, she explained. "It has very good results. But they have to be sure. And the sooner they begin the treatment, the better. You don't want to be wasting any time." I gather that it has something to do with an enzyme and the gut-brain connection, and how the body responds to inflammation. Too much for me to absorb, but a totally different angle than anything I've heard Joanie and Eric mention.

Diego drives me out to the airport, leaving Maria to make dinner. She said it would give the two of us a chance to get to know each other a little better. It was also her way of giving him permission to discuss her condition. He talks steadily all the way while I try to write down the key points, resting a notebook on my lap.

As a child, he explains as he drives, she had repeated bouts of illness somehow related to the weakness of her lower body. His hands fly on and off the steering wheel, making up for what his English vocabulary lacks. It makes me nervous, but curiosity is uppermost. In the end, the doctors decided her legs were too great a strain on her system, with the pain and inflammation. She thrived after that. Felix helped develop what he called her "flowerpot"—a contraption that she sits in, with artificial legs attached. She is able to stand and to walk a couple of steps by shifting her weight from side to side. "It makes her tired, but she loves to be up high, like other people," he says.

And then with an "Adios!" he drops me off and is gone.

~ ~ ~ ~

Yet again in an airport, my head trying to catch up with my body. Just two weeks ago, I recoiled from the crowds at Cape Town airport; now I'm undisturbed by the people around me. The rituals of checking in and handling luggage and finding seats have all become second nature again, the way they used to be when I was a globe-trotter.

Scrolling through photos on my phone, I find ones of snow angels in Connecticut, and one Eric took of Freddie in my arms, me finally looking a little more relaxed with him. And there is one from this morning, a selfie Maria insisted on, with her holding up the box of chocolates. I find Sam Parker's card and send the picture to him, with a smiley face and the words, "Staying in touch." There are also shots I took of the funny pictures of her and Felix in their fancy dress outfits.

There is an email from Joanie, asking if I got to Maria safely; nothing else. Her concern is welcome, but the terseness is still disturbing. I send her back a "yes" and a promise to write at length when I get home. She says nothing about how Freddie is doing.

This morning feels veiled in mist. When Deidre booked the flights for me, twelve hours in Barcelona seemed impossibly rushed, but now it feels as if Maria and I have been through a decade together. I'm relieved to be leaving, and sure she feels the same. I need to be alone to absorb all that has happened and all that's been learned—and the question still to be answered.

The ghost hovers at my shoulder, not saying anything but finally sharing with me the not-knowing that colored his whole life. Was this why he sent away for that pseudoscientific family tree stuff—in some final bid to find answers to the questions he couldn't bring himself to ask his mother?

~ 13 ~

It takes longer and costs more, but I ask my taxi driver from Cape Town airport to turn off the freeway and drive through the suburban streets of my childhood and youth. Numb with exhaustion and disoriented, I hope the familiar sights will help my soul settle back into the city.

We wind through the blue-shadowed avenues of Rosebank and Kenilworth and Wynberg, passing near to my parents' house, and the synagogue we attended on the High Holy Days, and the cinema where I met my first boyfriend, astoundingly still a theater. We pass hedges spilling with honeysuckle and hibiscus. Notice a brown tinge to trees that should be lush green, and the grassy verges are the color of straw. Drained swimming pools, glimpsed through wrought-iron gates, confirm that water is still being rationed.

The affluent areas give way to poorer neighborhoods with their dusty streets and neat ranks of pastel-colored homes, segregated by economics though no longer by race. The contrast is still depressing. They lap up against grimy pockets of decay and industrial ugliness. I spot the school where I did my student teaching, and the community hall where my pupils performed. The security walls are higher than they were back then, but most of the streets look peaceful, despite the recent upheaval and violence.

Behind everything, like a stage backdrop, rises the spine of mountains, hazy mauve today, as always providing orientation. They say you can never get lost in Cape Town, though this past year it hasn't felt that way.

When we finally reach Kalk Bay, I open my front door, bracing for the awful emptiness. Instead, there are yells and hugs. Edith and Roxie and Jacob and Nomse are inside and greet me with a chorus of "Welcome back!"

As they step aside, the first thing I see is a letter propped on the mantelpiece, from Charles. Turns out to be a kind of a handwritten cease-and-desist missive, sent via express mail. Why? —to pack more emotional punch than an email? Roxie says it arrived on Christmas Eve, three days ago. I guess yesterday's email was to demand why he hadn't yet had a response.

She signed for the letter, faking my signature. "You're glad I did that, not so?" she asks. Yes, I am, but she could also have burned the stupid thing. I skim the letter with its prissy script and can't bring myself to read it properly.

It's the day after Boxing Day in South Africa, our British-style post-Christmas holiday, and Edith suggests we declare this to be a second Boxing Day, and that we share a festive lunch of leftovers. Just what I need. Thanks to some quick shopping at the airport in Barcelona, I have olives and a great bottle of wine to contribute, and little gifts for all four of them.

Edith says I look like a different person. The others nod in agreement. I'm not sure why until I catch sight of myself in the bathroom mirror. My cheeks and the tip of my nose are pink. I must have gotten sunburned on Maria's balcony. It belies the fact that I feel shredded, but perhaps the nonstop emotion of these weeks has shifted my energy.

The meal comes complete with traditional Christmas crackers that Roxie says they've been saving for just the right occasion. We all put on the paper crowns that come inside them. The little strip of paper that is meant to produce a bang has lost its firepower, but the plastic charms and games and printed fortunes have us exclaiming like children. I get a miniature set of jacks, complete with a marble-size rubber ball. We take turns playing with them, seeing how many jacks we can scoop up with each toss of the ball, even Jacob with his enormous hands. His jubilation when he succeeds makes me laugh—and I catch sight of Edith watching with a benign smile.

Roxie tells me she and Jacob have been working together in my garden, and they compete to describe what they've planted and the new, tighter water restrictions. These people are interacting so comfortably, the sight almost moves me to tears. I wish Felix could see them, though he would have been less surprised than I am.

As Jacob is about to leave and head home with Nomse, he turns to me with his hand pressed to his chest and reminds me that the poodle vase got broken. I rack my brain to remember what it looked like and insist I don't care.

To work off the stuffed feeling and the stiffness from the flight, I offer to walk Edith and Roxie's pugs. They tug me down to Main Road, past the train station, and down to the harbor. There are too many vacationers around, and it's much hotter than where I've been. The sun grills my shoulders. Fish smell and diesel from the boats waft over me, and I have no clue what the time is. I just want to stand at the water's edge, letting the lapping soothe me, but the pugs are eager to get closer to the action. Fat, glossy seals are entertaining the tourists, hopping up onto the quay and then plopping back into the water, to screams of delight from the children.

The fatigue is so deep, I can barely summon the energy to give Mergatroid and Skelm a goodnight stroke, before crawling under the puffy comforter. A litany of tasks and worries clamor to be considered, but I shove them aside. As has become my habit, I send up a prayer for Freddie in case some force is listening and fade out. I'll start thinking again tomorrow. Unaware, simply repeating what I've done these past weeks in other rooms, I push all the available pillows together in the middle of the bed and sprawl across the entire space.

~ ~ ~ ~

In the morning, I carry my coffee—just one cup—out to the patio, together with a slice of toast, my phone, and my diary. The plants look great. They have really perked up. The protea bush has two tight, spiky pink buds, and the intertwined bougainvillea creepers are full of purple-red and orange blossoms. I suspect Jacob has been using more water than I did.

Something with flat, glossy leaves is sprouting in the trough by the fence. I don't know what it is—perhaps a baby hibiscus? —but it looks healthy. That's more than I can say about myself. I feel awful.

I am about to call Ethel in New York when I remember I must reverse the time difference. Seven hours earlier by her. It's frustrating. I want to make this call before my courage fizzles out, but it will have to wait. I want to speak to Joanie too, to hear what is happening with Freddie, but can't do that either. It's only three days since we parted, but the silence from her scares me. Is he sick? Is she angry? Has the news of Maria upset her more?

The sky has darkened, and the wind is blowing like a northeaster that should bring rain—but these days probably won't. I'm chilled and still tired, despite the long, deep sleep. All night my dreams kept looping through the same image, over and over, of Maria gliding away as I hurry to keep up, her feet like small wheels, with a file of crucial information on her lap. Is it because of the questions I raised about her father? A solid band of congestion stretches from one ear through to the other.

Not only might I have infected Freddie, I might also have endangered Maria. And her father. And the sweet elderly woman who sat next to me on the plane that night. And Roxie and Edith, and Nomse and Jacob. My coffee tastes bitter, and I have absolutely no appetite for the toast. Ugh, I know this feeling—emotional and physical malaise. Guilt piled on top of pessimism, adding to fatigue, and topped with pain. Or maybe it's just a sinus reaction to all the airplane air.

Charles wrote that his mother is battling pneumonia. She is in Lenox Hill Hospital. At her age, that's terrifying. I hope he was exaggerating. And I hope I'm not carrying the same infection. Back inside, wrapped in a blanket on the sofa, I reread his letter, forcing myself to focus this time.

Evidently, he gleaned from Ethel that she went out for lunch after her symptoms began, and with whom. He isn't blaming me—how could he?—but clearly that détente when we met up after *The Nutcracker* has crumbled. His tone is stiff and formal, how he becomes when he's feeling injured. It's just what his mother wanted to avoid, and she doesn't know the half of it.

Apparently, he called Gail Tennant—I can imagine his schmoozy, old-family-friend tone—and she told him all about the book project. She also provided my address and my email. Silly, indiscreet girl—but then she would have had no idea that she shouldn't. I remember how hard it can be to resist Charles.

In the impeccable penmanship I haven't seen in so many years, he writes:

I gather that the book is a collaborative effort. I have a very good idea who your collaborator might be. If you care to remember, from the very start of our relationship, I was impressed by your familiarity with physiological issues like those I have lived with all my life. I deduced that this expertise was thanks to your ex-boyfriend, the man you later betrayed me with.

If this is indeed the case, I think you can understand why I take exception to my mother helping you promote such a work. I have not said anything to her, not wanting to distress her when she is this ill, but I would appreciate you altering your plans. I am quite sure that with your distinguished record and with that other book you did, it should be easy enough now for you to find yourself a different agent. I wish you all the best with the project.

The fucker, like hell he does! I haven't used that word about anyone else in my life. His request, if such imperious crap can be called a request, has poked through my defenses. I don't want him to pressure Ethel about the book, but I also don't want to give him the satisfaction of complying. Old, old rage comes bubbling up, making my headache worse than ever.

I was such a wimp when we met. Charles was opinionated about everything and utterly sure of his judgment, and I found that attractive. After the years of struggling to find my way alone in Boston and then New York, it was a relief to let someone else take charge. Even when that awe had faded, I never did learn to stand up to him.

So, perhaps it's understandable that he expects me to go along with his diktat. He really believes he knows what's best for his mother, that she'd be horrified if she knew who my cowriter was. The letter gets even more insidious. He reminds me that he's writing almost on the anniversary of our first meeting, Christmas Day. I feel a momentary pang of nostalgia for the pleasure of that night, talking to this passionate, dark-haired guy with his lopsided stance, as we served meals at a soup kitchen, and then, feeling we had earned our pleasure, heading out together into the sparkling, icy night.

But then I recognize his manipulativeness. So much for goodwill to all men. Right now, I have none to spare for this pompous ass.

Odd to pity her, but his poor wife. Dorothea probably took herself off to Switzerland, not just for their son's sake but because Charles is impossible to live with.

Also feeling more charitable about Deidre these days. But if I'm kinder to those women, shouldn't I also bear Helga in mind and cool the connection with Humphrey? That thought simmers for a while and gets shoved aside. We're not doing anything very wrong, just communicating over issues that matter greatly to both of us.

New Year's Eve, my first since losing Felix, is just days away. It was our tradition to go down to the beach at midnight, to sit there with the stars overhead and the distant glitter of fireworks. I want to do that this year too—but please, not alone. Humphrey was the one who brought up the date, not me, and it would be so good to have his company.

Perhaps the whole issue is moot. I haven't heard back from him, not a word. Is he upset that his mother had an affair before her marriage? Or about Felix perhaps not being his full brother? Or with me for withholding that information? I've wanted to text or call, but first I need to know how he is feeling. And I'm scared that Helga will answer his phone.

A spear of shadow cuts across the light shining through the patio doors. My head pops up. For a split second I expect to hear, "How're you doing, Sally?" —the real voice of the man in my thoughts, but it's just Mergatroid. She jumps up on the couch and comes to snuggle under my arm. The rumble of her purring is soothing against my ribs. "Where's your son?" I ask, but she ignores me, focused on her own pleasure, kneading the cushion as I stroke her.

Where are you? I ask my ghost.

I haven't heard from him either, not since returning yesterday. Despite that, the house seems less empty than I feared. Perhaps it's because I'm still thrumming with the living beings I've been around—Libby and Ethel and Joanie and Freddie and Maria. Plus, there's this bowling ball thumping about inside my skull.

"Could you go do some shopping?" I ask Mergatroid. She turns her half-closed yellow eyes at me as if considering the request. If I'm sensible, I'll put on shoes and go down the street to the minimart now, before I feel even worse, to stock up on juice and chicken soup and more aspirin. But I'm too tired. Sleep first, errands later.

Bob Halpert wakes me. When I open the door for him, he's holding a small bouquet, a charming mix of rosebuds and baby's breath, not like Humphrey's hideous carnation arrangement. "Not from me," he hastens to say. "I found this on your doorstep." My heart does a little skip, thinking Humphrey sent it to make up for the other one, or to welcome me home. There's a card attached by the florist with a printed message from the sender. It does say, "Welcome home, assuming you're back," but it's from Sam Parker. When I see his name, I think of chocolate and him guffawing over that French comedy on the plane. I wonder if he's staying nearby or placed the order from a distance. Despite his tie-dye shirt, he has excellent taste.

I ask the good minister to sit in the leather chair on the far side of the room in case I'm infectious. That makes him speak louder and his cheeriness grates on my nerves. But he offers to mix me a hot toddy, which turns out to be surprisingly soothing, even with the cheap hooch he retrieves from my cupboard.

Somewhat revived, I tell him about meeting José. He leans forward, eyes wide, agog to hear whether this was in fact Felix's father. When I finish what I know, he gives a big sigh and leans back, his hands folded across his middle. "That is wonderful!" he exclaims. Really? I don't understand why he would think so. This is a story of extramarital sex and the possible duping of a young husband.

"Hmm, I don't see it that way," he says. "I was afraid that Felix's mother had an affair during her marriage, or—if it came before her marriage—that she was seduced by some cruel Casanova. But what we have here is a love story of two young people with a mutual passion. Understandably, she chose not to go against her parents, to come back to the familiarity of her own people and her own country. And they both found loving partners."

None of that is necessarily the God-given truth, even from this man with a closer connection than most. I point out that José led a strange, half-hidden life, and that Elsabet married someone who bullied her. Bob shrugs and tops up my toddy. I say, "Do you think it's possible Felix's father suspected that this wasn't his child? It would explain why he was so much harsher with his eldest than with his other children." Bob nods to that too. It's sad, but I do like his version, with the love uppermost.

Given that he's my friend, not my spiritual anything, I have never asked him for moral advice before, but I consider it now.

It would be helpful if we could chew over the Humphrey dilemma. I've tried to talk to Libby about it again but doing it by phone or text rather than face to face isn't the same. I can't get her to understand the attraction. Also, she is in the middle of some drama between her kids. Apparently, her son's new boyfriend is a Log Cabin Republican and has clashed with Bridget's avowedly socialist husband. The pre-Christmas standoff has turned into a New Year's them-or-us showdown. Even in the best families . . .

"Are you all right, Sally, aside from feeling sick?" Bob asks. "You seem rather down, more than before. You know you can tell me anything?"

Perhaps, but suddenly I can't bring myself to risk his disapproval by asking about Humphrey. However, I can ask him about Ethel. I've been dithering about that all day. I'm determined to call her, but I don't know what to say. I describe to Bob the book situation and my confusion, trying not to get too vituperative about Charles.

"My ex-husband is proposing that I make some excuse to Ethel—maybe just tell her I've hit a snag with the writing, that I've decided to put it on ice. If I do that, he says, he'll stand back, and Ethel and I can continue with our friendship. But," I insist, "I can't abandon the book."

Bob peers at me over his glasses.

"I gather I'm missing some link in this story, an episode that caused your ex-husband to feel resentment. No, don't tell me; I don't need to know. But hurt people tend to want to inflict hurt. What we need is a solution that neutralizes his ability to hurt either you or his mother. I'll pray on it."

"In the meantime," I butt in, "can I call her? I'm worried about her. And she was so concerned about Freddie, I want to tell her about the Portland visit. Would it be bad to lie—to tell Charles I'm still trying to come up with a good cover story that will satisfy his mother?"

He wrinkles his stubby red nose. "I wouldn't call that a lie, just an obfuscation, a little stalling device." Ha! I think. To Libby, obfuscation is the same as lying, but this very good man thinks otherwise.

~ ~ ~ ~

Thus encouraged, after he departs, I email Charles a curt, fake-angry response, indicating—as I know he'd expect—that I'm ticked off but will reluctantly do as he requests, on condition that he stays out of it. And before he can respond either way, I call the hospital number he has given me.

"Yes? Who is this? I can't hear you." Ethel's tone is true to form, but her voice is breathy. I answer with as much volume as I can muster, not a whole lot clearer. "Sally, oh, I am happy to hear you, my dear. Speak up, please." She gives a barking cough that makes me recoil from the phone. It sounds so phlegmy, my own chest hurts in sympathy. I tell her I am also not one hundred percent, but it's probably just a cold. She clucks in sympathy, and I switch the topic to Freddie.

"He is delicious," I tell her. "Maybe I'm biased, but I think he is very handsome and amazingly alert. He seemed to understand everything we said to him."

She sighs. "Ah, the magic of grandchildren!" She breaks off to clear her throat, and then resumes talking. "But tell me, what about his health? You mentioned that he had some

209

problems. It's heartbreaking to see a little one struggle so early in life."

I start telling her how the doctors are worrying about his weight and muscle tone. A cold hollowness opens as I speak. Picturing him, I remember the shadows under his eyes, and how his tiny doll legs would flop as if the will to live couldn't reach his extremities. I've pushed that fear into the background, but now, alone and tired, it sends out fingers of dread.

Ethel seems to read my mood. "Do you pray, Sally? You might remember my faith is somewhat unorthodox—but I do believe it helps to address our Maker. He doesn't guarantee any of us a set lifespan but talking to Him seems to help with acceptance."

I'm not sure who I'm tearing up for now, Freddie or her or Felix, or simply because acceptance has been a sticking point for so long. The tears make me gruff-voiced when I try to speak again. Ethel is perturbed. "You don't have this pneumonia, do you? You said it's just a cold. Oh heavens, I didn't give it to you, did I?"

All I can think of is how intertwined we all are. In that moment, I desperately want to confess about Felix and have a completely clear connection with her, but the more urgent need is to reassure her. "No, I've just got a case of exhaustion," I say, "and I'm a tough bird. I'll be back on my feet in a day or two. I have to be—I've got a big dance symposium to prepare for. I'm the keynote speaker."

"Bless you, Sally, that's wonderful," she exclaims, and I'm glad I said nothing else. "You brought us so much joy with your dancing and your music. Remember that Sinatra song I fell in love with, what was it called? You said the words were by a South African lyricist."

I'm touched that she still remembers.

"Yes, Hal Shaper. It's 'Softly, as I Leave You.'" Felix introduced me to it way, way back, actually to Elvis Presley's version.

"Oh my, yes! Did I tell you I heard Michael Bublé sing it live? Now, promise me you'll look after yourself. Let's speak again soon."

When we ring off, I do a little waist-up dance to the tune. I'm elated, though nothing has been resolved.

~ ~ ~ ~

Joanie told me, in a text that arrived overnight, that she has found some new information on Freddie's probable condition. It's a relief to have a longer communication, though it's very businesslike. The medical name Diego finally told me, driving to the airport, meant nothing to me, but she has been researching it for the past two days. She is confused about some aspects and asks if I can find out more.

I'm better today than yesterday, which makes me think my malaise has been exhaustion and nothing worse, but I'm not energetic enough to rev up the Harley. I take out my Volvo and drive all the way to the University of Cape Town. I need to go talk with my friend Mary about the conference—but first I have this mission.

The view of the city from the mountainside campus is as gloriously expansive as ever on this bright, windy day. With conditions so dry, that wind can mean fire danger, and just above the buildings are forests that can easily go up in flames.

But today all looks serene, and the parking, thanks to the Christmas vacation, is less congested than usual. I find a space on the same level as the library. Just as well. These shaky legs would not have fared well with the usual climb up or down the slope. Armed with my ancient alumni card from when I did my teacher training, I find the bioscience section and take a seat near the medical periodicals. Could probably have done the same research online, but given the choice, I prefer the old ways. I go through Joanie's text again, noting key words to look up.

She asked how I'm doing back in Kalk Bay, but also mentioned that she had taken Freddie to the doctor, that once more he was running a fever. She says that it could be from me, or it could be a bug picked up in the hospital last week. She writes: Everything seems to make him ill, including my milk. I don't know how much more of this he can survive. We're running out of time.

I feel included in her "we" and find that comforting, though the thought is blood-chilling.

But then, as if to block out her own thought, to distract us both, she asks if I've seen "delicious Uncle Boet" again. That part I ignore.

Instead, I wrestle my focus back to the medical data. Fortunately, she seems to understand the information I've passed on better than I did, and she is being careful not to jump to conclusions. She says:

It's rare. Was only identified as a separate phenomenon a year or two ago. There are lots of theories, but they think they've isolated the gene involved. They don't have a conclusive test for it yet, but they think it's like with Tay-Sachs, you can be a carrier and show no symptoms, or it can show up in the child if it comes through both parents. Turns out, after all, Eric's family does have a Spanish branch. Does mine?

That could explain what is happening with Freddie—or it might be coincidental. We need more leads.

If he does have what Maria has, there's an experimental treatment they can try, but it's risky, not something they'd do without clear proof. If it's not that, we're back to a blank.

I can almost hear her voice fade away through the typing. And then it snaps back:

If only we had Dad's damn DNA, we could see if it matches Jose's, and that would give us something concrete to go on.

If only we had your dad along with his DNA, I think. I am desperate to help.

~ ~ ~ ~

Next, lower down the mountain, I stop in at the College of Music. It's twice the size it was when I studied there. I sneak a peek into the concert hall where the event will take place. It's deserted, with rank upon rank of shadowy seats leading down to the half-lit stage. Spooked, I back out in a hurry.

When Mary invited me to take part, she asked if I was ready to face an audience again. It had been a while, but I had plenty of time to prepare, and Felix was urging me. I said yes to hush him, though I was nervous at the prospect. Now I'm not scared of being on stage anymore; the drama of the past few weeks has overshadowed lesser fears, burned them away. But I have no speech yet and very little time to set that right. The anxiety could come back.

Perhaps I still can squirm out of it, if a suitable replacement can be found. But what self-respecting expert would take on a gig like this at such a late date?

My footsteps squeak on the cement flooring. I should have put on proper shoes instead of these old rubber flip-flops. Lipstick might have helped too. To compensate for my slovenliness, I sweep into Mary's office, armed with a barrage of questions about the sequence of speakers and what kind of audiovisual equipment we'll have.

She's not fooled. Mary and I worked together when we first qualified as teachers, and we've been friends ever since. "You look tired, Sal, and you're even thinner! Are you all right? If you're worrying about the event, don't," she says. "The early registration is excellent, and we've had a lot of inquiries. We have this dynamic young publicist and she's worked wonders. Would you like to meet her? She lives out your way, in Fish Hoek. She said she'd be happy to come see you and record a little interview to put on YouTube or somewhere."

In the spirit of fake positivity, I say, "Sure. Why don't you tell her to pop in on her way home after work tomorrow?"

~ ~ ~ ~

By the time I get back to Kalk Bay, all I want to do is kick off those flipflops and sink back onto my couch. There's a message from Trevor on the home phone, eager to know about José and if he is connected to his dad and saying again how much he enjoyed our time together. That brightens my spirits. I'll try calling him later. But still no word from Humphrey— not a text, not a phone message, nothing.

And the ghost is still silent, as if all my traveling has left him suspended in some geographic limbo. He wanted me to ask questions, and I've been doing that, but I haven't found answers. How about a clue or two, Mr. Expert?

Half asleep, drained by my excursion, I take a cruise through mental albums. I picture my Tiger Man striding down our cobbled street with his just-off-a-horse cowboy gait, hat on head, or—with a different hat—prowling a farmers market to find me ripe granadillas, or—and this one I think I have a photo of—Felix crouching beside the wheelchair of a beaming child, telling him some nonsense tale that has made the little boy's eyebrows peak with skeptical amusement.

If I do have that photo, where would it be? For the first time since my return, I haul my creaky limbs up the equally creaky steps to the attic. It's as dust-free as every other room in the house, with everything just slightly tidier than I left it after showing Humphrey around. I'm lightheaded by the time I stand in the room, but with a pleasurable shiver I feel again the unexpected wave of lust that rippled between us.

I find the photo of Felix and the child pinned to my corkboard and turn to look at the old Panama hat on the rack. There is the gap I'd forgotten about, where the felt fedora used to be. I remember taking it from the hook and passing it to Humphrey through the beam of sunlight, and a single hair glowing in the light as he took it from me.

One hair. One last fragile thread of Felix. Not sure if this is fever or a burst of excitement that speeds up my heart. Is there any way that hair has survived use by the new wearer? Could one hair be enough?

My knees tremble as I descend the stairs and settle back on the couch. This could be it, the link we need. I could do more research, but I'm too wound up to do any typing.

Instead, I phone Humphrey. Screw him if he's sulking or his wife answers. But thank goodness, it's his voice I hear and his face that appears on my screen.

"Turn on your camera," he says. I demur, mutter about being a mess. "Just do it—for me," he insists, grinning, feline. "Look, you can climb back under a desk if you want. You seemed comfortable enough there when I called you at your friend's place."

I oblige—with the camera, I mean, not the desk—and immediately regret it. I look austere, marble-colored, compared to his tanned vitality. He is sitting outside in his garden and the sun is glinting off his head, so it looks golden. I find myself caressing my pendant with my free hand, trying to see the color of his smiling eyes. They are obscured by shadow.

When I comment that I haven't heard from him, he gives a quick, dismissive explanation about Christmas and the family being scattered. I mention the news about José, and he just says, "It's what I suspected—that she was in love with him. It makes sense."

I'm deeply relieved. After all the tension and second-guessing, no antagonism. He isn't nearly as easy to read as I thought at first, but I like his even-temperedness.

"Can you lay your hands on that hat I gave you?" I ask. He

looks puzzled for a moment, turns away, thinking, and then exclaims, "Oh, yes, I know where I put it."

I'm miffed. I gave him a treasure and this seems cavalier. Or did he not want his wife to see it? Either way, the pendulum is pulled a little off center.

As we're talking, he walks back into his house and through some rooms and produces the hat. He is about to put it on his head, but I yell out, "Don't. There might be a hair in it."

"A hair?" I see him frown, and then his eyebrows shoot up. "You mean one of Felix's? A single hair—what are the chances?"

According to what I read in the university library, a hair isn't of use if it's just the shaft. But Felix yelped when he took off the hat because the staple yanked on his scalp. If that hair I saw was pulled out with its root, we might have a DNA sample after all.

Somewhere above me, near the heavy wooden beams of the ceiling, I hear a jubilant *Aha!*—not at my brilliant deductive skills but because I've finally clicked to what he's been trying to tell me. I suppose being a ghost has its frustrations.

From the guy on the phone, I hear a hesitant response.

"Interesting. Okay, I need to find a magnifying glass. But how am I going to know now if I'm looking at *the* hair, or one of mine? The color is probably too similar to be sure."

"Has the hat attacked you and yanked a hair out of your scalp?"

"No. I was smarter than my big *boet*; the price tag had a sharp staple, and I took it out."

I start to smile, but then my heart plummets. The hair, if

it was still in the hat, would probably have been attached to that staple.

I tell Humphrey, and I become aware that my pale face has probably just sagged another five years.

But he is looking off to the side again, thinking. "Things are pretty messy around here. Helga's been away for a while, er—visiting her folks. I've kind of let things go. I won't show you. But there's a good chance that price tag is still lying around, or it's in the wastebasket. I'll go look. And if I find it, I'll take it to that lab that did my test.

By the way," he says softly, "I have to be in Cape Town tomorrow. I was going to ask, could I come stay with you?"

~ 14 ~

Friday, December 30. I write in my diary, on the second to last page: *The year is almost over. What will the new one bring? Anything could happen.*

A glimmer of optimism flares, before my intuition whispers a warning of potential disaster. Or is that just habitual self-protection?

The past twelve months have been the longest of my life, though looking back I remember only patches. A couple of wonderful months at the start, followed by a plunge over a precipice. Some brighter moments near the middle when the kids came. And then these past three weeks of helter-skelter kaleidoscope.

When I woke, I was curled up in the middle of the bed. Spread my limbs like a starfish, disturbing the two furry lumps nestled in the crook of my knees. Then I curled up again, sinking within to reclaim the fading impressions from this date last year.

I recall blue and gold summer glory. Felix and I took a motorcycle ride around the Peninsula to Camps Bay. We went to visit his long-ago boss, John Latimer, the man who foresaw what a fine scientist the flailing teenager could become. John was always immensely proud of that.

My knee had been giving me trouble and I was thinking I should give up my bike, but we hadn't seen the old man in months. It was wonderful to watch them together, still mentor and mentee after all this time. Felix was like a puppy, eager to share ideas and new theories, and discuss who was doing what in their vast collegial network.

We thought it might be our last visit. John was over ninety, and as he put it, "My days are numbered. Brain's still sharp, but more and more body parts keep buggering off into retirement." It never occurred to us that Felix's number would come up sooner.

He and I wound our way along the craggy curves of Chapman's Peak Drive and came home via the coast road, through quaint Simonstown and sunbaked Fish Hoek, first him in the lead and then me, gloriously carefree except where we got stuck in bumper-to-bumper holiday traffic.

It dawns on me that Humphrey might know John too, through his marine research work. And as that thought surfaces, I remember: He is coming today!

Clamber out of bed and into the shower. Wash my hair and shave my legs, and for the first time in forever, smooth moisturizer on all over. Will put makeup on before he arrives, whenever that will be. I swallow a fizzy glass of Vitamin C. I'm feeling much better, but I want total recovery.

The refrigerator is empty. I need to go shopping, to stock up on ingredients for dinner, and some wine. And maybe a bottle of champagne for tomorrow night, New Year's Eve. Buoyed by that prospect, I don jeans and boots and helmet, and take out the Harley. My route carries me over Boyes Drive, with its panoramic view of False Bay, to Constantia, to a thatch-roofed farm stall shaded by the twisted limbs of ancient oak trees. The produce is not picture-perfect, but it smells of earth and juice. Bees are buzzing everywhere. It occurs to me, riding home past Kirstenbosch Botanical Garden, that in this past week, I've seen more of this city than in the previous fifty-two. Maybe Humphrey would like a guided tour.

Riding the motorcycle after a break, that was easy. Getting back into cooking is way harder. It's so long since I made a meal for anyone else, every choice opens up another doubt. What to buy? Does this guy like spicy food? I love it; Felix didn't. My specialty is pierogi like my mother made, but will they satisfy Humphrey? I opt to make another old family favorite, veal parmigiana.

Back home, I check email and spot a note from Gail Tennant, the agent. Her name triggers a pang of anxiety. I still haven't come up with a way to appease Charles and get around Ethel. But perhaps Gail has solved the dilemma for me—with a rejection. If her partner didn't like the sections I sent them, they might not want the book after all. That would simplify everything.

It would be simpler, yes, but devastating. The market for my book is overseas, in Europe and America and Asia. From here, functioning on my own, my chances of finding another international agent are minuscule. How on earth will I summon the drive to write the rest, knowing it's been dismissed as not good enough?

Deidre wouldn't think this way. She'd say if one door slams shut, hunt for the next one and kick it open. Anticipate success!

As I dish up tuna for the cats and make myself a snack, I try to visualize addressing the conference next month. What if I tell that elegant assembly about our concepts of dance therapy—and, perhaps, about the book that will contain them? That might be another way to make sure I finish it.

So, sandwich in my left hand and phone in my right, I re-open my email and click on the agent's message, braced for whatever. Gail asks:

When do you think you can give us the full manuscript?

Why would she need the full manuscript of a book she doesn't want?

My partner Martin loves the idea even more than I do. He has a niece with cerebral palsy who is in love with dancing, and he can't wait to show her your book. We have a couple of suggestions, but we like your approach, and both found your writing extremely readable. I am sorry that he didn't get to meet you in person, but let's have a Skype session, the four of us, right after the holidays. We're very curious to know how you plan to conclude the book. It would be wonderful to have a real fun finale.

She adds:

> P.S. I hope you don't mind that I gave your contact info
> to Charles Smith. He said he had some suggestions for
> you."

Swearing and cheering and panicking, I start to eat my sandwich. So much for Charles's "suggestions." There is absolutely no way now that I am going to surrender this fantastic partnership. But did she say "the four of us"? Oh, shit.

Felix, help! This is for your sake too.

But he's absent again. Evidently, I'm going to have to work this out alone—unless Bob Halpert's prayers yield a solution. And how should I conclude the book? With all the doubts and dithering, I've never thought that far. They want a "fun finale," and I have nothing but dry, earnest facts.

~ ~ ~ ~

Up to my elbows in breadcrumbs as I prepare the veal cutlets for frying when the doorbell does its *ding-dong.* Already?! I'd assumed Humphrey would come later. I've got helmet hair and I'm barefoot, still in jeans.

I open the door blushing, ready to make excuses, and it's not him. Instead, there's a willowy young woman with dark, glossy skin, short bleached-blond hair and a clingy pink midi-dress.

"Hi, I'm Ama," she announces. I look up at her blankly, wondering if they have census-takers in South Africa like in the U.S. and if they're allowed to dress like this, or is she selling beauty products? Her accent is British overlaying something else. Nigerian? It's an unfamiliar but fascinating part of this new South Africa that people are coming here from all parts of the continent. "I'm the PR person from UCT. You said I should come around on my way home from work, yes?"

I can't send her away. And I can't ask her to wait while I go and clean up. I opt for my only other option: I talk her into having a large glass of chilled white wine and ask her to chop vegetables while I carry on breading the veal.

"Fire away," I say. "What do you want to know?"

She props up her phone facing me and starts chatting as she slices. It's only then that I remember this is for YouTube, not just print, but it's too late to back out.

Next thing I know, Roxie and Edith let themselves in. Ten minutes later, there is another invasion, this time through the side fence. The kids from next door arrive with their mom, June, to welcome me home. The eldest, Samantha, is carrying Skelm's ginger sister who, she tells me, loves to come visit her mother and brother. Not sure that's true. Mergatroid's offspring start hissing at each other, and the next thing, fur is flying. I manage to shoo them apart. They subside into low rumbles, keeping a wary watch from behind the various pairs of feet. I think they're jealous of Mergatroid's attention.

June tilts her head appraisingly. "You look different—so much better—almost like your old self. It's nice to see."

By the time Humphrey arrives, around seven, we're all relaxing on the patio. I have set out chips and salsa, and crackers and cheese. Ama and June are perched on high stools, and the kids are playing marbles on the slate. Roxie, Edith, and I are sprawled in the deck chairs. He must have heard our voices because he comes loping up the side of the house, with his Panama hat and a travel bag on his shoulder.

He casts me a raised eyebrow "Is this a good time?" look as I jump up to greet him. I assure him that it is and introduce everyone.

June looks from him to me, bug-eyed with astonishment.

"Like seeing an apparition?" I ask her, grinning.

"It's uncanny," she whispers.

But then he gets talking, and I know she is adjusting, the way I did. He doesn't really speak the way Felix did, and when the hat comes off, there's thicker hair, and at first, he's more formal. As he relaxes, though, he becomes chattier. He lights up just as his brother would have, surrounded by women like this.

I'm strung between the pleasure of seeing him and awkwardness about the fact that he has clearly come intending to stay over. A more poised woman might stress that he's family and this is normal hospitality, but the man is so bronze-tanned and flat-out sexy, who would that fool? I try to see him with detachment, just as this graying sixty-something-year-old, but he still has a glow.

Ama has put her phone away and given up on interviewing me. She says she's got enough anyway. Now, in response to a grilling from Edith, she starts regaling us with tales about celebrities she has met since going into PR. She tells us about Roger Federer and Prince Harry and Idris Elba and Charlize Theron, who've all visited South Africa. My no-nonsense neighbors turn out to be starstruck celebrity fans.

Finally, June takes her kids and heads home through the gap in the hedge, and Roxie and Edith heave themselves out of the deck chairs and go off in the opposite direction, the dogs waddling up ahead. Ama stands too, and as she does, Humphrey hands her his card. I can't hear what he says, I just see him lean in to say something and register the glance she gives him from under her eyebrows. It looks like a teasing put-down—maybe a reminder of their age difference—but not entirely dismissive.

~ ~ ~ ~

With just us two left, I go into the kitchen to retrieve the food from the warming drawer and toss the salad. Humphrey takes a bottle of red wine from his bag, a very classy Cabernet Sauvignon, and fills two glasses. He waits for me to set the dishes on the table, and then he puts his hands on my hips and pulls me around to face him. The heat from his palms loosens what had tightened since Ama's exit.

"I feel like I've been waiting forever for this," he whispers. "I thought you might not come back from the States."

"I considered it," I say, clutching knives and forks to lay the table with. "It was great being there, and my friend Libby really thinks I should move back."

"But—?" His eyes caress my face.

"I wanted to be here."

He pulls me closer, his pelvis against mine, and kisses me, softly and then harder. With hands full of cutlery, I wrap my arms about his neck. His hair is cut short up the back of his head, a style Felix never ever wore, and the bristles are prickly against my wrists, but I want more. I want him closer.

He pulls away first, drawing in a deep breath as if to reorient himself. "We were going to have dinner, weren't we? I'm hungry as a horse, and that food smells great."

We settle into eating and sipping and talking. It's amazing to think we've only met twice before—and yet this feels utterly comfortable, as if there've been decades of sharing. I tell him about each episode of the trip, even about the fearsome Deidre and my dilemma with Gail, the agent. He is especially eager to hear about Barcelona, and how the conversation with José unfolded.

"He really adored your mother," I tell him.

"Does he look like Felix?" he asks, his brows furrowed. It's clearly a tough thing to ask.

"Not really. He's very old and it's hard to tell, but then Felix—and you—look just like your mother. It's possible that Felix resembled Maria. She has similar coloring. But that's not enough to go on."

That brings us to the hair in the hat and whether it might be useful. "I should have told you," Humphrey says, "but I was rushing to tidy up before I left. Helga's going to kill me when she sees what the house looks like."

"And—? Did the hair have a root?" He is peculiarly offhand when I least expect him to be.

"Oh, yes. A quite visible white lump, the size of the head of a pin. I dropped it off at the lab this morning on my way to the airport. They said it should be enough to work with, but they are backed up and it could take a while."

"How do we get them to speed things up, to give it priority?"

He shrugs and we sink into a shared frustration. I find my phone and show him the most recent pictures of Freddie, sent that morning by Eric. He is looking up at the camera with what looks like a smile, and there is the curl in the top lip, just like his grandfather and his great-uncle and great-grandmother.

But even with that grin bunching his cheeks, the little face is thinner than a baby's should be.

Humphrey says, "I wish Felix could have seen him." It's exactly what I'm thinking. He gives me a lopsided grin and adds, "Or has he seen Freddie?"

We settle on the couch, thighs touching. He reaches over and draws my legs across his knees, pushes up my jeans and starts stroking my calves, down to my ankles. With his thumb he begins gently pressing the arches of each foot. How does he know it's just what I need to relieve the shadow pressure from the motorcycle footrests?

Then he stops with raised eyebrows, staring at my toes. They're still that exotic geranium color Joanie painted them; I'd totally forgotten.

"I wouldn't have taken you for a pedicure kinda girl," he remarks with a grin, running his fingertips across the nails and then squeezing my toes in his hand. I'm not that kind. In fact, I've never had a pedicure in my life, or a foot massage, and it's bliss. I tip my head back against the cushions. Every body part is melting.

His voice husky, Humphrey remarks how fast these past twelve months have gone, what a strange time it has been. I tell him about this day a year ago, how Felix and I rode out to visit John Latimer. "You don't know him, do you?" I ask. "He was like another father figure to Felix."

"Dr. Latimer? Sure, I do. Amazing guy." His hands go still. "I'd always known about him through Felix, and a few years ago our group got involved in developing one of his seawater-testing gadgets."

He sits up and exclaims, "He can help. I'm darn sure he knows those lab people. Call him, ask, now! Go on."

Usually, I don't take well to having orders barked at me, but I'm too mellow to object. It's late to be phoning, but John answers on the second ring, sounding quite bright. And he gets the urgency at once. "I'm not following this stuff about Felix and another man being his father, but I do know the fellow who heads up that lab in Port Elizabeth. I'll speak to him. You should have a result before the end of the weekend."

"Even with New Year's?" I venture, eager to believe that the old man knows what he's talking about but scared it's wishful thinking.

"These places operate around the clock," he replies. "Things growing in petri dishes don't care what day of the week it is. They owe me a favor. By the sound of things, there's no time to waste." Humphrey, listening at my shoulder, punches the air.

I put the phone down and we beam at each other, proud of our teamwork, bonded by our caring for this child. Humphrey turns, glides his hand from my knee up my thigh, pressing gently. I feel the warmth through the denim. His eyes are locked on mine, the pupils so large only a ring of green is visible. Then he looks down and scoops my pendant in his fingers, his knuckles nestling into my cleavage. "I've been dreaming of doing that," he purrs.

"We should stop," I whisper, but I do nothing to stop him. He undoes two buttons on my blouse and runs his fingertips along and under the edge of my bra. I feel like one of the roses in Sam Parker's bouquet, opening layer by layer, involuntarily rising to meet his touch. My breathing is quicker and so is his. I can hear it and feel his lips against my neck. I want them there, and on my mouth, and . . .

And at that moment my phone rings. We both jump. "Freddie?" Humphrey asks. Same thought. I grab the phone, expecting to see Joanie's number, but it's not. I'm relieved. She sent a message earlier to let me know that Freddie's fever had gone down. He still doesn't want to nurse, though, or take a bottle.

This is an American number, but one I don't know. Then I recognize the voice: Charles.

"Hello, Sally. I'm sorry to call you so late on your end. Six hours or seven?"

"Seven this time of the year. Yes, it is late. Why are you calling?"

"My mother. I thought you would want to know." His voice sounds stifled. My own throat spasms as I hear him gulp in air once, twice. I know what he's going to say as if I've been waiting for it, though I haven't. I want to stall him, to block his words. If he doesn't say it, nothing has happened.

"She went into cardiac arrest yesterday, and her lungs began to fail overnight. She was struggling to breathe. They wanted to put her on a ventilator, but her instructions were very clear—no extreme measures."

If I stop him right here, nothing has changed. But he goes on. "They made her comfortable. She slipped away about an hour ago. We were all there, my sisters and I, and my uncle, a couple of the grandchildren."

"Did she know? Did she have a chance to say goodbye?" I try to add voice to my breath, to reach across the distance.

"Not today. She was dozing through the last hours. But my sister Barbara was with her last night." He gives a half-sob, half-laugh. "She says the last thing Mom said was, 'Tell them to switch off that awful Muzak. Play me the 'leaving softly' song."

I whisper, "Did Barbara know the one your mother wanted? Did she find it?"

He says, "Yes, of course. You know Ethel always got her way."

I wish him long life and thank him for calling and disconnect.

"My mother-in-law," I tell Humphrey, and collapse into his arms with an inhaled howl.

He holds me, rocks me until the wails subside, dabbing away the wetness on my cheeks with his fingers. And when I can speak again, he says, "Tell me about her."

He listens as I describe how devastating the estrangement was, and how sweet it's been to have the connection again, how grateful I am for that, but how much more I'd hoped for. "I had a mother again," I say.

He asks about the song, and I find the CD that Eric and Joanie gave me for my birthday back in June. We sit snuggled together, listening. Thank goodness, thank goodness for his presence, not to have received this news on my own. I pull his arms tighter around me and feel him kiss the top of my head.

As the shock recedes, exhaustion sets in. We talk about his

parents, and mine, and life expectancy.

Eventually Humphrey notices me yawn and he rises to his feet. He reaches out a hand and pulls me up, saying, "Time for bed?"

I lead the way to the bedroom, my hand in his. The cats are curled together in the middle of the bed. I shoo them off with an apology and look across the expanse of the quilt at the pillows piled in the middle, feeling Humphrey behind me, his breath warm on my neck. My whole body is craving closeness, total embrace.

And I can't do this. Not now. Not in this bed. Not with him. I sink down on the edge and make him sit next to me.

Emptiness looms ahead of me. I want to resist it, but this is my reality. The absence is the absence is the absence, and this man, Humphrey, can't fill it. I want to cling, to hold on to the heat he offers, but it's not right. I don't want a one-night stand with another woman's partner. I've been in a theater, absorbed completely in the dream onstage, but the curtain has come down and the houselights are back up. It was, after all, an illusion.

"What's wrong?" he asks, stroking a strand of hair away from my ear and nibbling the lobe. That's not something his brother ever did. No one's done it to me in years. It tickles and makes the small of my back jerk. He pulls away and gives me the raised eyebrows look.

I have both my hands in my lap now. The tingle has faded and all I'm feeling is fatigue, from my crown to the arches of my massaged feet.

"I can't do this," I say out loud. "I'm sorry. I really thought

I wanted to. I'll make up a bed for you in the spare room."

"We could just cuddle," he says. "I hate to leave you alone, feeling so sad."

I get up and take his hand again, drawing him with me. "Let's get you some blankets and sheets."

He follows me back into the living room, where I have the chest filled with spare linen. He stands there looking around as I open it. And then he exclaims so suddenly I drop the lid, "Who are those flowers from?"

Sam's pretty posy is in a glass vase on the mantelpiece. It's where I had Humphrey's poodle with the carnations. I tell him how distraught Jacob was about Skelm breaking it, but he isn't amused.

"Who are those flowers from?"

"A very sweet man I met on the plane," I say, reaching for another blanket. "Are you jealous?"

Then I register that he's not joking. He mutters, "No, of course not. But how many men are there in your life these days?"

My solar plexus cramps. I whisper, "What the hell?"

"You heard me. How many guys are offering to bed the poor little widow?"

I round on him. "What about you? Where is Helga?"

"Don't start with that. My marriage is my business. She's been away—for a while."

"Well then, what about that girl this evening, Ama? I saw you giving her your card. What the fuck was that about?"

He glares at me. "She's in PR, isn't she? I gave her my contact info, asked her if she'd be interested in doing some work for us. Shit—what do you think I am? She's younger than my daughter!"

I flop down at one end of the couch. He thuds down on the other. And we both sit staring at our feet, silent.

Finally, I say to him, "How much did this—this interest in me—have to do with Felix?"

He turns and looks at me, his face wooden. "I was going to ask you the same question."

Minutes pass. The cats come padding in, look up at us and meander past to the kitchen. I hear the rattle of dry food in their bowls. The clock is ticking at what feels like half pace and double volume, punctuating my tinnitus.

Honesty was to be my new mantra, wasn't it? Full disclosure when possible.

I say to Humphrey, "It felt like a miracle when you appeared. The impossible was happening. I had Felix back. But the minute you took off your hat, it was clear you were someone very different." He gives a snort. "I don't know how much I still willed you to be like him. I've watched the way you walk and the way you smile, and even how you get excited about ideas. But I liked the parts that are different too—your laughter, your courtesy, the way your shirts are ironed. I find you incredibly sexy. But I hate the fact that you're willing to cheat on your wife, and that I was willing to do it with you."

He nods, his lips pressed together. "Felix didn't cheat on you? I always thought he was a big player."

"I did too. A few times when we were students, but he never ever pretended to be faithful when he wasn't." All these truths I overlooked. "He used to talk about freedom. But I don't think he cheated on Deidre—except once with me. And with his second wife, Nellie was the one who had flings on the side and then went off with someone else. He wasn't a player. It took me a long time to recognize that—too long."

"Shit, now I learn this." Humphrey rubs the bridge of his nose, staring at his knees. "He was a better man than I am. I make big resolutions, but once in a blue moon I meet someone who's just beautiful and they're interested too. . ." He looks up at me. "Helga got wind of you. That's why she's at her parents' place. Not just you. She's been dredging up every suspicion she's ever had."

I feel sick that I've added to her unhappiness. That should always have been uppermost, and it wasn't. Oh so reluctantly, I ask, "Do you think we can be friends, just friends?"

He shrugs and sighs. "I suppose so."

It's after midnight by the time we call goodnight to each other from the adjoining rooms. As my eyes adjust to the darkness, I see a tall figure appear at my doorway. My resolution wavers. I don't have it in me to push him away again. If he really only wants to snuggle. . .

As I am about to pull back the blanket, he says, "I just wanted to let you know I'm going to leave very early in the morning, see if I can get a flight to East London, to my in-laws. But I'll call you the minute I get word from the lab."

He adds, "If you're not awake when I go, just know it's not one of those 'Softly as I Leave You' sneak-aways, okay?"

~ 15 ~

Last day of the last year when Felix was still alive. I poke my way back to consciousness with the sun glittering off the sequins on the red fabric wall hanging above the bed. It's transmitting sparks to the far wall like an urgent Morse code I should be able to decipher and can't. Without needing any code, the house signals its vacancy. Just me and the cats.

For a few moments I try to keep at bay the double recognition that I'm going to be alone tonight after all, and that this stupid dance with Humphrey—the delusion that my loss has been erased—is over.

And then another fact presses down further, squeezing the air out of my lungs: Ethel. It's as if my body knew before my mind recalled. Charles phoned, didn't he? That really happened. How could I not have anticipated it? She was in her nineties, with pneumonia. But just days ago, she was lively and looking forward to the future, to reading my book, to throwing that party. We were going to have years more to catch up on what we missed. How can all that be lost, gone?

You never know how much time you have, I remember ghost-Felix saying. Take it from me.

Other losses lurk in layers of hurt behind this one, losses that came long before Felix's exit: my mother, my father, my baby even before she made it into the world. Ethel was with me through all of those, loving and comforting.

Freddie—no, I don't want to think of Freddie in this company. Joanie said he was doing all right, kind of. Please let that be true. Continue to be true. Whatever or Whoever is in charge, please make him strong.

Would it help if I get down on my knees on the fluffy rug and press my hands together? I wish I believed that prayer could alter anything. Ethel said we aren't guaranteed an answer. But this tiny being doesn't deserve to suffer, to struggle because no one knows how to help him. How can all our efforts fail this child? I can't bear to think about that or anything else. I don't want to think.

I pull on jeans and Felix's old gray T-shirt and leave the house without even having coffee. I need to get away from where the argument happened last night and from the unwashed dishes, even from the phone that delivered the awful news about Ethel. On Main Road there are too many cars, too many loud people talking and laughing, walking merrily arm in arm, blocking the sidewalk. Head down, I push my way past them and cross over to the subway, under the train tracks, to the beach.

Our beach, where one crazy evening Felix and I made love,

counting on the darkness to conceal us, and barely caring, perfectly in tune even as our aging bodies struggled to match the lust drawing us together. I can still hear him chuckling afterwards over a silly joke we shared, about the chicken and the egg, and which came first.

No Felix on that beach now, nor anyone else except a pair of drunks sprawled together against the back wall. It's a humid, ugly day. The sky is overcast and glary, and the sea is as flat as hammered steel. The water is barely lapping onto the damp, littered sand, the normal rhythm suspended.

I take off my flip-flops, roll up my jeans, and walk into the ocean. Warm as the air is, the water is icy and hurts like hell. I'm glad. It's what I wanted. My ankles feel arthritic. I walk in further, stepping on rocks and fragments of shell. The cold soaks the fabric around my knees, and they ache worse than my ankles.

What now?

I keep walking, pushing against the weight of the ocean. Strange that the little minnows darting in the brown shadows below experience that pressure like air and would find this emptiness up here leaden against their gills. Neither medium seems right for me.

A swell pushes the water past my pelvis to my belly and the small of my back. I am too lethargic to hop and yelp. I stand as still as I can, absorbing the punishment.

In the strange hush that comes from the absence of waves, a male voice rises above the chorus of birds and distant cars: "Sally! Sally Paddington, what are you doing?" I turn and see a figure in black, arms out like wings, a shoe in each hand, wading into the water. It's Bob Halpert.

"My dear Sally, don't do this," he yells.

I turn and stare. And then I try to reach him, to save him and his clothes from further soaking, but the receding water holds me in place. I push against it, annoyed with him and not ready for any pep talks. At last, an incoming wave shoves me back into the shallows.

I feel as if I've washed ashore from a very long journey.

"Can I take you home?" he asks. His eyes are mournful as a bloodhound's.

"No. I don't want to go home."

He presses both hands against his sweating head and turns brusque. It's an aspect I haven't seen before, but I suppose you can't head up a congregation as large as his without having some power to compel. "Then you're coming home with me. No arguments. I'll find you something dry to change into, and I'll make us a nice cup of rooibos, just the way you like it. Come along now."

He's angry with me, and I can't work out why. So, I simply obey and follow him back to where his old Morris is parked, a little askew as always. I hesitate before climbing in, not wanting to get the seat wet, but he's holding the door and urging me in. He seems to think I might make a break for it if he gives me any space. Perhaps I should. That would be a sight to amuse the tourists—a skinny crone loping along the sidewalk, chased by a tubby priest in soggy socks.

I go peacefully. At the rectory, I get out and follow him inside and obediently close myself in the bathroom with a bag of clothes from his charity bin. He's given me a collection of kids' clothes, but that's probably smart. The stuff is creased but it all smells freshly laundered, and I find a sufficiently large pair of checked Bermuda shorts and a blue T-shirt with Teenage Mutant Ninja Turtles on it.

Bob cracks a grin when I enter his dining room. "Well, I must say you don't look anything like your usual self."

"It'll do." Right now, I haven't a clue what my usual self is. The only familiar part is the self-pity.

And then, with my hands clutching a thick-walled mug of tea on my knees, I announce, "Ethel is dead."

I'm not sure he will remember the name and who she is, but he does immediately. His eyes bulge. "Oh my, er—good heavens! That's not what I had in mind."

What he "had in mind"? I had expected a blankness or sympathy, not guilt. "Remember I said I would pray for a miracle for you?" he says. "Didn't you want to be able to move ahead with your book and not have to worry that your ex would rat you out to his mother and tell her your coauthor was his nemesis?" I nod. "Now you can do as you please. He has no more power to hurt you. But, oh my ..."

This line should be his, but I can't resist. I say, "The Lord works in mysterious ways."

"He does indeed." Bob's face is pink. "You did say she was very elderly, didn't you? Must simply have been her time."

He gives himself a little shake and then looks hard at me. "I understand your sadness, but that's not why you decided to walk into the sea this morning, is it?"

~ ~ ~ ~

Eventually, I have to go back to the cottage. The cats wind

and twist around my legs, mewling their sweet reminders of what a shit I am, going out like that without feeding them. "You won't starve in one day," I tell them, but I know they're right.

It had been a long session of 'fessing up. I told Bob why Charles hated Felix, and about the flirtation with Humphrey. He sat in his big wingback chair, hands clasped over his paunch, head to one side, taking it all in without saying a word, just nodding now and then.

"I'm fucking miserable—sorry—but I am," I told him at last. "But I wasn't planning to drown myself."

"Sometimes it doesn't take a plan," he replied.

"You've had a parishioner off themselves on impulse?" I was being flippant, but he didn't react.

"No. A person who was very dear to me, a young man." I've wondered about Bob's romantic preferences; all he has said in the past is that he never had a grand passion like Felix and mine. I knew that mentioning that man was a measure of how deeply I'd alarmed him.

"I know he didn't intend to, not in any thought-out way. He would have written me a note, and left his place tidy, or at least have made some plans for his pets. He was such a conscientious human being—too conscientious. Things just escalated—a bad call from his boss, another cruel attack from his family, too many bills, a bottle of painkillers that should never have been prescribed."

I reached over and grasped his hand. He squeezed mine back and asked with a little smile if I had fed Mergatroid and Skelm. I hadn't. Or made my bed. But then really, I wasn't going to kill myself, and I insisted he acknowledge that. "I just don't know what to do with myself tonight, or tomorrow. And I'm terrified that Felix's grandbaby won't survive, or maybe even worse—that he is facing a life of suffering, because we don't know how to help him."

He got brusque again. "I know you're not in the habit of praying, and—well, sometimes prayers work out in unintended ways—but I am going to ask you to sit with me while I pray for little Frederick. And tonight, why don't you come with me and Roxanne and Edith, and perhaps some others, for a walk up to the viewing place above Boyes Drive, to watch the fireworks at midnight. It is a spectacular view."

How could I refuse him? I sat in silence as he asked God for his blessing on Freddie. He didn't actually ask that he be healed, which puzzled me. When he'd said "Amen," I asked about that. "It's not for me to question God's will," he said. "I'm merely expressing our—my—love and seeking the grace to understand whatever outcome He deems best."

A bit wishy-washy, if you ask me; I was hoping to hear something fiercer, along Deidre's lines, but given his success on the book front—I hadn't yet absorbed the full implications of that one—I didn't complain. Ethel too had talked about acceptance.

"Will we see you later, then?" he asked as I gathered up my damp clothes.

"Maybe. I'll let you know."

I made my way home through the sweltering midday heat, hands shoved in the pockets of my shorts, praying not to bump into anyone I knew while garbed in that outfit.

~ ~ ~ ~

It's a stupid thing to do after all Bob's effort to uplift me, but I turn on the music system and again slip in the CD of Ethel's song. Well, my song—and Felix's. He used to play it— quite recognizably—on a tiny harmonica I gave him the second year we were together.

When I hear it, I hear Felix exhaling and inhaling those notes, with all their longing and regret. It's about an asshole who sneaks away while his lover is asleep. Felix didn't choose to leave me. Humphrey did, even if it was the right thing to do.

I don't want to think any more about either of them or anyone else. A half-empty bottle of wine from last night is on the coffee table in front of me, its cork barely inserted enough to stay upright. Our used glasses are in the sink, and with the music weaving around me, I'm too lazy to get a clean one from the cabinet. I take a swig from the bottle, and then another. It tastes sour but not awful.

What was discussed at Bob's? Didn't he bestow some words of wisdom that should help me not want to end this all? The morning is lost in shadows.

What a cheap way to get drunk! All I've had is the tea at Bob's, and an empty stomach proves a good facilitator. There is no point in wasting the last inch or two, so I drain it before the song ends and find another bottle in the kitchen, almost full. Before the last number on the CD, I'm feeling somewhat blurred.

This coming year, I turn seventy. How can that be? I'm older than my mother. Older than my father. They both died in their sixties. Isn't one supposed to be sorted out and serene by seventy? Some of my favorite pop stars, the wild boys of my youth, are in their seventies. Are they wiser now? Anyway, they're rich and that has to make up for lingering idiocy, and they still have their groupies. Me, I'm not rich or adored.

When Humphrey phones minutes later, I burp and say, "Hi, Feliksh." I realize my mistake and burp again. "Whoops, Freudian slif. Humph, what can I do for you? Have you found your wife?"

"Sally?" He sounds surprised. Why, I don't know. After all, I offered him whisky the second time he visited me, and well before noon. This, at least, is after pub-opening time. My heart is fluttering, whether from the alcohol or hearing him. I'm wondering if he's still angry about the flowers or that I wanted him to be like Felix. "I was calling to tell you about the lab result, but this might not be the right time."

Already? That's like a splash in the face. I ask him to hold on a moment, put down the phone, and pour myself a cup of cold, leftover coffee from yesterday morning. It's disgusting, but I start feeling slightly sharper.

"Wow, that was fast. Tell me. What did they say?"

"Special favor to John Latimer. The hair isn't one of mine, but there's a partial match, so yes—it's Felix's DNA."

He sounds gruff, as if he's fighting back emotion. "Are you okay?" I ask.

"Yeah, no, I'm all right. It's just—I'm glad we can give Joanie and Eric this information, for whatever it's worth. But it also means Felix was right about Dad, that he wasn't his father. That Mom had this secret all those years. That Matt and Olivia and I aren't his full siblings."

"Will you tell them?"

"I don't know. Liv has always said our family is full of secrets; maybe she's suspected something like this. She was the closest to my dad."

"Do you think your father knew?"

He gives a "Whew" and is quiet a moment. "I hope he didn't. Or maybe I hope he did. It would explain a lot."

The next step is to send Maria the results. She has been talking to doctors involved with the foundation she runs, and she has arranged a gene test for her father. We've spoken twice since I got home, and it's been clear in her voice—usually so ebullient—that this whole matter is deeply distressing.

I try to convey her concern to Humphrey. "She wants this not to be true. If the link is there between Felix and her father, it probably means Freddie has the same thing that she has. She's hoping for a mismatch."

"Yes, I understand," he says, and I hear the methodical mind at work, cool and practical, like Felix's. "But if they can confirm the diagnosis, they can take action. Didn't you say the sooner they act, the better?" That's true. In fact, Maria did too. But how long will this next step take?

Another aspect taps my attention. It provides a detour away from the gut-knotting "if" about Freddie. I say to Humphrey, "You mentioned that there might be money involved. I gather from Maria that her father had quite a lot and was generous with it, but he doesn't seem to have much now. I was wondering if the money in your mother's account could be sent back to him . . ."

I've touched on it with both Joanie and Trevor, and this

was their suggestion. But of course, there are other grandchildren, and Humphrey might take exception to my depriving them of funds. "That'd be fine," he says. "I can talk to the bank about it. It really wasn't a big deal. I just brought it up because I thought you might be more motivated to help work out who that Josie was."

Darn him. As always, he goes from sweet to sour in one beat. I snap at him, "So did you get what you wanted from me? Have I served your purpose?"

"Whoa, hothead, lighten up! I never said you were a gold digger."

"Don't tell me to lighten up!" Now I'm stone-cold sober and feeling mean, but he defuses my fuse.

"Hey, silly Sally, I thought you might want the money for Felix's kids. You did a great detective job, and we all wanted these answers. It might make all the difference for Freddie. You're glad about all that, aren't you?"

Deep breath, and another. Of course, I'm glad—if it can make that difference. The results could still go either way.

We agree to speak as soon as Maria gets back to me and say goodbye. I watch his name disappear off my screen and sit there staring at nothing, till I remember the next task. I email Maria to let her know Humphrey will be sending the profile.

~ ~ ~ ~

In the middle of the afternoon, I force myself to eat a bowl of cereal, and strip to have a shower. My skin is sticky from the salt water and looks papery. I'm glad Humphrey never saw me naked. My hair is snaggled in knots from not brushing last night or this morning. My arms grow tired, trying to drag a comb through it.

Without rational thought, just impatient to be done, I grab scissors and chop off the bunch caught in the teeth. The chain around my neck snags in the blades. I take it off and hang it alongside Felix's abalone shell. And then I clasp the next bunch and the next, snipping above my knuckles, snip, snip, until I can't find another clump long enough to grasp that way. Then I turn on the shower, spurt shampoo into my palm, and rub it into a lather. My hair feels like fur. I've never had it this short ever, not even as a kid.

Feeling clean and steadier, without looking in a mirror— because who cares? —I call Libby to wish her a happy New Year. Also, I want to let her know I've stopped the nonsense with Humphrey.

She gives a whoop of approval. It's just the reaction I need right now, a metaphorica pat on the back. There is no one else who can provide that, because—thank goodness—no one else (except perhaps Helga, and I hope not her) knows how close I came to crossing that holy line. "But he was good for me. He was a catalyst," I tell Libby. My lips are wobbling, tears threatening, but I inhale and keep my voice steady.

"How is the weather there?" Libby asks, changing the subject. I tell her it's muggy and hot, and she groans, tells me to thank my lucky stars. "It's miserably cold here," she declares. "And everyone is in mourning about the state of the country, except Bradley's Howard, who thinks this is the best thing since Ronald Reagan. He keeps telling us to buy shares, that the stock market is going to boom."

I tell her about Ethel, and now we both choke up, and the

line is silent for a few moments. We reminisce about the times she came with me to their family's beach house, and her last encounter with Ethel after the theater that day.

And then hesitantly Libby puts into words, with an apology, what I haven't let myself dwell on even when Bob mentioned it: "Now you can make your book the best it can possibly be, giving Felix a wonderful tribute." I'm a bit shocked, but coming from this sweet soul, it doesn't sound as cold as it might. "You don't need to worry about Charles or about Ethel's loyalty to him."

"Maybe I'll dedicate it to her," I say.

"That's a beautiful idea." She points out, with business savvy that always takes me by surprise, that it will also give a boost to the marketing. "Ethel's friends will all want to show their support. And Charles won't be able to say a thing. Didn't she have a foundation for children's health or something like that?" It wasn't Ethel, it's Maria who has the foundation, I tell her. "That's just as good," Libby declares. "You can donate a portion of the proceeds. Ethel would have approved. Then he really can't get in the way."

This feels right. I had planned to donate a portion of the proceeds to a related organization, and this will work perfectly. I could even ask Charles to organize the donation in his mother's name. Our issues aside, he truly is a lover of dance and always fancied himself a philanthropist. Now I'm getting excited, tapping a rhythm with my bare feet. I know his ego; if anything could help him transcend the old pettiness, it would be the prestige of a role like this. In fact—and this thought brings moisture to my eyes, blurring my vision yet again—

maybe the book will inspire him to find a way to dance.

It's a disturbing reminder: In all our years together, it never occurred to me that he might crave to dance too. I still despise his self-centeredness and how high-handed he was about the book, but the part of me that loved him long ago when he was young and eager suddenly wants this for him.

I tell her, and she sighs. "That's beautiful. Isn't there a way to bring that thought into the book—without the personal details? Go write it now, before you forget!"

As we're talking, a flash bleaches the view outside, followed moments later by a deep drumroll. It's been so long, I almost don't recognize the sound of thunder. Drops of water begin pelting the window.

Pleased but nervous, because the room has gone so dark, I tell Libby what's happening. The curtains billow, letting in a gust of rain. "Do you want to close the windows?" she asks. I don't because the moist air smells so good. "Doug says it's called petrichor," she tells me. I trace the word on my thigh in an effort to imprint it: PETRICHOR, heralding the end of the drought? Perhaps not yet, but it is the scent of hope.

And then we go back to family talk. I fill her in on Freddie's medical odyssey so she can update Doug and Bridget. She makes me repeat things a couple of times, to help her get it all straight, and then she exclaims: "What a miraculous world we live in! Here's something that happened many years ago, and no one could know what the truth was—until now!"

She's right, if finally, we do get the facts. Elsabet probably didn't know—couldn't know, so José didn't, and neither did Felix, or his supposed father.

"We still don't know for sure . . ."

"But we will, and then Freddie will be on his way to recovery!"

That optimism scares me. It runs counter to the frozen caution Joanie and Eric have enforced and my own, but right now it is helpful to hear. It opens space to breathe.

I stretch out my legs and wiggle my toes, trying to match her bubbliness. Next thing I know, Skelm scoots out from under the couch and pounces on them. He tumbles about my foot, trying to turn it into a worthy opponent. The prickle of his claws makes me squawk. I tell Libby about cutting my hair, and she pleads for a photo. I search for my phone to take one, before I realize that it's at my ear. Now she's cackling. I tell her about the flowers from Mr. Tie-Dye, which delights her even more.

I ask what she and Doug are going to do tonight. She says, "Probably fall asleep in front of the television even before the ball in Times Square drops. What about you?" I tell her Bob Halpert has invited me to come up the mountain with him and our friends, but that I plan to sit alone on the beach. I don't mention this morning's dip.

"Don't do that," she pleads. "Promise me you'll dress up in something sparkly and go join your friends." I feel better for our chat, but still can't imagine doing that. In any case, I don't possess a single sparkly garment.

~ *16* ~

Inspired by Libby and the goodwill towards Charles, quickly before it fades, I make a new resolution: This book is going to get finished!

To reinforce the vow, I clamber up the steps to the attic. Turn on the computer. The bay is a dark mass of gray, dotted with white caps lit up by the slanting rays breaking through the clouds. Pull my attention back to the screen and open the book file. No more external roadblocks, no more excuses; the onus is all on me. With a bit of fussing, I manage to import and incorporate the new, polished first chapters, and—thinking of opening and closing acts—I turn to the rough outline of the final section.

And almost shut the file again. My brand-new determination wavers and collapses. How on earth do I give Gail and Martin that upbeat ending they want? There is something missing—I'm not sure what—there are so many dilemmas I can't answer definitively

That's a problem? I hear over my shoulder.

You're back again?

You don't need neat solutions, not to this or any other problems, just possibilities—as you see them.

Sounds good, but what can I do with that? What would you do?

I'd have fun.

Fun? For the first time in my entire life, I'm going to be alone on New Year's Eve. Maybe I'm still a bit drunk, but I yell out loud, in this silent house that last night felt so filled with life: "Why aren't you here?"

When I listen for an answer, the rafters are deserted.

Downstairs, the phone starts ringing. It's probably Bob calling to nudge me about tonight, so I ignore it. But maybe it's Maria, responding to my email. I leap up, half losing one flipflop, and skitter down the steps, clutching the handrails to steady myself. Three steps from the bottom, my heel slips off the wood, and my foot hits the floor at an angle that shoots an electric shock up through my wonky knee.

The phone has stopped ringing by the time I hop towards it. I tap-tap on the screen to see missed calls, and yes, it was Bob. I don't bother to call back. I pack some ice cubes in a dish towel, wrap it around my leg, and lie down, winded and resigned. Each time I shift my weight, pain radiates from the knee. I don't really mind; it's a distraction from the inner mess. There'll be no going up the mountain or down to the beach this evening.

Have fun, he said. This isn't fun.

Bob calls again, and I can't not answer. "I'm not coming. I've just reinjured my knee," I tell him.

The man of God sounds positively uncharitable. "Nonsense. The rain has stopped, and we're all going. I'm sure you went through many sprains in your years of dancing. You won't be able to climb up the mountain, but bandage it firmly, take some aspirin, and I'll come get you in fifteen minutes. We're all having dinner at Edith and Roxie's. We'll drive up to the viewing spot about eleven o'clock. I have some crutches. I'll bring them." He disconnects without letting me answer.

Cornered, with no way out. I hop to the bathroom, put on lipstick without looking in the mirror, and spritz on perfume I haven't touched in ages. Its fresh spiciness slows my ragged breathing. In the bedroom I find a gray silk blouse and manage to hop and wiggle into some black pants. They're baggier than before but drape quite easily over the Ace bandage. But the combination is funereal. I put on a pair of silver earrings, but they barely help. Look around for something else to add more glitz. The sequined wall hanging sparkles back at me.

Copper Girl, what are you up to? He sounds astonished—for once.

Without stopping to debate the move, I squirm up onto the sore knee, shift onto the other foot and push myself up. Come to think of it, the knee isn't all that bad. I might have just nudged it back into place. Now I can reach up and dislodge the hanging off its hooks. It tumbles onto the pillows. I slide the rings off the rod and sweep the red fabric about my shoulders, rings and all. Finally check my reflection in the full-length mirror—and freak out! There is this totally unfamiliar person with a coronet of short white curls. She looks like a cross between Queen Elizabeth and Scarlett O'Hara, draped and ready for her grand entrance.

My new image garners a "Good heavens!" from Bob, and "Wow!" and applause from Edith and Roxie. There are other people at their place whom I've never met and who simply accept this eccentricity as my normal style. They don't know me, don't inquire how I'm doing, as everyone else in this community does, and only ask about the crutches.

"Very temporary," I tell them. Halfway through the evening, I give them back to Bob. I can manage without them.

Up on the mountainside later, we can see the golden spread of lights and the sprays of red and green and gold erupting from dozens of celebrations. Wetness from the rain sparkles on the rocks and plants around us. I check in with my ghost. Don't hear any words, just feel his embrace in my sequined wrap.

With my phone, I take one fuzzy picture after another before finally snapping a perfect moment. It captures five simultaneous rosettes of color along the dark curve of the bay. Very proud of it. And I also ask Bob, who has a fancier camera, to take a picture of me in my finery.

As I'm about to stash my phone away, I notice an email from Maria. For a moment I turn away from the revelers and try to concentrate. It has two attachments, one apparently giving José's gene report, and one providing a comparison with Felix's from the Port Elizabeth lab. But it's hopeless. I don't know how to make sense of them, certainly not perched on a damp rock with people passing around plastic flutes of champagne. I send her a thank-you, with much love and best wishes.

And then I send the whole email to Humphrey with a note, uncorrected: Yu understnd thissstuff beettr than me. Help pleas. And happy NYear.

Sign it: Silly sAlly.

~ ~ ~ ~

Sunday, January I.

Awakened by the cats stepping very deliberately across my stomach. When I open my eyes, they are both staring straight into my face, quite indifferent to the date or when I fell asleep. No getting away without catering to their needs today. And no sparks hitting the far wall in this morning's patchy sunlight— because the wall above my head is bare, blank. When I stand up, my knee is tender but not electric-sore. Nothing is torn, I don't think. Hobble to the kitchen, turn on the coffee machine and feed my companions.

I make myself a strong cup of espresso, for a change, take out my diary, and check my phone. There is a message from Humphrey: Herewith, my analysis of the results. Happy New Year, SSS (Silly Sister Sally) LY, Boet.

I don't know what "LY" means, assume it's one of his typos, and move on to the two-column chart he has copied, comparing data. The numbers mean nothing to me, but I understand what he has written below it: Beyond question, parent and child. José and Felix are father and son.

~ ~ ~ ~

I send the whole chart to Joanie and Eric, along with an edited version of Humphrey's message to me. I think about phoning, but I want them to be able to absorb the information at their own pace. Just tap out a gushy note to wish them everything good for this fresh new year, only now about to begin by them.

On Monday, they can take the charts to the specialist, the "top guy in the field," according to Deidre.

Next, I send a note to Trevor, with Humphrey's news and the best image of the fireworks. I'm expecting we'll talk later and discuss what it means regarding him and Felix. I know he will get a kick out of being one part Spanish, in addition to all his other ingredients, and I hope it will soften his heart towards his father.

Just moments later, my phone rings and it's my beautiful boy himself. What he says makes me choke up with tears so I can barely squeeze out an audible response.

"Sal, you know how January 1 is Imani, the last day of Kwanzaa?" I do, but I can't remember what it stands for. "It's about honoring the best about the community, or about us, ourselves, as members of a family. Remember I told you how much Dad loved the idea? It's weird, but I feel as if he set up this whole crazy thing so that it would all come together just in time, like a big present, as if he's watching over us with that big grin of his."

~ ~ ~ ~

Finally, deep down in muscle fibers that have been tight since the call about Freddie's arrival, I feel a loosening. Relief billows upward, like a crop of hot-air balloons. At last, my beloveds have their starting point. Now they know what to look for, where to seek the treatments that might be Freddie's salvation. As challenging as it all could be, the next steps are clear.

Those two words— "next steps"—give me a fist bump of pleasure. I know good things await this child. If only I was still in that house in Portland, I could run down the stairs and hug Joanie and discuss it all face-to-face, and pick up and squeeze that beautiful little cleft-chinned grandchild of mine.

Calm down. Listen for my Tiger Man in the bright, breezy air and hear only the tinkling of wind chimes—next door, not inside my head.

Soon enough, José will know for sure what he sensed for so long. I wish Elsabet could have known the truth too. Or perhaps not. The certainty might have been more than she could hide for the rest of her life. But I wish Felix had known.

Then his words come floating back—was it only three weeks ago? —*Freddie will flourish.*

Perhaps, just maybe, he knew already, and it was only us living folks he had to steer towards the information. Happiness floods through me. Without standing up, I do a two-step sashay within, and imagine—or feel? —a warm hand on my back.

Ready to dance now?

~ ~ ~ ~

Around noon, Bob Halpert appears at my door. He has just conducted his morning service, the first of the year, and is going for a walk. Would I like to come, to help him set in motion his New Year's resolution to exercise more? I point out that I'm not really up for a long walk and it looks likely to rain again, but if he will put off his new start until later, I can probably make it as far as the corner. If the café is open, we can have brunch.

He agrees a little too readily. I will need to support him in his new resolution, but not today.

As I'm pulling the door shut behind me, he gives a yelp. "Oh dear, how could I do that? Sally, please forgive me, I totally forgot to tell you."

"Tell me what?"

"The other reason I came looking for you yesterday at the beach."

Skelm slips through the door. These days his mother is content to stay in the yard, but he is constantly trying to head out on an adventure. I corner him and shoo him back inside. There is no way I'm going to be able to keep him closed up. This is a risk I'll have to live with, and just hope he always finds his way home.

"I didn't set out to visit you," Bob says, "but as I passed by here, I encountered someone looking for you. He said he had tried your bell, but there was no response. So, I tried. When you didn't answer, I became rather alarmed, you know, remembering how very downhearted you seemed last week. I took the car out, thinking perhaps I'd see you taking your constitutional along the Main Road. And then I thought to look on the beach . . ."

"Who was the person at my door?"

"Well, I believe it may have been the admirer who sent you those pretty flowers I found on your front step the other day."

"Sam Parker?"

"That's his name? I didn't ask. Seemed like it would be too

nosy."

"What did he look like?"

"Well, a bit like an American version of me, but with a very colorful shirt. Perhaps a tad less stocky. And a very nice smile."

"And a terrible haircut? Definitely Sam Parker! I'm sorry I missed him."

"Yes, a pity. He seemed like a delightful fellow, if I say so myself. And impressive hair, actually, rather like President Kennedy. He might still be around. Said he was staying at that new bed-and-breakfast place, the very spiffy one. Perhaps we'll bump into him."

Evidently the grandkid haircut has grown out. I'm curious to see what he looks like now. Bob and I set out side by side, at a gentle pace.

The rowdier tourists must be indoors nursing hangovers, because the people we pass are calm and friendly. As we make our way along the street, they exchange smiles with us.

Timing can be such a delicate thing. I'm scanning for a particularly bright T-shirt, not in a rush to see it, but also not wary.

Yesterday, if I had spotted Sam, I'd have ducked out of sight. Today I'm ready to wave a greeting. Tomorrow might be even better; it will give me a chance to have my hair shaped a little.

You look fine. Go for it!

Oh, hello!

Strange thing about Felix: He was never possessive, or not that he'd let on. Not even about his brother.

Why would I be? I'm Numero Uno with you, always will be. Who do you think sent Boet your way?

Really? I'm not sure what to make of that.

~ ~ ~ ~

As we're parting after our brunch, full of salmon and mimosas, Bob remembers another thing he forgot: He takes out his phone and shows me the picture he shot last night of me in my glitter special. It looks totally mad. What possessed me? Even he laughs as he sends it to me.

After he's gone, I dry off a chair on the patio and settle down with my phone and my diary. It poured while we were in the restaurant, and the air is fragrant. Drops are glistening on the yesterday-today-and-tomorrow and the fuzzy centers of the pearly pink proteas. There's an empty space where Jacob removed something, I can't remember what. It would be a perfect spot for another spekboom bush; they're said to be resilient and edible. Grow it from a seed or get a plant from the garden store? Either way, worth giving it a try.

I add "spekboom" to the January 2 shopping list I've squeezed into the December 31 page. If I'm going to continue this recording process, I'll need to buy a new volume. Start to add "diary" to my list but cross it out. No great need to record my days. They're pretty memorable anyway. Mergatroid hops up and settles on top of the open page, purring. I switch to my phone.

Along with the fireworks photo, I send the red shawl shot to Libby and Doug, with an all-caps message:

THANK YOU VERY MUCH FOR THE FASHION GUIDANCE—NOT!

I'm beginning to regret that I didn't have Bob take one of me in the baggy shorts and Ninja Turtle T-shirt. I could have started an album of Silly Sally looks.

And *kaboom!*—the finale of the book presents itself.

I want to get back upstairs to the computer. Or maybe not today. Give the knee another day to calm down, but tomorrow. Meanwhile, I make mental notes. The last pages will showcase an array of wild, try-anything images to make my point— *our* point, Felix and mine: Dance isn't all toe shoes and tight buns. Within the traditional disciplines, there's room for play that opens up all kinds of fresh pathways.

The photo of Felix in the flamenco outfit will work, and the one of Maria in her bunny suit, dancing with arms and torso and floppy ears. My long-ago student Winston still loves clowning around and will surely give me a picture. And I have contacts in the States with some bona fide stars—four or five come to mind right away—whom I can cajole into giving me fun shots.

And suddenly I can't wait for Monday, to call the duo in New York. I want to tell Gail and Martin about this rogues' gallery that will fill my last chapter. And I'm impatient to describe my coauthor, the late, great cornball, Dr. Felix Barnard. Come to think of it, I could show those pictures to the conference audience too. Imagining already the live response resounding in that big lecture hall.

I told you we could do it, Copper Girl.

No, you didn't. But this is good, isn't it?

Good enough.

Ha! I swat at the air and laugh out loud, definitely like a crazy lady. This is better than good enough—and I don't need him to tell me.

At that moment, I recall the line from Humphrey's email this morning, and comprehend what "LY" means. A grin bunches my cheeks. Felix, neither in the flesh nor in spirit, has ever used the word with me. I've learned to trust that he felt—feels—it anyway. But this Barnard does use it, with me.

Mergatroid, disturbed by my glee, climbs off my diary and jumps down. I squeeze one more entry onto the last page: *Sally Paddington has a brother who says he loves her!!!*

I rise from the chair, diary in one hand, phone in the other, and start to sway. With eyes closed, to an inner soundtrack of "Here Comes the Sun," I let the joy ripple from my core, through my arms and my hips and my feet, out into the world.

I don't hear Felix, but I feel him beaming.

About the Author

As a journalist, Elaine Durbach was fascinated by what drives people and shapes their perception. As a fiction writer, that is still her passion.

Her own perception was shaped by a childhood in various parts of southern Africa, including Zimbabwe, Zambia, Lesotho, and South Africa. She earned a journalism degree at Rhodes University and started her career in Cape Town.

She was awarded a Cape Times Journalism Scholarship as a student, and as a reporter won a World Press Institute Fellowship, which brought her to the United States. Elaine returned to New York as a correspondent for the South African Morning Group, and then worked as a freelance journalist in the city and wrote for the United Nations. After moving to New Jersey, she worked for seventeen years for the *New Jersey Jewish News*, along the way winning another three press awards.

LAF – Life After Felix is her second published novel. The first was its prequel, *Roundabout.* She has also written two nonfiction books, *With Mixed Feelings* and *South Africa: The Wild Realms.*

She lives in Maplewood, New Jerssey, with her husband, Marshall Norstein, and their son, Gabe. When not writing fiction, she edits other people's writing, takes photographs, makes jewelry, and draws portraits all over her notebooks.

Staying In Touch

If you would like to schedule an interview, set up a book talk, or simply ask a question or share your views, you can do so via the contact form on the author's website: www.ElaineDurbach.com,
or email her at ElaineDurbach@gmail.com

You can also send a message or respond to posts on Facebook on the Elaine Durbach Author Page.

If you enjoyed this book, please share your opinion in reviews and with friends and family. If so inclined, ask your local library or bookstore if they have it, or can get it for you.